Elif Shafak is one of the leading novelists in Turkey. Born in France, having lived in Spain, Jordan, Germany and the United States, multi-culturalism has been a constant theme in her works. Shafak studied political science in Turkey. She held teaching positions in Turkey and the United States. She is now Assistant Professor in the Department of Near Eastern Studies at the University of Arizona.

Her publications include both novels and essays, among them *The Flea Palace* (shortlisted for the *Independent* Foreign Fiction Prize 2005) and *The Gaze*, which won the Turkish Writers' Association Best Novel of the Year Award in 2001. She is a columnist for two major Turkish newspapers and has contributed to various European and American publications, including *Berliner Zeitung*, *The Washington Post* and *Wall Street Journal*.

Brendan Freely is a freelance writer, editor and translator currently living in Istanbul.

Praise for Elif Shafak

'Her literary success and journalism mark her out as a figurehead of a new generation of writers, who use literature to reconfigure Turkish identity, and its relationship to the country's history' *The Independent*

'Ms Shafak is well set to challenge Mr Pamuk as Turkey's foremost contemporary novelist' *The Economist*

Praise for *The Flea Palace*

'A hyper-active, hilarious trip with farce, passion, mystery and many sidelights on Turkey's past.' *The Independent*

'Take special notice of this multi-populated, enchanting work set in dilapidated flats dominated by an overpowering stench. It is wonderful' *The Bookseller*

The GAZE

Published in Great Britain and the United States in 2006 by
MARION BOYARS PUBLISHERS LTD
24 Lacy Road, London SW15 1NL

www.marionboyars.co.uk

Distributed in Australia and New Zealand by Peribo Pty Ltd
58 Beaumont Road, Kuring-gai, NSW 2080

Originally published in Turkey in 1999 by Metis Yayinlari as *Mahrem*

Printed in 2006
10 9 8 7 6 5 4 3 2 1

A CIP catalogue record for this book is available from the British Library.
A CIP catalog record for this book is available from the Library of Congress.

With thanks to the European Commission Euclid Culture 2000 for assistance with
the translation of this book.

ISBN 0-7145-3122-7
13 digit ISBN 9780-7145-3122-9

Set in Bembo 11/14pt
Printed in England by Bookmarque Ltd

The GAZE
by Elif Shafak

Translated from the Turkish by Brendan Freely

MARION BOYARS
LONDON · NEW YORK

'There are inquisitive eyes behind each lattice screen;
It can be said that every lattice screen is a
spy-hole shaped like a piece of *baklava*;
Thousands of lattice-framed eyes watch the
neighbourhood.'

Refik Halid
Üç Nesil-Üç Hayat

Istanbul – 1999

I was dreaming about a flying balloon. I couldn't make out the colour, but because the sky was charcoal-grey, and the clouds were snow-white, and the sun was bright-yellow, it was definitely a colour other than charcoal-grey, snow-white or bright-yellow. The flying balloon in my dream existed for as long as I could see it, but ceased to exist the moment I couldn't.

The flying balloon rose rhythmically, the snow-white clouds floated coyly by, the charcoal-grey sky darkened little by little, and just as the bright-yellow sun was setting silently and without echo, a violent wind blew up. All at once, we were shaken by the violence of the sudden wind. Lime, tar and clay; sticks and twigs, bugs and dusty earth rained down on us. I had to close both my eyes so that the storm wouldn't take away what I saw. As I shut them, when my eyelashes touched, a noise like the sound of boiling oil coming into contact with water was heard. Air was escaping from the balloon; it was spraying emptiness into the emptiness for each moment it was out of sight. Anxiously, I opened my eyes. I was too late. It didn't exist after all. I existed. I was awake.

B–C was sitting on the edge of the bed, with his eyebrows raised, looking at me angrily.

'Enough already. I've been shaking you for some time now, but I couldn't wake you. You were sleeping so deeply.'

Without giving me a chance to answer, he roughly pulled the blanket off me. With the blanket gone, my body resembled a rowboat that had been stranded, rolled up in its nets, in a sea from which the water had been drained away. I was deprived of the warm darkness of water. I emerged fearfully into the daylight, but not fast enough for B-C. While I slept, I was able to move my limbs this way and that, taking pleasure in the fact that I was hidden from view by the blanket, and now I was trying nervously to compose them. B-C's insistent call was pulling them to him like a magnet.

'Everything is being shaken loose outside, all hell is breaking loose, and her ladyship is still snoring away. Come on, get up. Get up and watch the commotion.'

The terrace door was wide open, and the wind was gently wafting in. As the curtains were being blown here and there with a terrifying effect peculiar to the curtains in haunted houses in films, the sky was visible through the gap between them. A starless, cloudless, moonless night; a pitch-black filter had been placed over our eyes in order that they might not be dazzled.

I stood well away from the window.

I saw what I saw with B-C's eyes.

Well away from the window.

What I saw with B-C's eyes was this:

At the foot of the hilly street…in her fifties…meaty…pale-faced… docile…a woman…a housewife…her night-gown is flannel…her slippers have pom-poms…thrown out in the street…under the street light…watching the flies…swarming around the light… blocking the light…everything lost…at this time of night…her eyes fixed…on the wings of the flies… In her fifties…with fifty tosses of the ball…aching…ready to celebrate her suffering…complaining every step of the way…ready to do a belly dance…married and with a family…mother of three children…breasts like desiccated lemons…her womb dried up early…yet she wouldn't have loved her blood…she would never have imagined…the fact that she had been missed…but accepted quickly…though she was always that way… always sociable…and quiet as a mouse…no one would have made… spinach pastry like she did…she could fit nine dumplings onto a spoon…would have rolled them as thin as a pencil…her grape-leaf *dolma*…her writing was like pearls…when she was in school, that is…everything was fine in those days…like warm milk…life slipped easily down her throat…warming her inside as it did…in those days…everyone around her a propeller…at her orders…her rough husband-to-be…him above all…how he ran after her… 'the rough one doesn't even talk much'…after all these years…without feeling the least bit of shame…without considering his age…you get up and go…such a lovely nest…wife like a rose…the children along with her…sacrifice it all…and for whom…the girl could be his daughter's age…she was a real coquette…when she got tired of him…when she spent his money…out…she would get rid of him…grit your teeth…the male part in any event…later on he'll come to his senses…endure for the sake of your children…besides you weren't the only one…we've all been down that road…it's not as if your late father didn't make his share of mistakes…I didn't say a word all this time…do your duty…cherry sherbet…of course it will pass…it's a passing phase…like everything…this too will pass…of course he'll come back…he'll get on his knees and ask forgiveness…who else but you can make…your spinach pastry…and who can fit…nine dumplings onto a spoon…as if that slut even knew the way to the kitchen…she has other skills…her kind of womanhood is like the flame of a match…it extinguishes as soon as she gets out of bed…in that case you…your womanhood was legendary…too…

Flannel night-gown…slippers with pom-poms…even if she's peevish sometimes…she's forever sweet…like warm milk…as it moves down her throat…softly losing itself…in the moment…a rancid taste…perhaps the milk is spoiled…she spat it out anxiously… that disgusting stickiness…it was the cream on top of the milk…it turned her stomach.

One of the pom-poms…is very loose…like dead skin torn from the lip…it attempted to leave…its own flesh…the bird's home…the place where it belongs…it dangles…it's clear it will come off…it's clear it won't last…but what about the other one…the pom-

pom that's still sound…is it really sound…or is it just pretending to be sound…is it mimicking something it isn't…a truth to be understood…the pom-pom must be pulled forcefully…but if it comes off anyway…even in its sound state…openly…the best thing to do…not to try to do the impossible…but that's curiosity for you…she wants to know…and see…whatever her eyes can see… she takes off her slipper…the one with the sound pom-pom…the flies are far away…like vultures after carrion…like a black cloud devouring the light's flesh…everything is exactly the same…but the woman knows very well…which one she will choose.

'Whore fly! Whore! Whore fly!'

The woman's voice cuts through the air.

Well away from the window.

This is what I saw through B-C's eyes.

Quite late at night, in one of the two sides of Istanbul, in a neighbourhood where morally upright families and freethinking single people frequently lived side-by-side, at the top of a steep hill that was difficult to ascend and descend, a woman, probably in her fifties, the mother of three children, was leaning against the lamp-post, shouting to the flies that she wanted her husband back. Dogs were howling, doors were opening, lights were burning, babies were crying, and the gossip of the next few days was being composed. The neighbours had gathered on the balconies and at the windows; they'd spilled out into the street. Their eyes, shining brightly with the heat of the commotion, were as wide as saucers from surprise. There was enough material to feed the gossip mill of the neighbourhood all winter. Everyone was eagerly taking in as much as they could.

If I said everyone, I meant excluding the inhabitants of the house!

The inhabitants of the house, among them children, sisters, nephews and in-laws, surprised at what had befallen them, ran out barefoot, in pyjamas and night-gowns, with cream on their faces and rollers in their hair, and surrounded the woman, pinching and pulling and begging her, trying to get her inside. 'Let's go home so she can do whatever she wants, cry and shout as much as she wants, let's get her inside so the neighbours won't see her. It doesn't matter if they hear her so long as they don't see her.'

The fear of embarrassment shows on the faces of all the inhabitants of the house except for the youngest in the family. He is a loveable rascal who at the age of five least accepts this commotion as part of his lot. The others wear their fears as if they were on a string, like a bracelet or a necklace. They jump around looking for new fears. The elders are not aware of what the young one is doing, they're too busy trying to get the woman under control but it's not easy, not easy at all.

They can't get this woman who's someone's aunt, someone's sister and someone's mother because she has the strength of a madwoman, they say that a crazy person has the strength of ten people.

They saw that they weren't likely to succeed, they saw that she was completely out of control, so they manhandled her into a taxi. They had their own car, but once again someone had parked on the pavement and blocked their way. Indeed the car that was blocking them was probably owned by one of the people who was watching and it wouldn't have been difficult to find him, but they thought it best not to bother. It was best just to take a taxi as soon as possible to the nearest and farthest hospital.

The taxi driver…a young hunk…newly married…allowed his wife… to work…until they had children…praised for being progressive… but by the time they got married…they were already up to their necks in debt…there are advantages to having your wife work…a man younger than the taxi driver…will take over the taxi later at night…and work until morning…as soon as it's morning he'll turn it back over to his friend…both of them together…work for someone who won the lottery…seeing the man later…a big, strapping man…like a barrel…still dreams that he's poor…gives thanks when he wakes…in a loud voice…still counts his pennies…asks for his penny...in a low voice...so God won't hear...the taxi driver and his friend...whether they earn money or not...always count out the same amount...into their boss's palm...but the taxi driver's friend is not progressive...he won't allow his wife to work...even if he did who would hire someone like her...she's not a lady but a kind of monstrosity...she gave birth to five children one after the other... and all five looked like her...twisted mouths and noses...all of them misshapen ...though our man's wife isn't at all like that...she's slender...thin and fresh...though a bit lacking in height...in spite of that the girl looks like a model, honestly...she's wasting herself working in boutiques...she said so herself...this guy is bothering her...with the excuse of buying sweaters and shirts...he drops by the shop every day... The taxi driver is going to go by tomorrow and put a stop to it...when he thinks of his wife...he sometimes feels the itch...a couple of times he couldn't stand it...he pulled his cab up in front of the house...while the whole neighbourhood laughed up its sleeve...but he doesn't even go much to the district where he lives...he has to work without a break...he does work, for God...to tell the truth he was thinking of having a little adventure tonight with his wife...maybe when he gets rid of these customers...he looks at the passengers in the rear-view mirror... 'What a pity,' he says to himself... 'The poor thing has gone round the bend...it isn't easy with things getting so expensive...prices going up every day.' Indeed it was for this reason alone...that he started working nights...night customers...don't add up what the driver makes... the way day customers do...night customers talk about different things...you'd think...that a person either talks about serious things or about total nonsense...but night customers...are nonsensical when they talk about serious things...and serious when they talk nonsense... 'For instance just the other day...I had a customer just like that...his face misshapen...pickled as a newt...almost dawn... five in the morning...the guy insisted..."Come on...let's find Sultan Mehmet the Conquerer's tomb...let's have a word with him...what the hell did you conquer this city for?...dragging your ships over the hills…so many men martyred…all for this stupid place?" '…he was drunk…he was stubborn…he was determined…the taxi driver didn't say anything of course…but he looked…the drunk had stuck his head out the window…shouting at the top of his voice… 'Mehmet Sultan! Sultan Mehmet!…Where are you?…Get up and look around!…Look what a state they've put your descendants in!'…there was no shutting him up…true Moslems going to pray at that hour…were terrified…looking at the taxi…the taxi driver was bewildered…he couldn't cope with it…so he pulled up in front of a police station…he left the drunk in the hands of the police… later he regretted it…Mehmet the Conqueror's descendant was a good-natured drunk…as they manhandled him into the police station…he turned and asked…'They say he wore an earring. Is that true?'…the taxi driver's curiosity was aroused…he wanted to ask around about Mehmet the Conqueror's earring… 'Get a grip on yourself,' he said to himself…'don't be as crazy as that madman…as if it were possible… The great Mehmet the Conqueror…what's it to you anyway?…as if we didn't have enough troubles…to waste time worrying about Mehmet the Conqueror's earring?'…he heard on the news the other day…that the population of the insane asylums…has risen dramatically…this year… 'It's clear that the woman in the back…has gone out of her mind too…my poor country…we're all going to die mad…or insane!'

While the ones in the back were trying to get the woman under control, the one in the front lit a cigarette with shaking hands, and with a couple of puffs filled the taxi with smoke, the windows were closed tight, they wouldn't open them, but the man was getting his troubles off his chest, 'This is my sister-in-law, my sister-in-law, she left her house and has been staying with us since last summer, insisting she wants to get divorced, she has three children as big as herself…as if at her age it will be easy to be divorced, these women have never provided for a household, they've always been looked after by their husbands, they think it's easy to make it to the end of the month, they'll have nothing to eat or drink when they divorce, I told my wife they deserve whatever befalls them, I couldn't explain it to her, anyway that's what happened, day and night they talk and talk, my sister-in-law cries, my wife cries, my sister-in-law cries, how many times have I told her, don't do that…you're not helping, look, your sister is getting worse, talk to her about something else, why don't you go out to the spa, you can bring your mother, it will do the poor woman's rheumatism good, whatever I said I couldn't get her to listen, day and night the house is full of women and girls, talking away, these women have more relatives than you can count, turning it around, bringing up the same subject again and again, no one could convince her, she insisted on getting a divorce, in the end she went to a lawyer, this morning a paper came from the court, good I said let's celebrate, she looked at me as if I'd crawled out from under a rock, my God I understood then the woman was going mad, but if I told my wife she wouldn't have believed me, her older sister can do no wrong, I said I hope nothing goes wrong tomorrow, I saw that my sister-in-law had calmed down, after dinner she washed the dishes and went off to her room, her favourite television show was on, she never missed it, she didn't even glance at it, she drank glass after glass of warm milk for her upset stomach and went to bed early, anyway she hasn't dreamt at all since she was a girl, she used to fall asleep the moment her head hit the pillow at our house too, she always got up earlier than anyone, she prepared a flawless breakfast, eggs with yolks like apricots, I mean even tea tasted better when she made it, she did it perfectly, no one could do things in the kitchen the way she did, my wife never had anything resembling that kind of proficiency, she doesn't take after her older sister at all, but what good is proficiency to someone so unlucky, of course my brother-in-law is very much in the wrong, you don't do something like that after so many years, honestly I'm embarrassed to talk about it, a girl her age, he set her up in a fully furnished house, the girl was a dancer in a sleazy night-club, her name is Sinem, he introduced her to us last year, she's just a little slip of a thing, I didn't say anything because I thought it was just a fling and it would pass, how could I have known then that it would become so complicated, that it would go as far as divorce, when the television show was over we went to bed, I didn't know my sister-in-law wasn't asleep, that she was waiting for us to go to bed, the moment we were in our bed she jumped out of hers, threw on her night-gown, put on the slippers with the pom-poms, opened the door and went out into the street, a passer-by might have thought she was a slave in our house, we were woken by the commotion, we looked out and saw her in the middle of the street shouting at the top of her voice, and as if that wasn't enough she was doing a belly dance at one point, we didn't know what the hell was going on, what had happened to her, just drop us off at the nearest hospital, how humiliating this is for us, in all that panic we didn't even bring any money with us, I'm sorry about that brother, with everything happening at once, all of us tumbling out in our pyjamas, I didn't bring my wallet, they'd driven me out of my wits, I'm going to get a divorce too, let her keep her crazy sister and her rheumatic mother, let them do whatever they want from now on, my life is finished, these women have squeezed the life out of me drop by drop.'

'Don't worry about the money, brother, no one is going anywhere! After all, we all live in the same neighbourhood,' said the taxi driver.

Colours are fa-ding, movements are slow-ing. The man is chewing something. The words tumble out of his mouth: 'You're always in this neighbourhood, but, after this humiliation are we going to be able to continue living here?'

He takes a cigarette pack from his pyjama pocket. He suddenly feels guilty. He wants to tell the taxi driver why it is that he brought cigarettes but not his wallet. He can't speak, his throat is completely dry. He can't find the lighter in his pocket. He must have dropped it in the taxi. Or else…he hadn't had it with him from the start. He simply can't remember how he lit his last cigarette. Or is this his first cigarette? This distresses him even more. While he's waiting for the car's cigarette lighter to pop out, he glances towards the back seat. His sister-in-law isn't shouting any more; she's just breathing heavily. Also, from time to time she moans as if she's in pain. Without taking his eyes from the rear-view mirror, the taxi driver lights a cigarette from his own pack. He considers turning on the radio. He changes his mind, it would be inappropriate. The women are embracing their sister and crying silently. Little by little the night is becoming dark-er; step by step the road is getting steep-er. His chest has congested. He opens the window all the way. It's cold enough out for snow. The cigarette smoke that has built up in the taxi pours out of the window like an ash-coloured kite swinging its tail back and forth.

Sounds are fading, the wind is dying down.

Sounds faded, the wind died down. As they were being closed, the curtains were blown here and there with a terrifying effect peculiar to the curtains in haunted houses in films, 'They're going to have to move at first light tomorrow. They're not going to be able to bear it here,' said B-C. He added with a twisted smile:

'When your privacy is gone, you should leave at once!'

The Gaze

'I was dreaming about a flying balloon. It was in the charcoal-grey sky, among the snow-white clouds, in the shade of the bright-yellow sun. I'd climbed up onto the roof. I'd been watching the flying balloon from below, when a violent wind suddenly blew up. All at once, we were shaken by the violence of this sudden wind. Pitch-black dust swirled up from the ground. The flying balloon was being swept away. I was running as fast as I could over the rooftops to keep it in sight. As I ran, roof-tiles were rolling down. I leaned over to look at where the tiles had fallen. Below, the avenues of the city were sparkling and crowded. Cars had crashed because of the tiles rolling along the road. A bright red, squeaky-clean car was swerving angrily down the middle of the road. The tiles had cracked its windshield. A huge spider had woven a web over the crack. The thin, transparent threads stuck to the glass were waving about here and there. The driver was looking for me, without knowing it was me he was looking for. He could see me, but he didn't suspect me.

White snow was falling on the pitch-black dust. I started walking along the pavement. I walked very slowly in order to avoid stepping on the little threads. Suddenly, my eyes fixed on my feet. I was wearing woollen baby shoes with a bird design on them. I must have forgotten to put on my shoes when I left the house. I was embarrassed. I had to find shoes somewhere before anyone saw me. The window displays in the shops were lively. There were ballet slippers, shoes lined with fur, sandals, laced boots, high-heeled women's shoes, round-heeled men's shoes, gaudy children's shoes.

The labels described what they were. All of the shoes were made of ice-cream. I went into one of the bigger shops and bought mixed fruit flavoured shoes. When I came out, the driver of the car with the cracked windshield had narrowed his eyes, and was watching me carefully. I tiptoed in front of him. He didn't follow me. As I returned to the pavement, I saw the flying balloon in the shade of the bright-yellow sun. It moved along half-heartedly. The bright-yellow sun came out. I looked at my new shoes with alarm. Drop drop, drop drop…'

'Come on mother, say something to her!'

I jumped because of the pain in my knee. Again I'd fallen asleep, in a place where I shouldn't have. I was sweating. As I tried to pull myself together, the smell of my sweat reached my nose. I looked around to see if anyone else could smell it. I was in the minibus. When I got on there was no one else but me. At this hour of the afternoon, it was rare for anyone to be going in that direction, and I knew it wouldn't fill up easily, and that it wouldn't leave until it was full. That's why I was comfortable enough to fall asleep. It wasn't enough that I'd overdone it at lunch, I'd had two portions of pudding on top of everything else, and I didn't have enough strength left to walk. I must have slept for quite a while. When I woke, the minibus was completely full. There was only room for one more passenger. When that person came, we'd get under way.

The woman next to me was watching me out of the corner of her eye. She probably noticed the smell of sweat. The girl on her knee kept kicking my knee with the brass buckle of her strawberry coloured shoes. I have no doubt that the child is doing this on purpose. She's doing it just to wake me up and get me to slide over a bit. And she is the one who keeps whining, 'Come on mother, say something to her.' And I had sprawled out in my sleep too. I had to pull myself together right away. I close my legs and slide over toward the window. I take my backpack from the seat and put it on my lap. When I lift the backpack I see a paper bag full of spiced, yellow roasted chickpeas. I'd bought them to nibble on while waiting for the minibus to fill up, and had forgotten them. When I pick up the paper bag, there's quite a bit of room for the others. But they're still not happy. Especially the woman, who makes exaggerated movements to show that she's not going to be able to get comfortable; she keeps crossing and re-crossing her legs; makes rustling noises as she rearranges her packages, first on her lap then under the seat. She squeezes the child on her lap to her breast, saying, 'Come, darling,' as if there was anywhere the child could go. She keeps turning and eyeing the last narrow empty seat with worry, and as she does all this she keeps huffing and puffing in complaint. I know this type well. I know why they behave the way they do. I'm used to it. These kinds of things happen to me all the time.

Of course the best thing for me is to take a taxi, or to catch an empty bus. But going everywhere by taxi reduces my budget, and, as you know, it's not really possible to find an empty bus. Usually I take a taxi to the first stop for the bus I'm taking. But this isn't convenient for all routes. If the bus is crowded, I rarely get on. And whenever I climb up those stairs and push and shove my way down the corridor to find a place for myself, I regret it a thousand times. A voice within me tells me to get off the bus immediately and go home. As if that were possible. The force of the crowds moving back at the driver's ill-tempered commands pushes me further from the exit. I see that there's no escape, and try at least not to make eye-contact with any of the eyes that examine me with curiosity, and point me out to one another. To tell the truth, a lot of people offer me their places. But this doesn't make things easier for me. Every time, my face gets flushed with heat. I sweat as I struggle into the empty seat. Naturally I always sweat at times like this. Whether it's summer or winter, the moment I even get a little distressed, ice-cold sweat begins to pour off my back. As soon as I've sat down, I sit as straight as a ramrod, so as not to touch the person next to me if I'm in a double seat, or the people standing nearby if I'm in a single seat. At the same time, I try to ascertain whether or not the people around me can smell my sweat. Though there's nothing I can do about it either way. Anyway, I always sweat more when I try not to sweat. I like sitting next to the window. Next to the window, I'm less aware of the other passengers, and can spend the trip watching people outside.

Sometimes no one offers me their seat. Sometimes it's impossible to get near the windows either. Then, in order to escape the stares of the people surrounding me, in order not to guess what is on the minds of the people who are looking at me, I look for a spot that I can stare at vacantly until I reach my stop. As much as I can see through the window between their heads, the passengers' shoes, shopping bags squeezed between legs, the covers of the books in someone's hand, the bus's warning signs, the buttons on the automatic doors, the levers to be pulled in case of emergency, folded newspapers, rings on hands grasping the straps...these are my choices. I'll pick one of these, and won't take my eyes off it until I reach my stop. Whether I sit or stand, it's very difficult for me to take a bus from one place to another. But if you're as fat as I am, minibuses are even worse than buses.

The child next to me is squeezing the money she wants to pass forward tightly in her palm; despite her mother's insistence she's determined to give it to the driver. This child, one of those children whose bedroom was flawlessly prepared when her birth was still just a distant possibility, who was born late and with difficulty, who was prayed for, who wore out the doors of fashionable clinics, the instructions of famous doctors being carried out to the letter, the subject of many tests, expensive treatments, boring arguments, on the threshold of divorce, 'otherwise we'll produce a child', after their consolation, they succeeded only a moment before they lost hope, even a blood clot was considered cause for celebration, her mother didn't take her eyes off her for a moment, more toys than she could have imagined, tens of photographs taken of her every moment, her every smile inspiring epic poems, her every remark recorded in notebooks, her photographs in every family album, decorating frames and wallets, constantly praised, constantly spoiled, never left alone, never lonely. To me this is an ugly child. On top of this her eyes bulge. She's wearing glasses like the bottoms of jars, the kind that make a person's eyes look three times bigger. The child keeps turning and looking at me. Both of us wearing sour expressions; examining each other as if we could turn to vinegar at any moment. In any event, the chirping voice of the schoolgirl reaches us.

'Ah, don't say that. I'm sure she's a well-behaved child,' she says. Then, as if she's laughing to herself, she adds: 'I wish I knew this beautiful girl's name. Go on, tell me, what's your name?'

The bug-eyed child forgot me right away. She turned and concentrated on listening to the schoolgirl. Now, with her lips tight and her eyebrows raised to give her an even more sour expression, she stubbornly refuses to give her name. The child's unexpected resistance goads the schoolgirl into action. She has to find a way to make her talk.

'All right then, let me ask something else. Come on, tell me, do you know how to count?'

The bug-eyed child nodded her head emphatically. But she still doesn't open her mouth.

'No, nooo!' says the schoolgirl. 'If you knew you'd have counted aloud. You're such a big girl and you still don't know how to count. What a shame!'

There's a sudden silence in the minibus. All of us passengers are captivated by the schoolgirl's insistence. The housewives in the back stop their gossip, the irritable estate agent stops making calls; the driver closes the window and turns off the radio; sounds from outside are muffled, and even the rain falls more quietly.

'Yes!' chimes the child's voice. 'I know!'

'No! You don't know.'

'I do too know, I do too know.'

The bug-eyed child starts stamping her feet. As she stamps her feet, her pudding-white socks, the teddy-bear ribbons in her hair, her thick strawberry-jam coloured shoes, and her skinny legs, covered with new and old wounds from unhealed mosquito bites, swing back and forth before my eyes.

'She knows, she knows,' says the driver, who'd been watching through the rear-view mirror.

'If that's so, let's hear her count,' says the schoolgirl archly.

As is my habit when travelling on buses, I begin looking for something I can stare at vacantly for the rest of this difficult trip. I don't know how I didn't notice it before. Hanging from the rear-view mirror, there's a toy doll wearing only a tasselled skirt and a straw hat, with silky blond hair down to her toes, trying to cover her full breasts with one hand and holding a basket of fruit in the other. When the driver hits the brakes, a light flashes on and off in the doll's left eye. At the same moment, the bug-eyed child begins to count.

'One. Two, three…'

Then suddenly she falls quiet. All of us hold 'four' on the tips of our tongues. The driver and the young man sitting in the single seat next to him, me, the child's mother and the schoolgirl, the housewives in the back and the ill-tempered estate agent, all of us wait with tense smiles. Even the man in the very back corner next to the window, exuding the smells of flowers and perfume, has formed his lips as if he's about to say 'four', and has stayed that way. As if by doing that, the numbers would follow by chance, and he would get to his important appointment more quickly. A while later, the ugly, bug-eyed child, casting a coy glance around, certain now that she has the attention of everyone on the minibus, leans delightedly against her mother and continues counting.

'One, twoo, threee, one, twoo, three, one, two, three…'

My brain is throbbing. The numbers demons, with lamps on their waists and brooms in their hands, their tongues cut off and their eyes poked out with hot irons, banging on the door as they jump up and down tak tak donk donk there's no one here, they don't hear my voice. Hunched over, I look out the window, dreaming that I don't see what I see. Meanwhile, the child is counting faster, losing her shyness and becoming more bold. She's enjoying holding everyone captive.

'onetwothreeonetwothreeonetwothreeonetwothree'

I want to get off. To get off and catch another minibus. No, another minibus won't do. A bus won't do either, or a taxi. I can't tolerate any of them now. No matter how much my body objects, it's surely best to proceed on foot. And before I start walking I can stand and have a bite to eat. A nice sausage sandwich with ketchup and potato salad would be good for my nerves. Perhaps a lemonade to go with it. I could escape this minibus at a convenient spot. It's still not too late to get off. But then the man will get confused. The person who paid two fares for one and a half places will become the person who paid two fares for nothing. On top of that, if I get off the minibus, the mother will definitely move her ugly, bug-eyed child to my place. I change my mind.

I'm hungry. But traffic is heavy, the rain is falling faster, and there's a long way to go. I'm hungry. But the child is ugly, and bug-eyed, and the numbers are awful. I am hungry. But I shouldn't overreact. This trip will last long enough to count to three; just from one to three.

'One, twooo, three, one, twoo, three, one, two, three, onetwothree, onetwothreeonetwothree...'

ONE
'CLOSE YOUR EYES!'

Pera – 1885

After the evening call to prayer, the westward-facing door of the cherry-coloured tent at the top of the hill would open for the women.

Indeed that was when threes and fives and tens of women would start entering the westward-facing door of the cherry-coloured tent at the top of the hill. Bringing their noisy commotion with them. Part of the huge tent had been assigned to the women. Carrying swollen bundles and with their fussing children beside them, they crossed the threshold pushing one another and grasping their long woollen coats. Hundreds of women of every temperament and nature would come here. It didn't matter what nationality they were, what language they spoke or what religion they professed. It was enough that they were women; and, also, that they came together. This was the condition that Keramet Mumî Keşke Memiş Efendi had placed: No woman was to arrive at the tent alone.

Keramet Mumî Keşke Memiş Efendi knew that the westward-facing door of the cherry-coloured tent was open to the bright side of the moon.

And he would tell this strange story about her. What the bright side of the moon feared most was not being loved, and also being alone when she wept. She combed her hair with a silver comb. The inlaid teeth of the comb collected the shiny strands of her hair with great care. Later she would secretly leave every single strand on another person's shoulder. She believed that she would be unforgettable in the eyes of whomever the hair was with. She was not far wrong either; those who carried the strands of her hair, not understanding at all why their hearts were so distressed, would stare absentmindedly at the dome of the sky, unaware that their worries and their pupils were growing together. They felt deeply that what they sought was there, but they couldn't translate their feelings. Indeed some of them found themselves so caught up in the celestial passion within them that they could no longer eat or drink. Fortunately, the bright side of the moon soon tired of her playmates. She would erase new relationships in two breaths, swallow all affection in a single gulp, devastate every friendship she formed. No one was strange enough, no story was sufficiently poetic. Yet she still couldn't give up on people. Because she was afraid, so afraid, of being alone, and of crying by herself.

Once, leaning into a well and looking at herself in the water in a copper bucket, she said, with deep admiration, 'How beautiful I am. In that case, why am I unable to be as happy as an ugly person?' The well grumbled, the water became cloudy. 'How radiant I am,' she said abstractedly. 'In that case, why can't I be free of the darkness in my heart?' The copper bucket cracked, and water trickled out of each of the separate cracks.

Since that day, the bright side of the moon has avoided wells. When unanswerable questions come to mind, she powders herself with the silver powder compact that she is never without. She always wanted to be unique, peerless and unrivalled. She could not stand a female who shone more than she did, if one day she should meet someone like this, there is nothing she wouldn't do to get rid of her.

Keramet Mumî Keşke Memiş Efendi didn't tell this story without reason. Because he knew well that women were each other's enemies above all. Whenever women came together in the same place, they'd first start examining each other from head to toe, trying to discover each other's troubles, then move on to asking after each other's health. As the conversation deepened, wherever there was a rip or a stain, a dark room or a garbage heap, they'd discover them one by one and file them away secretly. Their friendships were like sleeping cats, keeping one eye on each other, and pricking up their ears at the slightest sound. The mortar that held their friendships together became diluted by suspicion covered with egg white. Even the soundest of friendships was shaken by the first pang of apprehension. However, the silver comb was useless without a silver mirror. As Keramet Mumî Keşke Memiş Efendi knew, the women became uglier in each other's reflections. This is why they were not to turn their backs on each other, but had to arrive side-by-side, arm in arm. Climbing up the hill together, they had to be as crowded as a cherry tree as they entered the westward-facing door.

Some of the women were accustomed to being together. Most of them enjoyed socialising, or wished to appear as if they did. They'd climb the hill laughing and joking. They'd start up the hill together in a crowd, and the same crowd would arrive at the entrance to the tent. And some, knowing well that in the end they would all have to come together, preferred to climb all by themselves until the last step. Most of them were reserved by nature, or wished to appear as if they were. The fountain on the hill was a turning point for them. When they arrived at the fountain, they had no choice but to come together. The fountain put on airs; it sprayed out water with enthusiasm. The women wet their mouths, foreheads and necks with the ice-cold water. Those who had come that far by themselves would come together in small groups, and would enter into complaisant and unavoidable friendships as they continued on their way. The rest of the way up the hill would be spent getting to know each other. From then on they couldn't be separated from each other; from then on strangers became friends, and friends became travelling companions. With each step they became more cheerful and open. As they walked arm-in-arm some of them even began to lose their fear. For Keramet Mumî Keşke Memiş Efendi's orders were strict; even if she was fear itself, no female should be excluded from the crowd of women entering the tent. For this reason, after the evening call to prayer, carrying swollen bundles and with their fussing children beside them, they crossed the threshold of the westward-facing door of the cherry-coloured tent pushing one another and grasping their long woollen coats.

Most went on foot. Because those who insisted on going by carriage could be the victims of mysterious accidents. Sometimes nothing went wrong; even if the horses were sweating profusely, they went straight up the hill and succeeded in making it to the top. Sometimes the carriages would overturn for no reason. Sometimes they would slip on the ice, sending the passengers rolling back down at great speed. When these incidents were spoken of, it was with much exaggeration, and the addition of a sprinkling of mystery. When this was the case, the women who were accustomed to detecting the warning of a disaster usually caused by carelessness, preferred to leave their carriages at the foot of the hill and climb on foot, for there was no need to anger the saints buried on the hill. From time to time, there were also some groups who arrived on litters. These, pale complexioned women from elite families, would climb the hill with dignified expressions on the shoulders of their strong powerful servants. But as is the way of the world, these too overturned from time to time.

Those who turned and looked back when they reached the top of the hill could see the sea. The sea was blue, bluer than blue; it was hostage to its own clear stillness. Once in a while some women got a crazy idea. The sea was a breast, gently swollen, aching, calling softly from afar for a mouth for its milk. Now…without regret for the past or concern for the future; as if…just by relaxing, opening their mouths and closing their eyes, it would be possible to be filled with time by sucking deeply on the present moment. In any event, their responsibilities were ready and waiting to be wrapped up. The loose string would quickly be re-wound. Children would take care of their mothers, mothers-in-law would take care of their daughters-in-law, and friends would take care of each other; those who were still captivated by the sea would be reminded that they had to reach the cherry-coloured tent before it grew dark. It worked. Once those who were lost in empty dreams were reminded of who they were, they would come on their own. In any event, as Keramet Mumî Keşke Memiş Efendi often said: if the ship of womanhood were to sink, it would not be from a slow leak in the cargo hold of womanly duty motherly responsibility, but from a resounding and heavy rain of cannon balls of dreams. Women were susceptible to the lure of dreams.

Even though in time this area came to be called a swamp, no one who had ever smelled the heady fragrance of the fig and lemon trees, or seen their delicate purple buds would want to believe it. Here, sparrows would chirp merrily, peacocks would strut around showing off, and nightingales would compose melodies to roses of unsurpassed beauty. For all of the women, if the area surrounding the cherry-coloured tent was a part of heaven, then that steep hill was the bridge which the righteous will pass over and from which the unrighteous will fall on the Day Of Judgement. But no one bothered their heads much about this question. It wasn't the outside of the tent that was important, it was the inside. And if anyone knew the truth of the matter, it would be Keramet Mumî Keşke Memiş Efendi.

Here, it was possible to meet women of every temperament and nature. Matchmakers eagerly cast their eyes about for marriageable girls, irritable old women who constantly moved their lips as they cursed everything, cunning and foul-mouthed cloth peddlers looking for customers to corner, widows wrapped from head to toe in grief, cheap sluts who had aged before their time, greying whores who looked older than they were, fresh young girls whose pink complexions showed that they'd spent the whole day at the baths, professional midwives who knew at a glance what cure was needed for anyone's troubles, swan-necked dancing girls who never danced, never even smiled without hearing the sound of money, poor Jewish women from the miserable shacks of Balat, Gypsy women who carried their babies on their backs and their secrets in their bosoms, spoiled, pink-skinned Circassion girls, Arab women with mascara and jet-black hair, brides-to-be who tied silk handkerchiefs to the branches of the trees around the tent, rich Armenian women with palanquins inlaid with mother-of-pearl, Persian women who smelled of hot spices, French governesses who taught etiquette to the children of elite families, multi-talented concubines who were raised to be given as gifts to the palace, pregnant women with swollen bellies, Italian actresses who couldn't share with their troupes, deeply religious grandmothers who were forcibly dragged here by their grandchildren and the grumbling of their daughters-in-law, ladies who were the toast of Pera society, house-proud Greeks from Tatavla, Russian women of slight and graceful build and languorous looks, successful English dance teachers, usurer's wives who had new clothes made each time their husbands made a killing, self-sacrificing nurses from the hospitals of Beyoglu and so many others…young, old, children, everyone imaginable was here.

There was one only reason these varied women, who did not mention each other in their prayers and who did not let each other exist in their dreams, struggled up the hill to meet at the westward-facing gate of the cherry-coloured tent: in order to see the ugliest of the ugly, that wretched, plagued creature, the Sable-Girl!

Keramet Mumî Keşke Memiş Efendi was responsible for all of it. Indeed no one but him would ever have thought of all these things. Keramet Mumî Keşke Memiş Efendi was a clever and agile man. His strangeness was apparent from birth.

Keramet Mumî Keşke Memiş Efendi came to this realm in the following manner:

His mother, whose life would not have been fulfilled if she had died before giving birth to a son, and who had poured the blood of sacrificial victims onto the earth in the hope of this good fortune, who had even sought the help of a sorceress in order not to leave any spell untried, who had given birth to six girls one after another, and after so many miscarriages, finally, having learned this in a dream one night from a hairless, beardless dervish, tied locks of her hair to the thin branches of the blackberry trees in the garden and arranged candles in concentric circles, and her husband, who she'd pleaded with, shaking with embarrassment at having to undress in the innermost circle, not saying it was not because of the cold but because 'the neighbours will see and we'll never live it down,' was made to believe her, and not change his mind. Towards dawn that night she became pregnant with Memiş. After nine months and ten days of not lifting a finger about the house, on a violently windy autumn evening, the poor woman gave birth to Memiş with a stillness and patience that amazed the midwife.

Although in truth the name was not given to her in the dervish dream, she was absolutely certain that Memiş was the most appropriate name for such a generous-hearted person. Living up to his name, Memiş wouldn't even hurt a fly. Indeed, as a baby Memiş didn't even utter a sound of complaint to his mother. Unlike his elder sisters, throughout the pregnancy he did not cause his mother to drown from her tears, to cook unmentionable foods, or to have awful nightmares. Even stranger was the fact that the birth was painless. He wasn't born but rather slid out; he didn't slide out but virtually flowed out. He flowed from one shell to another without panic or hope. As if all he wanted was to establish himself here without bothering anyone, he slid himself into the midwife's hands without causing any trouble or inconvenience. After six girls in a row, the first boy child!

The poor woman was so certain that this time her child would be a boy, she didn't even feel the need to ask the child's sex when it was born. Burying her head in the pillow, she drew in the dense smell of the room. The room had a smell that she wasn't used to: it smelled as if, somewhere nearby, they were using the smoke from different kinds of tree barks in order to get rid of termites. 'Strange thing,' she thought to herself. She had to tell them that there were no termites in that room. 'When I wake,' she said to herself, 'When I wake I'll tell them.' After a last smile of delight, she closed her eyes and never opened them again.

Because the midwife couldn't take her eyes off the baby, it was some time before she noticed that the mother had left them. There was something unsettling about this tiny, tiny boy, but she couldn't quite understand what it was. Thank God, there was nothing wrong with his body; he did not start to cry, but it was possible to take care of that with a little slap. There was something else about this baby; some…thing…else…a little later one of the neighbour women came in and handed the midwife a bowl full of the blood of a ram that had been sacrificed. Just as the midwife was about to dip her finger into the blood and dab his forehead, she started to chuckle. Finally she realised the cause of her uneasiness: it was the baby's face.

The baby Memiş's face was virtually transparent. His mouth-nose-eyebrows-eyes were both complete and incomplete. His mouth-nose-eyebrows-eyes hadn't come in person, but had sent their shadows instead. The midwife's anxiety transmitted itself to the others in the room, and now everyone leaned over and carefully examined the face of this baby who didn't cry or move and who seemed to greet the world with an indifferent smile. All of those who were examining this face that had just come into existence found nothing extraordinary about its features, but at the same time couldn't take their eyes off of these extraordinary features. As if every feature of this baby's face had been scattered randomly, but there was still a hidden order in this randomness. Because of the state it was in, they couldn't quite understand what the face resembled, or decide whether it was ugly or beautiful. The blessed baby's face confused them so much that, except for the midwife who didn't like the gloominess one bit and stood up all of a sudden, no one could leave the cradle's side.

Confronted with the boy in the cradle and the dead woman in the bed, the midwife asked God for strength and said to herself: 'There's surely a miracle here!' In this way, Keramet was added to the baby Memiş's name.

If it were up to the midwife, there wouldn't have been reason to delve into the matter too much. Indeed if there was a miracle involved, there was no point in worrying to such a degree. But the baby's aunt was a bold and fearless woman; very intelligent, and stalwart too. That day she sensed immediately that things were going wrong, but because she didn't want to go out of her room unless the house was deserted, she sat in her room for hours, reading the Koran and waiting for a sign. Then, when at last things became quiet, she took the baby into her lap, and looked it over carefully. She agreed with the others about baby Keramet Memiş having flowed out rather than being born. But the way he flowed didn't quite resemble the flowing of nocturnal rivers vengefully scooping out their beds, or of wild waterfalls cascading loudly, or of endless seas agitating sadly, shabby, heavy rains pouring down indifferently or of melting snow in the first warmth of the beginning of spring. It would be more accurate to say that he dripped rather than flowed.

Moreover, there was a difference between dripping and dripping. Water drips too, and blood; oil drips, and time; and tears also drip, for instance. But each one drips differently. Some of them could become steam and dry themselves with the desire to rise into the sky, some of them stayed in the place they'd landed, some of them could come to the top of whatever hollow they had been put into and show off, some of them could depart from their eternity and arrive at endlessness; some of them could leave behind deposits of anguish on the paths they'd travelled. When it came to the baby Keramet Memiş, his dripping didn't resemble any of these. He looked as if he would stay where he had dripped, in the state in which he had dripped; that is, he was more like a drop of wax rather than of water or blood, oil or time, or even tear drops.

For a long time, the aunt smelled this baby that still didn't cry, or move, but simply remained where he was, and how he was. And when she determined that the smell wafting from the baby was definitely that of wax, she became frightened. Because a drop of wax stays where it flows and hardens where it stays as soon as it is far from the source of heat. Because the wax cannot become liquid unless it can return to the bosom of heat from which it came. But the warm womb that had brought the baby Keramet Memiş into the world had long since begun to grow cold. Soon, as the source of light that was his mother's body became as cold as ice, the liquid would solidify and then become rigid. And once something had hardened, it was impossible for it to take shape. So the baby's face needed to be shaped. It was as if a curtain of wax, half transparent and half mysterious, had been pulled between the baby Keramet Memiş's face and humanity. At that moment the poor woman realised that she had to pull herself together and do something.

Since this strange baby had dripped into this world instead of being born, from moment to moment he was hardening just like a drop of wax where he fell and in the state in which he fell; and since he was completely deprived of the source of heat that would warm and soothe him, and by soothing melt him, if she didn't intervene at that moment, the baby's face would freeze in its transparent immobility. If she hadn't appreciated this and taken it into hand quickly, Keramet Memiş wouldn't have had a face for the rest of his life.

Immediately, the aunt took a piece of hazelnut shell and burned it in the fire. Later, she began to shape the baby's face even as it began to harden. With the black of the hazelnut shell, she drew the eyes and mouth, the eyebrows and eyelashes, the chin and forehead and the cheeks and temples. When it came time for the eyes, the dead woman in the bed was about to freeze and the wax-drop baby was just on the point of hardening completely. From that moment on, it very definitely wouldn't take shape, or come to life. Indeed time was so short that, with her hands tangled up by panic, she could only draw two thin slits for eyes. There was no more time for the eyes.

That day, the baby was not only left with the face his aunt drew with the hazelnut shell, he was also left with a name: 'Mumî!'

After that they showed Keramet Mumî Memiş to his father. The poor man was so very delighted that he finally had a son after all these years he swore to feed all the poor of seven neighbourhoods and to bring anyone who hadn't been washed since birth to the baths for a good cleaning, But before he had finished saying this, a lump formed in his throat. He sensed some kind of misfortune. With the terror of a sparrow whose wing has been caught by a cat, he ran with his heart in his throat to the room where his wife slept. He couldn't find the courage to open his eyes. Feeling his way in the darkness, he found the now completely ice cold body. He buried his nose in his wife's hair, which as always smelled of walnuts and cinnamon and the north-west wind. But it was as if another smell had been added to these. As if... the smell of wax was hanging in the air.

He laid the baby Keramet Mumî Memiş next to his mother. As he left the room he didn't even turn and look once; either at the mother nor at the baby. In his mind he had buried the two of them together, side-by-side. As the door closed, he murmured something, perhaps a farewell.

'If only!' he said, 'If only she'd lived, if only she'd given birth to a girl again.'

So that's how Keramet Mumî Keşke Memiş came into this world. The rest was left to time. Later on, when his form had grown, Efendi was also added to these famous names.

Keramet Mumî Keşke Memiş Efendi was very clever and agile. Every night he wrestled with a different group of demons. He climbed mountains no one else had the courage to climb, he was quick to develop a thesis in his mind, but once he had developed it he grew bored with it. If he wanted, he could squeeze blood out of a stone, or imprison the wheel of fortune within itself. Then leaving the poor wheel of fortune as it is, he would be seized by lust in sinful hidden places. Everybody knew that he regularly visited houses of ill repute. According to rumour, he loved listening to the stories of the regulars and the working women; he distributed gold in exchange for the stories he heard and for the pleasure he had received.

From time to time he also went out hunting. The aim of hunting was not to gallop across the meadows with a bow in his hand, it was to spend the whole day painstakingly and delicately laying the completely undetectable traps he'd spent such tremendous effort preparing; but at the end of the day, because he hadn't the motivation to return to collect whatever had fallen into his traps, he always returned from the hunt empty-handed. He'd long since been as rich as Croesus and as wise as Solomon. Nevertheless, if it crossed his mind, he'd give everything he had at hand to charity, and be left without a penny. Later, he'd straighten things out again. If he wanted, he could sell a crow as a nightingale, or an old horse as a donkey, could even fool the devil himself and gather seven neighbourhoods for his show. He also loved to surprise people, but grew cold toward them when they were surprised by the unsurprising. However, it wasn't Keramet Mumî Keşke Memiş Efendi's intelligence or proficiency that people found odd, it was his eyes.

His eyes were already like that when he was a child. They were always like that.

His eyes didn't give away what he felt. Perhaps he didn't feel anything.

His childhood passed like this. On one side there were his elder sisters. The sisters who found new games every day simply so he wouldn't get bored, who lit rows of oil lamps day and night, winter and summer in every corner of the wooden house to replace the warmth of his departed mother, who gathered in his room and set up a shadow play for him that would last until morning, on the evenings when the child was being punished, who went from door to door in every corner of the city in order to collect the best tales, not hesitating to give away their favourite parts of their trousseaus; who would get sick with envy if one of the others told him a tale that had never been heard or told before, who continued to love their youngest brother above all else even after they'd married and started families, despite their husband's beatings and their children's reproaches.

On the other side there was his father. The father who, once night fell, didn't hide the fact that he didn't like to see his son; who until his last breath slept in the bed in which his wife had died, and never touched another woman; who some nights would wake up suddenly and smash all the oil lamps in the house to pieces; who forever opposed the affection the girls showed this little boy; who would fly into abrupt rages, and take out his cherry-wood stick; who would ask after his son as soon as he came to his senses the next day; who would feel pangs of regret and beg forgiveness when he saw his son's bruised and purple flesh; but who before a few days had passed would fly into a worse rage, and give him an even worse beating; who drank constantly, and swore constantly; who was not good at anything…

So he spent his childhood lurching between these opposites. On the one side his sisters' undying affection, and on the other his father's passing rages. Indeed Keramet Mumî Keşke Memiş Efendi's strangeness was already apparent then. But whether he was treated with respect and deference or whether he was put down and treated with contempt; whether he was fed more than he could eat or whether he was taught a lesson with dry bread and water, whether he was loved or whether he was beaten, it had no effect on his expression. Not once did his eyes ever give away what he felt. It was as if those two narrow, slanting slits of eyes were devoid of any emotion. He was like that as a child and he's still like that today. Even when he married, and saw his fate before him, his eyes, as always, were as mute as ever.

Then, there was a difficult turning point. On his wedding night, he broke the mirror that reflected him. And he looked at himself harder and longer than he'd ever looked before.

It was like a shaman's patched and threadbare cloak
Reflected in the broken pieces of mirror
Ready to unravel, it was like a piece of unravelled thread
Scattered randomly,
There was order in its randomness.

Time was without end, space was without limit
So why did it end up squeezed into this form?
He took the scissors and
Cut up the story on which the name had been stamped;
Scattering the pieces through time and space

In another time
Either much later or very soon
And in another place
Very far away but also just here
On the point of returning to the world
It had immediately to cease existing.

~

He was here but didn't want to exist, and when he saw that he was trapped here in this form, even though he didn't want to exist, his days became difficult. He was torn apart like a mad laugh. But he lived. And much later, early one morning he went out into the streets again. Not as before though, there was something altered about his going out into the street. He looked at his surroundings. Not as always though, there was something different about the way he looked at his surroundings. His pupils were pincushions. They were covered with holes made by evil eyes and evil words pinched into their halo. Water leaked from some of these holes. This was how he wept.

It had been so long since he'd walked that he could neither keep his legs from trembling at each step nor determine where he was going. It was as if every direction was the same, as if every passageway led to the same dead end, and every street looked exactly like the other. Life was as he'd left it; it was aware neither of how long Keramet Mumî Keşke Memiş Efendi had been absent nor of the crisis he had passed through.

A woman was passing along the street; young and healthy, and a bit flighty. Keramet Mumî Keşke Memiş Efendi planted himself in front of the woman like a thief blocking the way to the fountain.

'Where are you going like this?'

'Home,' said the woman. Gesturing with her hand as if she lived just over there. Keramet Mumî Keşke Memiş Efendi drew himself up very close to the woman. He felt an urge to see the woman's lips, and to kiss them, but before he'd even finished thinking this, he tasted a sweetness in his mouth.

'The walnut man,' explained the woman. 'I made walnut *baklava*. The sugar stuck to me. I've become like *baklava*, sticky and sweet. Soon I'll be as wrinkled as pudding. I didn't want to end up like this.'

'All right, then how would you have like to have been?' shouted Keramet Mumî Keşke Memiş Efendi from behind as the woman walked away from him.

'Ah! I'd like to have been like the sweets in shop windows. They're so bright and colourful.'

She said other things, but she was so far away now that he couldn't understand what she said. Just as she was about to disappear from sight around the corner, she stopped to rub her sprained foot. Keramet Mumî Keşke Memiş Efendi took this opportunity to ask another question.

'Where can such sweets be found?'

The woman had bent over while rubbing her ankle, and as she did so the wind teased her. Sometimes the wind came slyly from the front, plastering the woman's scarf to her in such way as to show off her body; sometimes it played to the left or right, trying to loosen the woman's hair; sometimes whistling from behind to grasp her hips. The woman let herself free for one moment; for one moment she revealed whatever had remained hidden. It all happened in the blink of an eye; it was all a deception of the eye. By the time the woman's answer reached its destination, she had long since stepped off on her way.

'In Pera! To Pera! Pera!'

That was when Keramet Mumî Keşke Memiş Efendi understood that something had happened to the women of his country. Had they changed during his withdrawal into solitude, or had they been this way for a long time, and it was he who was late to see it? Was life really as it had been when he left it, or had things changed a great deal in his country while he was experiencing his crisis at home? In any event, he understood well on that day when he went out into the street and looked around in a different manner, that there were new things happening. Indeed anything new or European was very much in demand. It was clear that the trays of sweet walnut *baklava* paled in comparison to the deceptive attractions of the colourfully wrapped gelatine sweets. *Baklava* was served in large portions; sweets are served one by one. *Baklava* was to be eaten and finished; sweets were to be savoured. Sweets were to be enjoyed alone; *baklava* was what was served to neighbours and visitors. Sweets were unfamiliar; *baklava* was known. However you sliced it, *baklava*'s taste and essence was the same; but one understood even from the different coloured wrappers that the sweets were all different from one another. Once a person has become used to the taste of *baklava*, it becomes dull; when it comes to sweets, one is always in pursuit of taste without ever reaching it.

One addressed the stomach first; the other the eyes.

Keramet Mumî Keşke Memiş Efendi didn't care that this was only one woman among many. How many more women would he have to meet in order to have met enough women? How many books did one have to read in order to be wise, how many lands did one have to see in order to be a traveller, how many defeats did one have to suffer in order to become discouraged? How much was too much and how much was too little? Since the mirror had been broken, one was enough for Keramet Mumî Keşke Memiş Efendi. One could be divided into a thousand; decreasing drastically through famine and drought, one can be multiplied by a thousand and become abundance and plenty. Indeed, he found the number One to be extraordinary,

Wherever a person hurts, that's where his heart beats. Keramet Mumî Keşke Memiş Efendi pressed his fingers on his eyes. To no avail. It didn't stop. His heart beat in his eyes. And suddenly, the pieces were riveted together. He found a way to unite women's suffering with his own suffering. Because everything was dependant on everything else.

His inner thoughts took their proper shape just like dye poured onto water to make marbled paper. Just as his eyes were the sole reason he had been thought strange since childhood, from now on he would address only the eyes. However much he had lost because of his own eyes, he would gain even more from the eyes of others. And in order to succeed he would observe carefully the winds that were blowing in his country. He wouldn't flee from the wind's rage, nor run after it in order to kiss its hands and skirts, nor gather the pieces it had dropped and scattered. Keramet Mumî Keşke Memiş Efendi's intention was to go right up on top of the wind and look into its eyes.

Because when the wind blew wildly in a person's face it wove a curtain of lime, tar and clay, sticks and twigs, bugs and dusty earth in front of open eyes. The curtain caused so much pain that anyone foolhardy enough to want to look was obliged to close his eyes. For this reason everyone believed that the wind couldn't be seen with the eye. However, Keramet Mumî Keşke Memiş Efendi's eyes, the very eyes that were the cause of his strangeness and unhappiness, those two narrow slits that had been drawn on his face, that is, the eyes that had never opened, could look at the wind comfortably. When he looked straight into the wind he could read the state of his country and understand the way things were going, and know what to do in order to take advantage of what was going on. With this discovery, the eyes that until now had been a source of suffering would be the source of fulfilment.

For the first time since he'd deliberately broken the mirror on his wedding night, he'd found a reason to live. Wherever a person hurts, that's where his heart beats. Now, Keramet Mumî Keşke Memiş

Efendi's heart beat in his eyes. Now the pain of the loneliness that his eyes had caused him would be relieved by drawing thousands of people around him. The life that his eyes had made distasteful would become sweet. The eyes that had seen what no one else could see would cause every glass raised to be filled with an elixir distilled from the contagious blindness of the people. For this reason, he would first ascertain the situation of his country, so he could gather those who believed in this situation as if he was picking mushrooms.

Keramet Mumî Keşke Memiş Efendi had made his decision. Since the women of the Ottoman State only thought about appearances, he would present them with a world of spectacle. And since the answer to the question he had asked was Pera, then that's where he would do whatever he was going to do.

~

Theatres were already popular, and competition was fierce and heated. To start from nothing and reach your goal took not only time, but effort. But Keramet Mumî Keşke Memiş Efendi had to see the results of his efforts right away. It was clear that the clothing business was very profitable, but this isn't quite what he meant by establishing a world of spectacle. At one point it had occurred to him to start a circus of a thousand faces that would be a feast for the eyes and painful on the pocket, but he quickly changed his mind. After collecting quite a few ideas, he spent a long, long time thinking them over and then finally made his decision. He would erect an enormous tent. A tent the like of which would be remembered not just for days or for years, but for centuries. A tent that, like a snake swallowing its tail, would begin where it ended.

The colour of the tent would be the colour of cherries.

In the cherry-coloured tent he would present a world of spectacle to thousands of women. Keramet Mumî Keşke Memiş Efendi, who was born to a woman who paid the ultimate price in order to have a little son, who was raised by his six older sisters and crossed the border that separates the two sexes; who for a long time had found himself observing how each of his elder sisters managed her own husband, and thought that there was no coincidence in how these methods of management resembled each other, and that there were rules that all women knew but never mentioned, and understanding that he had been brought up according to the same rules, and could never forget the morning of his wedding night and having since birth possessed extraordinary intelligence, clearly had little trouble envisioning this world of spectacle he would present to the eyes of women. He was aware that women were deeply pleased to see women uglier than themselves. He was going to show them what they wanted to see. In the cherry-coloured tent he wasn't going to display ugly women, or the ugliest women, but ugliness itself.

~

There was one only reason these various women, who did not mention each other in their prayers and who did not let each other exist in their dreams, struggled up the hill to meet at the westward-facing gate of the cherry-coloured tent: Sable-Girl! The women had come here to see her, the ugliest of the ugly, the strangest of creatures, the despicable, plague-ridden Sable-Girl.

~

In order to understand what the Sable-Girl was seeking in Pera, in a cherry-coloured tent that had been pitched on the top of a hill, while the Ottoman Empire was Westernising with the panic of a boy who'd stolen an apple from a neighbour's garden and hadn't the courage to look back, it's necessary to go back some way. Back past all of the glazed secrets. It's necessary to travel in time and space. Not that far back; about two centuries earlier. Not that far away either; to the lands of Siberia. Because it is two centuries ago in Siberia that the story of the ugliest of the ugly, the strangest of creatures, the despicable, plague-ridden Sable-Girl begins.

But to tell the truth it is possible to skip this part altogether. It's possible not to write it; and not to read it. You can jump ahead to the next one without tarrying here, the next number, that is. In any event they may not even have lived what happened. No matter how ugly she was, she might not have become a spectacle, and had the right not to be seen, and keep herself distant from curious eyes. Indeed she wouldn't have been so ugly if she hadn't been seen.

(Anyway, if we're going to see what we could have passed over without looking at, we have to go to the Siberia of 1648 now.)

Siberia – 1648

God was above, and the Czar was far away.

The witches were wandering about. The witches were blowing the mouldy poison they hid under their knotted tongues onto the hops. As the villagers fell one after another, the acrid stench of death could be smelled for miles. Wet snow blessed the rows of corpses lying in the ditches who had opened their mouths hungrily. Indeed it had been going on for a long time. Czar Alexis had forbidden the sale of hops. But the witches had to find another way to spread the poison they kept under their knotted tongues. There had to be another way, this deluge didn't ebb, this massacre didn't end. The plague was rampaging through Russia.

The year 1648 was as famous for the plague as it was for its evil consequences. That year, the Voyvod of Belgorod found himself ordered by Czar Alexis to capture the witches immediately. He quickly rounded up the known witches in the area. Fires were lit in the square, and they smoked for days, and the soot was somehow impossible to wipe away. They caught fire, and so did their poison. Their rotten breath became mixed with the air. The air became heavier; as if it was going to vomit – murky and leaden. It enveloped everything. It was not the witches who were spreading the poison, despite the hundreds who were so hastily captured, but the air itself, which could not be grasped, and therefore could not be captured. Those who still managed to stay alive faced one of two possible deaths. Those who didn't catch the plague were burned as witches; those who weren't burned as witches had the plague.

The air was spreading poison, but it wasn't possible to see it spread. The air was an invisible place. It was at the same time boundless and small enough to be consumed in a single breath; at the same time far away and right under one's nose. 'Take care not to breathe!' said the guardians of the Czar. The villagers were obedient. By no means did they breathe when they were outside. They worked away all day, picking edible plants, draining the pus from the corpses, sitting on the graves, sweeping up the witches' ashes, and then, giving the day to the care of the night, closed themselves into their houses. It was then that they drank in the air as desperately as the lungs of the victims of accidents at sea, urgent and pitilessly longing for air, deep under the sea and struck with the terror of not being able to get out, as they rush to the embrace of the surface of the sea. The sickness was spreading rapidly.

The young Czar's chief preacher was from the Defenders of the Faith. 'Your Highness, it's time to grant them permission so they can come,' he said one day. Indeed the Czar had been on the point of thinking this for some time. 'Yes,' he said, nodding his head thoughtfully. 'I grant permission. Let them come.'

They came. They came in order to root out the renegades within their ranks and put an end to dissent in the Russian Church, to purify great Russia and to standardise religious rituals, and to fan the spiritual torments of the ignorant peasants and wipe out idolatrous practices once and for all. As their numbers increased, so too did the number of those who were proclaimed to be enemies; as the number of their enemies increased, so too did the number of their victims. Because 1648 was as famous for the plague as it was for its evil consequences.

That year the Salt Revolution broke out. It was during the first days of June. A mob that somehow couldn't reach the Czar took revenge by burning down the boyars' houses, looting their possessions and attacking their wives. The fire started on the third of June. The flames spread quickly, and the grumbling crowd besieged the Kremlin.

One of the rebels stripped naked, climbed on the shoulders of his comrades, and shouted as loud as he could:

'I'm so hungry that to make room for what I could eat in just one sitting I would have to build a road from here to Siberia.'

~

Siberia wasn't concerned about these events. He'd been deaf since birth anyway, and couldn't hear anything that wasn't aimed directly at his eardrum. He was aware neither that God was above nor that the Czar was far away. He was doing his own thing, playing his own game with loaded dice of mammoth ivory. The story of the Sable-Girl was rooted there; in Siberia in the first half of the 17th century.

Siberia wasn't concerned about these events, but for some time many people had been concerned about Siberia. Beketov, who with his thirty Cossacks had founded the city of Yakutsk, wrote a report to the Czar: 'Your Highness. After following the length of the Lena river, I reached the lands of Yakut, where I built a small tower and took the necessary defensive precautions… I have shed my blood and stained my soul for you, I have eaten horse meat and roots and pine cones and all manner of filth. Your humble servant.'

This is what he wrote in his report. This is how he and others gained their enormous wealth. From the summits of the daily growing mountains of furs, they cursed poverty and challenged nature. They didn't care about anything except fur. The furs were so soft… Soft and warm, furry and bloody sacks of gold. The conquerors of Siberia accepted all kinds of fur. They were mostly after squirrel, fox and ermine; but especially sable. The hunters made huge fortunes from this small, nervous animal. Every day, sledges full of dead sables were piled up in the Yakutsk customs house. Every day, hundreds of sable furs were given a value of thousands of gold coins. Those who had arrived at the beginning of the season had long since filled their money bags. Nor did one often meet any who had decided they'd made enough and that it was time to go back. These hunters couldn't get their fill. More furs, more protection money, more power... Siberia had more, and they wanted more.

In wide squat cabins built of huge tree trunks and with transparent fish skin stretched across the windows, the hunters waited months for the coming of spring, and the melting of the snow. The beds next to the brick stove belonged to the strongest. The strongest were the cruelest. The rest warmed their beds with prostitutes. But if they continued to feel cold anyway, they would secretly take the dreams being dreamt by those next to the stove, and cover themselves in their warmth. Those whose dreams were stolen would wake up shivering, listen to the snores, mutters, moans and gnashing that broke the silence of the night, and wait for their eyes to grow accustomed to the darkness. But no matter how carefully he looked, he couldn't determine who the thief was. In any event, everyone here was more or less a thief.

Rancour spread insidiously like a disease, and because revenge waited like an animal in ambush for the right moment to strike, the gambling around the stove every evening would be the cause of vicious fights. Sometimes the fights would subside by themselves. Then, the game would be resumed where it had been left off. Because for the hunters a broken arm or a broken leg was worse than death. Sometimes, too, even the simplest argument could end in murder. But even so, the friends of the murdered man wouldn't make too much of a fuss, because they preferred not to risk being crippled. In any event, everyone here was more or less a murderer.

The smell in these cabins was so heavy that it even covered those who were sleeping here for only one night. Even from the first days, the fur trappers who spent their nights in these cabins began to stare in the same way, at the same vanishing point. Far away, farther away than could be seen, the snow would be melting drop by drop. By the time the roads were clear, they'd long since finished making their preparations. The hunters would set out with the intense impatience that follows months of waiting; they would gather the tax the natives within the borders had to pay the Czar, and gifts for themselves. Natives who had never seen the Czar's face or heard his name had to pay him a tax and had to give gifts to the hunters whose faces they didn't like and whose names they couldn't learn. If they didn't, they faced heavy punishment. The fur hunters decided how far they would venture into the interior of Siberia.

In fact all of the hunters had come here with the intention of getting rich as quickly as possible and then going back. But now, with lands to be conquered lying naked and defenceless before them, they didn't feel like going back to the cities of Russia where it was much more difficult to make a living. Every time they unloaded their sleds at the customs house and filled their money-bags, they turned around and dove once more into the whiteness, the solitude, the boundlessness. When there were fewer places left to discover, the yet undiscovered places increased steadily in value. Now everyone was coveting north-east Siberia. They said it was a paradise; a paradise of furs for the ambitious sons of poor mothers who had gone out into the world without ever having been wrapped in a fur. By 1630 the Cossacks had already set sail on the dark waters, having decided the north-east of Siberia could be reached by sea.

Their so-called boats were made of oak branches strapped together; they used no tar or nails. The sails were made of deer skin, and without a wind behind them they couldn't continue their journey. The constantly shifting icebergs cut the leather straps and smashed the boats to pieces. The crew were constantly suffering from hunger, filth, and attacks of scurvy. Those who died were buried with their dreams, and the rest continued to nurture their dreams.

The sailors used to tell a variety of stories about Siberia. About ice formations that from afar resembled swords, glittering brightly as one approached, and about strange plants that were invisible when you were right next to them; plants that fed on the songs of insects, and that swallowed themselves when they couldn't find the

voice of an insect to suck. Mother-of-pearl mermaids who called
out the name of each sailor's mother from the tops of icebergs, the
wonderful play of lights when ice-floes bade farewell to each other
as they broke up, eye-fish who watched the world from beneath the
icebergs, and whose presence was never felt if they weren't trapped,
repulsive reptiles who climbed onto the ship and gnawed at the
noses of the sailors. Primitive natives whose heads looked as if they
might roll off at any moment because they had no necks, and whose
sex was impossible to distinguish…

~

There was a man in one of the ships sailing to north-east Siberia.
His name was Timofei Ankidinov. He was a sable trapper, like
hundreds of others. He wouldn't listen to the stories the sailors told.
He only cared about one legend: Pogicha!

The legendary Pogicha River was beautiful enough to believe
in and more beautiful when believed in. It would smile delicately
after a fog like the fading face of a lost lover. It was always far away,
eternally far away. As one approached it, it drew further away. Those
who arrived in north-east Siberia, scattering sable carcasses that
wouldn't fit into their sleds behind them was they went, swore that
they wouldn't return until they'd heard the roar of the Pogicha River.
And perhaps once they arrived, they wouldn't want to return. There
had to be thousands of sable wandering the banks of the Pogicha
River, with their coal-black eyes and their coal-black enchantment.
There were paths lined with walrus tusks leading to hollows full
of emeralds. The waters of the Pogicha were quite warm, in places
to the point of boiling. The waters of the Pogicha were restorative,
and it was enough to bathe in them once to cure all wounds. After
flowing warmly and gently, the waters emptied into a placid lake.
The lake glittered brightly from a distance, and its bed was full of
enormous pearls. The shadow of a mountain that seemed far by day
and near by night was constantly on the surface of the lake. From

time to time, silver boulders rolled off the mountain. When two silver boulders collided, it would rain on the lake. The drops would leave phosphorous stains behind them. Isolated from the rest of the world, the rain would write aimless poems on the Pogicha.

Timofei Ankidinov sincerely believed everything that was told about the Pogicha. He didn't simply believe that the Pogicha existed; he believed it existed for him alone, and was waiting for him. Timofei Ankidinov was a sable trapper, like hundreds of others. He believed that, as his life had been so bland, and as his face was of a type that was so average and left so little trace on the memory, and as since birth he had had to wear himself out simply to be noticed by others; of everyone on the face of the earth, of every member of the human race, no one had more right than he did to see the Pogicha. He was so caught up in the legend that he referred to the Pogicha as 'my elegant lady', and whenever anyone else mentioned the name, and he saw that they were nursing dreams about it, he went mad with anger. The legend was promised to him and to him alone.

Indeed it was for this reason that even when the ship in which he had travelled for weeks was sinking into the dark waters he knew he wouldn't die. He was so sure he wouldn't die before he found the Pogicha that he didn't even struggle to swim to the shore. He was waiting for a magical hand to reach out from among the ice floes and pull him out. When he finally reached the shore, he encountered one of the sailors from the ship. The two men, as a consequence of having emerged unscathed from a terrible accident, embraced each other and kissed each other's cheeks with shame and delight and turned to look at the sea with surprise; where not long before a black whirlpool had been sucking down the wreckage, white bubbles were now being thrown up with the remains of the wreckage.

Meanwhile, blood from the wound on the sailor's head was filling his eyes, and lumps of black, clotted blood were forming in his hair. Nevertheless, the sailor didn't seem to be in a state to feel pain. With a sweet smile on his face, he was looking at the sea. A wave with a mischievous heart, a pale countenance and a lisping tongue was walking right up behind him. Under the wave, hundreds of hollows and thousands of depths had entered it and were increasing with passion; that's why its heart was mischievous. Within the wave, hundreds of sables had joined hands with thousands of shadows; that's why its countenance was pale. On top of the wave, hundreds of voices and thousands of echoes were screaming to the point of choking; that's why it lisped. The wave was washing gently over his toes, sweetly tickling whatever it touched.

Timofei Ankidinov was aware that his friend was about to freeze. Because freezing was that kind of thing. A death that didn't end. Not the kind whose progress is punctuated, nor the kind that one can come to prepared; neither an end to life nor the beginning of another time...only, but only a flowing away into the distance, from here into the distance...because freezing was that kind of thing; that is, to flow, that is not to stop while flowing, that is to flow as far as being unable to stop. Without threshold, without stages, without inconvenience. And because it was fluid in this way, it was the only death that drew a person's blood without injuring them. It would spread a warm feeling of consolation concerning life's final puzzle with its icy palms. On top of this, it believed what was believed about it. Freezing was a death that was fundamentally denial, and rebelled against its own existence. It whispered softly into its victim's ear. With delight it would tell stories that were woven from lies. Then, it would suddenly fall quiet, and try to leave with its story only half told. The victim would hurriedly embrace the warm consolation spread by the icy palms; he would not give it permission to leave. Freezing was the only death that asked its victim's consent.

Freezing was the only death that made one smile as it killed.

The sailor was smiling peacefully.

Timofei Ankidinov was watching him anxiously.

~

While this was happening on the shore, a little further away, in an overturned basket, a beardless youth was facing the most difficult test of his life.

The beardless youth was attached to a native tribe, and had been waiting in the basket for all of three days. For all of three days he had been combing this blind darkness. He would not have said that he missed the light. Just as a person would not want to eat something new in order not to lose the taste of something he had eaten, he didn't want to see anything new in order that his eyes not lose the image of the last thing he'd seen.

The last image his eyes had seen was that of his elder sister's lifeless body. It was stretched full-length on the ground. Her very long, jet-black hair waved in the wind that rose from the frozen ground. The whole tribe was in mourning. They didn't even have a single shaman. The elders thought that the migrating soul of the shaman might take its place in her brother. The look in the boy's eyes was like that of a sable familiar with death. They were as black as a sable's eyes. Looking deeply into his pupils, it was clear that he could be the new shaman. But no one knew yet if he was the right person. In order to know it was necessary to test him.

Once the boy learned that he was to be tested, he would run away from people and avoided asking questions. At night, before leaving the village with the others, he cut off a lock of his sister's hair, and ate a slice of her flesh. This was the last thing that had entered his stomach, which was now gathering together like an empty sack, becoming smaller as it did so, and, as it grew smaller, gnawing at the emptiness within him.

Drums were played along the entire route. Later, when they reached the shore, they lit a huge fire and arranged themselves around it; women on one side and men on the other. The boy, next to the fire, dove into the body of his mother, who was beside herself, and whose body was as tense as a bow, and whose looks pierced him like an arrow. As dawn broke, the fire went out, and the basket was placed in the centre. When he emerged from the basket three days and three nights later, he would either be a shaman or a nothing.

When he stroked the walrus-tusk necklace his mother had given him, he was overcome with despair. They'd gone by now, all of them had gone. The boy remained all alone in the snow, inside an overturned basket. Since then he hadn't eaten a single bite or uttered a single word. Until He arrived, not a bite nor a word would pass his lips. He was waiting for Him; his soul's equal, the visitor who was the soul of his equal. The visitor he was waiting for could be a human or an animal or a plant. The visitor would either grant him superhuman powers and make him a shaman just like his sister, or the complete opposite, indeed he might even be punished for his presumption. Whatever happened, whatever the risks were, he was waiting for Him. If the visitor was human He would arrive on foot, if a bird, flying, if a fish, swimming, and if it was a plant it would emerge from the snow, see the basket and come. He would come and decide whether the boy was to be the tribe's new shaman.

The beardless youth couldn't keep a strange sense of distress from eroding his courage. Even if he hadn't admitted it to himself yet, and even if he didn't know the reason for it, he felt a terrible fear of being seen.

~

The sailor was smiling peacefully.

Timofei Ankidinov was watching him anxiously. On one hand he couldn't rein in his jealousy at the thought that the sailor might be dreaming about the Pogicha, and on the other he was looking for some way to keep the man from freezing.

~

The visitor hadn't come yet. The beardless youth was thinking neither about his elder sister nor about the name he would be given when he became shaman. He was miserable from hunger, weariness and fear. He could change his mind at any moment, but he didn't have the strength to change his mind

At that moment his whole body shook. Something had entered the basket. For a while he stood waiting for his eyes to become accustomed to the darkness, as if he hadn't been living in this complete darkness for three nights, and as if when the visitor came He wouldn't bring yet another curtain of darkness. An indistinct figure slowly became apparent. It was a big sable. It was at least five times bigger than other sables. When the boy saw it he couldn't keep from smiling. This meant that the visitor he'd been awaiting so long was a sable that was his reflection in this world, a mirror of his face. This meant that, just as their eyes were identical, his soul also resembled this agile animal.

The boy and the sable stood eye to eye.

The boy and the sable looked at their resemblance. Both of their eyes shone with the knowledge of death. They were like two mirrors facing each other. As they looked, they flowed into each other and strengthened one another. Then they shut their eyes tightly. Then, in a manner that was both relaxed and energetic, and as if they were out in an open field rather than in that narrow basket, they began to dance the ancient dance of the shamans. The sable licked the boy's wounds. Every wound healed as soon as the animal's tongue touched it.

Without taking their eyes off each other, they spun at the same moment and at the same speed in the snowstorm of their hearts. They spun so much that they made the world's head spin. As they spun they were beside themselves. In that dark, narrow basket they discovered the boundlessness and the brilliance of their souls. And they loved each other. Later, when they emerged from the basket, each would go to the place where his body belonged, but their souls would not part. This, this was their secret. And this moment was their moment. The intimacy of the shaman and the animal.

~

Timofei Ankidinov had made a sledge from scrub and branches and he lay the sailor, who by the way his smiling face was growing pale seemed in danger of freezing, onto this sledge. His aim was first to get away from the sea and to find shelter. The rest he would think about later. Not that there was much to think about. He had a feeling he was going to make a fortune in these still undiscovered lands. This had to be a sable heaven. And who knew, perhaps it was even close to the Pogicha. Perhaps he was very close to that magnificence of which he'd always dreamed, to the boundless plenty, to his elegant lady.

As Timofei Ankidinov walked, pulling the sledge behind him, he kept his eyes on the land onto which they'd not yet stepped; his friend on the sledge, his eyes wide open, silently watched the road along which they'd passed.

Suddenly an indistinct shape passed in front of them. It was a sable, at least five times bigger than other sables. It passed without noticing the men and a little further on disappeared from sight.

When Timofei Ankidinov saw this enormous sable he was so surprised and so excited that he had difficulty keeping himself from crying out. He didn't say anything to the sailor. He changed the sledge's course, and started following the sable's tracks. The tracks dwindled, and stopped in front of a small mound. As the sable trapper approached noiselessly and began brushing the snow off the mound, he understood that it was a large, overturned basket. This discovery excited him even more. Perhaps under this basket was a door that opened onto the Pogicha. Perhaps all the sables in Siberia were succeeding in hiding from the trappers by passing through this door. If it could swallow such a big sable as that one, there was definitely a priceless mystery inside it.

'Perhaps it would be better if we didn't look. It could be a trap for trappers. Or a Siberian curse.'

As the sailor said this, he was trying to straighten out. Timofei Ankidinov look sourly at his face. He would never allow the Pogicha and its enormous sables to belong to anyone else. He pretended to stop looking, returned to the sledge, and suddenly attacked the man lying on it. The sailor, who was very weak and who was not expecting an attack like this, was so astounded that even as his body was being stabbed he didn't put up any resistance.

bloodinthesnowbloodinthesnowbloodinthesnowmansnowman.

Trembling wildly with excitement, Timofei Ankidinov looked around. There was a lot of blood around. Everything he saw had turned red. He cleaned off the blood that filled his eyes. He flung the bloody dagger far away and approached the overturned basket. He opened it and looked inside.

Sable and boy, two twin souls, two existences linked by blood, two balls of sadness, two strange faces, two confused hallucinations, boy and sable… Their two souls, causing each other to increase, were on the point of melting into one, but their union was left half completed. With the opening of the basket the daylight dove in with a brazen smile, followed by the stranger's avaricious stare. And at such an intimate moment. They had to be far from watching eyes; they definitely ought not to be seen. The spell was broken. It was all left half finished, and temporary. Now the boy and the sable were struggling to bring back the half that was each one's own body. Since there was only one body present. Because the spell had been broken right in the middle of their union, they could neither step back and return to their former states, nor could they step forward and complete their transformation.

The light that had torn that darkness, that counted intimacy for nothing, disappeared the way it arrived. Timofei Ankidinov's mouth hung open with surprise, and his eyes grew to the size of crystal balls from terror as he looked at the creature under the basket.

~

The military governor of Tobolsk was lying on his back, gulping his drink and picking at the scabs of the wound that had appeared at the end of his nose several weeks ago and somehow wouldn't heal. After all, Tobolsk had become the most important city in Siberia. Because the Russians saw Tobolsk not only as a commercial but also as a religious centre, they'd built a convent and a monastery side-by-side, as well as a religious school. The missionaries who sought to teach God's name to the primitives and to uproot idolatrous practices were entertained here for a while before setting out into the wilderness. When it came to commerce, all the merchants saw it as an important place to visit regularly. Tadjik and Tartar tradesmen in particular used to bring valuable goods from the east to the markets of Tobolsk.

The military governor of Tobolsk looked at the blood on the tip of his finger. The wound had bled again when he had picked at it. He filled his glass again. When he came here he'd had fifty servants, five prostitutes who were always bickering among themselves, three priests, and hundreds of barrels of wine and drink. If things continued to go the way they were, he was sure that he would leave with nine or ten times more. The trapping season was about to reach its end. Soon, all of the native tribes along the border would deliver their tribute. Any day, the Cossacks who ranged further would be turning back, with their furs. Furs! The military governor of Tobolsk smiled as he crushed between his fingers the scab he had picked. He loved fur. If it wasn't for fur he wouldn't be able to stand this cursed place for a single day.

He started to do the accounts in his head. Indeed his favourite thing was to go to his room at the end of the day and gulp his drink while adding up what he had made. This time he'd even succeeded in fooling the devil. When he'd thought of kidnapping the children of the troublesome Tunguz tribe, who hadn't paid their protection money for some time, he'd solved the problem once and for all. Now he was selling the children back to their parents for sable furs. To tell the truth, kidnapping the leaders of the tribe was very difficult, but quite profitable. He could get sledges full of furs in exchange for them. When some of them unnecessarily tried to resist, the military governor dealt out their punishment himself. He branded them with an iron whose capital letters had dropped off. He always branded them in the same place; right between their eyes. Wherever the prisoners went in the future, none of them would ever pick up a mirror again, and they would remind everyone who saw them of the military governor's power.

There were also shamans among those who were kidnapped. They were quite strange. They made such startling sounds in their cells at night that none of the guards liked to watch over them. They would ululate until dawn and stamp their feet, and they'd spin for hours, tearing their rattling chains and jingling walrus tusk necklaces to pieces. Sometimes the military governor would go down and watch them from a corner. He would throw maggot-infested meat that had been put aside for the sledge dogs in front of them. Until now, none of them had refused it. They'd chew heavily on the repulsive, stinking meat; the colour of its rottenness wrapped itself around the eyes. Every time he saw this, the military governor became nauseous and rushed away.

It was not long before he'd be free of this cursed place. He was going to leave in the near future. If he'd sunk his teeth in just a little bit more, he would have been one of the wealthiest men in the country when he left. His train of thought was broken by the pounding on the door. It was his orderly.

'Sir, there's a sable trapper outside. He says he has something very valuable in his sack. He won't show it to anyone but you.'

'All right,' said the military governor. He sighed in distress. 'Let him come in. Let's have a look and see what he has in this sack.'

A little later, Timofei Ankidinov, with a haughty expression, followed the orderly inside. He had straightened his back and was about to recite the pretentious sentences he'd prepared days before, when the military governor cut him short with a harsh expression, and asked for the sack to be opened at once. Meanwhile, the military governor was unable to speak for a moment because of the pain from the wound he'd made bleed again by picking at it. When he came to himself, the first thing he did was to pat Timofei Ankidinov on the back with one hand and raise his wine glass to the honour of the sack. Quickly filling every empty wine glass he saw, he repeated the same sentence no one knows how many times.

'This kind of ugliness is something everyone has to see.'

~

In a low, airless cabin in Tobolsk, the Sable-Boy used to get up and dance on top of a round wooden table. The overflowing crowd around the table would consist of merchants, trappers, adventurers, exiles, outlaws, holy men, Cossacks, prostitutes, the Czar's spies, high officials and their underlings, that is, everyone chance had set on the road to this distant land; shouting, cursing and insulting one another as they gulped their drinks, watching the Sable-Boy. Every evening the military governor of Tobolsk would drop by and look things over; he'd count the number of spectators. Since he'd managed to get Timofei Ankidinov out of the picture with a little money and many threats, it was all his. No one could interfere. Every night, he earned the value of at least two sledges full of sable furs from the people who came to see the Sable-Boy.

What had happened was that the boy, who hadn't become the tribe's new shaman, had become stuck somewhere between being a human and being a sable. Indeed he was a sable-person, because he had a sable for a soul-mate. And inside that overturned basket, when the moment came for his soul to embrace its twin; that is, at the moment when he was about to draw the sable's soul into himself and blow his own soul into the sable; I mean, at the moment when he was about to complete the transformation he had to undergo in order to become the tribe's new shaman, first becoming two beings in one with the sable, then later becoming one being in two; everything remained half finished simply because a hand had opened the basket from outside, and a pair of uninvited eyes had seen what they shouldn't have seen and the light from those eyes had shredded that intimate moment to pieces. The soul-mates had become separate within the same body. Indeed he was a sable-person. He was half sable, and half human. He was an unfortunate creature, imprisoned in order to display his unfortunate ugliness.

By day, the Sable-Boy sat in a circle defined by the length of the chain attached to his ankles, gnawing at the food that was thrown to him. When he'd eaten his fill, he'd sniff at the edge of the circle, trying to understand what kind of world he was in. In the evening he would get up on the table in the cabin and display himself. He was so ugly and so strange that there were those who changed their routes in order to pass through Tobolsk. People laughed when they saw him. Even though his appearance was wild, he was very obedient.

He never stood up for himself. He did exactly what he was told. Sometimes he would jump up and down on the table, sometimes he would approach the edge and let the spectators touch him, and sometimes he would turn his back and draw circles in the air with his tail. And he would also often get on all fours and run around in circles chasing his tail. Whenever he did this the spectators would crack up laughing. Whenever this happened, they would throw things onto the round, wooden table; either the curses on their tongues, or the boots on their feet, or the drink that was left in their glasses, or the prostitutes who wandered from lap to lap.

He was a Sable-Boy. In time, he earned the military governor far more than he could have earned in years in the fur trade. Then, one night, as he was showing himself off on top of the table, he collapsed to the ground. Faces and sounds became confused. He'd fainted. He'd become ill. In the following days, the military governor brought all of the physicians of the city to the cabin. Yet none of the physicians could put a name to the Sable-Boy's sickness, or find a cure. In the end the military governor, seeing the patient wasting away day-by-day and being seized by a mind-shaking panic, finally sought the help of the shamans in the cells. Of all the shamans, only one had a sable as a soul-mate, and agreed to look after him.

The Sable-Boy's condition improved somewhat, but the military governor became frightened that something might happen to him and his source of money would dry up completely. So as not to leave things to chance, he had to get some offspring from this strange creature. They would have to be half-human and half-animal just like himself.

Before long, they put the Sable-Boy in the arms of a prostitute. The Sable-Boy first sniffed the bed, then the prostitute, then, lying in the bed with the prostitute, sniffed himself. From among the smells of sweat and urine, faeces and drink, smoke and exile, he picked out and lay aside, as if he were plucking the finest of hairs, his favourite smell in the world, the only smell he loved; the smell of the cold! While he filled himself with the smell he loved, he gave the prostitute no trouble. He was as obedient as always.

Months later, early for humans and late for animals, the prostitute gave birth to twins. The first born had nothing strange about it. The military governor, who had refused to wait outside and was pacing back and forth next to the bed, scowled as he looked at the baby. His nerves were shot. Just then the second baby came. Its head emerged first; it was a human head. And then, finally, below the waist, a puny, wet tail appeared. The lower half of its body was sable. Screaming with delight, the military governor picked up the sable-baby and threw it into the air. He squeezed some gold coins into the prostitute's hand. Leaving her and the first-born baby there, he set off for home with his new treasure in his arms.

For centuries, all sable-children were born as twins. Each time, one of the twins was human and one was a sable-person. The sable-babies were sometimes boys and sometimes girls. The human twins had little chance of surviving, and no one knew what became of them. Those that were born half-human and half-animal would survive, and continue to provide an ever-increasing fortune for the military governor, and later for his children and his grandchildren and the grandchildren of his grandchildren.

And so, the destinies of the two families were intertwined like two vigorous vines that had met by coincidence. For centuries, the descendants of the military governor and the descendants of the Sable-Boy were always together. In every generation, those carrying the military governor's surname were the ones who displayed; those who inherited the Sable-Boy's condition were the displayed. And perhaps these two lineages might have remained linked forever. That is if one of the military governor's grandchildren's grandchildren hadn't loosened the last link in this very long chain.

The truth of the matter was that this man, one of the military governor's grandchildren's grandchildren, wasn't very enthusiastic about the business he had inherited from his father. Although the Sable-Girl in his possession was among the ugliest of her lineage, so he could earn much more money, this wasn't what the military governor's great great grandson wanted. Instead of carrying on the profession of his forefathers in the land of his origins, he wanted to move to a new continent that everyone said was enchanting and attempt what had not yet been attempted. He was passionate about this dream, but somehow couldn't rid himself of the Sable-Girl or of the profession he had inherited.

Then, one day, a messenger knocked on the military governor's great great grandson's door. Without saying a word the messenger held out the sealed letter he'd taken from his shirt and then stood aside to wait for an answer. In the letter, someone with a strange name who had heard about the famous Sable-Girl wanted to buy her, and he was making a very generous offer. The military governor's great great grandson didn't hesitate for long. He felt that God had finally answered his prayers. He settled the matter quickly. As the messenger in the cherry-coloured gloves counted out the coins, the other man was writing a statement granting all rights to the Sable-Girl to the man with the strange name who had written the letter.

That very evening, the messenger and the Sable-Girl were about to set off on the road, when the military governor's great great grandson came up behind them. He was curious about where the Sable-Girl was being taken. The messenger, who until then had not said a word, answered out of the corner of his mouth.

'To the west! To Istanbul!'

Pera — 1885

After the evening call to prayer, the westward-facing door of the cherry-coloured tent at the top of the hill was opened for the women.

It was then that in threes and fives the women started to enter the westward-facing door of the cherry-coloured tent at the top of the hill. Bringing their noise and their togetherness with them.

The opening would be performed by a masked woman. The mask she wore, with its eyes frozen as if they'd witnessed a moment of terror, the tongue swollen as if it had been stuck in a beehive, a nose that had started to grow straight out and then had changed its mind and grown down as far as the lower lip, and a pointed chin covered in hair, was truly frightening. The masked woman said nothing and did nothing, but simply stood stock still on the stage. As if she'd been told to wait her entire life, and had obediently waited, without knowing why, or for what. Then, at a completely unexpected moment, she would lower the mask. Exclamations of surprise rose from the audience. Because the face they saw now was exactly the same as the face they'd seen before. From far away, very far away, barely audible, came the sound of a violin. When the violin stopped, the woman whose mask was her face, and whose face was a mask, greeted the audience in a graceful manner. On her signal, the purple curtains with the threadbare fringes began to open slowly.

On the stage, at the foot of a steep drop, in a pitch-black cauldron with a fire burning brightly under it, surrounded by fearful creatures, a tiny, ugly woman began to sing a cabaret song. Her name was Siranuş; her voice was very thin.

'You were so beautiful, you were so lovely
If you'd been a *börek* I would have eaten you
With few onions, and much meat.
I got lost in conversation, you stuck to the pan and burned
At once I lost my desire.'

When the song was finished, the creatures pulled Siranuş's cauldron to one side, as well as the fire underneath it. While she suffered the punishment of the whimsical, dripping beads of sweat, the Three Ugly Sisters appeared on the stage. The three sisters, each uglier than the other, were Mari, Takuhi and Agavni. One of them had one breast, the second had two breasts, and the third had three. Side-by-side, they bounced their breasts up and down as they did a belly dance. They were so busy following each other out of the corners of their eyes to catch each other's mistakes that they forgot about the audience, and even that they were on the stage. Mari hated Agavni because she felt she'd stolen her missing breast. Agavni hated Mari for causing her to carry an extra breast. Both of them hated Takuhi more than anything in the world. They hated Takuhi who with her two breasts threw her sisters' deformities in their faces, and who, shining darkly like a pearl in mud, was ugly but not deformed. Some evenings Mari and Agavni couldn't control their tempers and stopped in the middle of their belly dance to start slapping Takuhi. When the audience saw them hit her, when they saw their belated revenge, their worn out enmity, their hearts melted, and they began to relax. Disagreeable to the tongue but pleasant to the eye, the hellish fire under Siranuş burned furiously; thick and languorous smoke would fill the western part of the tent. Finally, when the sisters took Takuhi by the arms and led her off the stage, the audience felt regret for having taken pleasure in the pain of others.

Right after the Three Ugly Sisters, Snowball Vergin would emerge onto the stage. Or rather he jumped out onto the stage. With him jumped the open syphilis sores all over his body. His mother, who was a famous Galata whore, caught the sickness from a famous sweet little gentleman who lived from his inheritance. The poor woman tried everything she could to get rid of the burden in her womb, but she gave up when she realised the baby, who was nourished not only by his mother's blood, but the also by time itself, clung to her womb like a mussel clinging to its shell. The wealthy gentleman swore that he would undertake the treatment, but a few months before the baby was born he found that both his fortune and his desire had been consumed. Vergin was born gasping for breath and with sores all over him. He was a half-wit from birth; he could not understand the clumsiness he saw. But Vergin grew anyway, not little by little, but by leaps and bounds. He grew so quickly that when he stopped to catch his breath he could see the changes in his body. He bent over and looked with curiosity between his thighs. Amazing. There wasn't even a single sore there. None of the festering wounds that had pierced his body, none of the aches that left his mind shorn, nor the memories that gripped the heart...none of them, none of them had touched him there. He was pleased.

He called his crotch snowball. No one asked him the meaning of snowball, and he didn't explain it to anyone. Indeed all of the personalities around him hadn't been given their share of gratitude from the world, but had been given too many nicknames. Vergin's nickname was accepted without question in the sidestreets of Galata.

He didn't grow much after that day. Because he'd already grown enough. He grew just like a snowball rolling down a hill, and the more he grew the further downhill he rolled. And he lived in his own haggard, tattered world, with his low and untamed dreams, just like a snowball that melted itself with its own warmth. While the shouting of passers-by echoed off sinister houses on the streets of ill-repute and broke up, happy faces, young, tender bodies scattered one by one; lifting wine glasses as they slowly chiselled names on tombstones, only Snowball Vergin, only he remained the same. He was neither bound to life nor was life bound to him.

Just then, Keramet Mumî Keşke Memiş Efendi appeared. When they sensed that this man, about whom all of the whores of Galata loved to tell strange stories, wanted Vergin instead of any of the beautiful women present, there was a commotion. But because they had long since become inured to all of the strange things in the world, the commotion soon died down. Snowball Vergin took his sack and left this damp and dingy place that he considered home.

When he first stepped out onto the stage, his eyes were as wide as saucers as he looked at the crowd before him. Hundreds of eyes were on him; they were spread out in groups in the darkness. He was quite pleased with the situation. From that day to this, every evening, he would wait his turn impatiently in the westward-facing section of the cherry-coloured tent, and when the time came he would rush like an arrow onto the stage.

After Snowball Vergin it was the snake-charmer's turn. When the ladies saw the snake-charmer, with a silver amulet on his arm, hoop earrings on his ears, and a cummerbund around his waist, they went pale with fear. Those of them who were pregnant closed their eyes tight. By now the snake-charmer would have reached the centre of the stage; he would greet the audience by raising his eyebrows slightly and gently nodding his head, and open the basket. The ladies held their breath, and clung to each other to keep from fainting. The snake would emerge from the basket, slither to the edge of the stage, and stare with its emerald-green eyes. As it stared and was stared at, the audience began to see.

The world was reflected in reverse in the snake's eyes.

In the world shown in the mirror of its eyes, virgins were widows, and masters were slaves. It was crawling with life under the black earth; it flowed into those who stepped on it. Among the thirsty tree roots, its rotten bones, its evil vipers, its useless structure, wasted seeds, among the wriggling worms, satin was sackcloth, shining copper coins were worthless. The worms gnawed at the young and the old, the rich and the poor with equal appetite. They were everywhere. They made a faint crunching sound as they gnawed; they could destroy the world with this faint crunching sound. If a sacrifice was performed on the dome of the city, and divided into pieces, with equal portions being placed in bowls in front of them, it wouldn't even begin to satisfy their appetite. When death takes a person's life, it leaves behind his cloak; when fire consumes a new-born baby, it doesn't touch the gold it's wearing. In a world like this one would rather be a cloak than the person wearing it; or be born as gold rather than as the baby wearing it.

It was a description of hell; not a hell after death, but a hell within life's bosom.

At this stage of the show, the women who couldn't look into the snake's eyes any more, jumped screaming to their feet. Nauseating, bright yellow bugs were crawling around their ankles, their throats and their earlobes. The women would hastily begin taking off all their jewellery and throwing it onto the stage. Everyone wanted to purify themselves; to purify themselves as quickly and easily as possible and get away from this hell.

Then, the mirror closed just as it had opened. The snake-charmer bowed with a slight smile, deliberately picked up the jewellery that had been thrown onto the stage and put it into his basket, and then, in contrast to his slowness of a moment before, rushed off the stage as if he was fleeing. The snake slithered after its master like a whistled melody.

After the snake-charmer, Madame Kinar would come out with her puppets. She had little puppets on each of her ten fingers. She would represent the natural world through them. For a deluge, she would spray the place with water; for hail she would break the branches of young trees; for a wind storm she would tear apart a bird's nest; for a flood she would sweep the crops away; for drought she would burn the soil; for famine she would empty the granaries; for a typhoon she would spray on whoever was in front of her; for a cyclone she would swallow all living creatures; for fire she would roast; for an earthquake she wouldn't leave a stone standing. There was no evil that nature did not inflict on mankind.

When the dust settled, an anxious silence would fall over the audience. Seeing all of these natural disasters one after another had unsettled the ladies and spoiled their fun. On top of that, everyone knew there was worse to come. Because it was the Sable-Girl's turn to appear on stage.

When it was the Sable-Girl's turn, darkness would fall inside the cherry-coloured tent. Pregnant women would writhe in distress, babies would start to cry, elderly women would recite all the prayers they knew one after another; virgins and widows, believers and unbelievers, poor and rich, all of the women came together, and held their breath. In that momentary darkness, it would cross their minds that the door of the tent must still be open. That is, they could get out; right now they could get away. Changing one's mind was certainly possible. But how was it possible to change one's mind when the moment they'd been waiting for had arrived?

Some of the women who'd come to the tent for the first time couldn't sit still; they would approach the stage with trembling steps, trying to imagine what this demon would be like. But such terrifying monsters appeared before them that they were shaken out of their dreams, and pulled back. Indeed, for the few minutes before the Sable-Girl took the stage, every single woman combed her most secret fear out of her hair, and out of the tangles of her brain. With every passing minute it became less tolerable, as fear incited fear. It wasn't the object of fear but fear itself that was so frightening. And fear was everywhere; it leaned against every corner and grew everywhere. It could attack from the ground at any moment. In these moments the women didn't have a chance to look at the stage because they were busy protecting themselves from the fear before them, behind them, beside them and around them. If they'd looked, they could have seen that the Sable-Girl had long since taken the stage and was watching the trembling audience with her sable-black eyes.

A little later, a huge fire was lit on the stage in order to draw the spectators' attention in that direction. And then all of the women who just a moment ago had been knitting sweaters from the letters of fear all screamed for help in unison. The Sable-Girl was before them, the show had begun.

The Sable-Girl greeted those who watched her in terror in an indifferent manner. Of the thousands of eyes upon her, she only valued a single, watery eye.

Every evening when she took the stage, she watched this eye that was watching her. She watched its watching. The mallet would come down, the drum would resound. The Sable-Girl would start a laboured belly dance. The furs she was wearing were long enough to sweep the ground, and ample enough to cover her body completely. They were definitely made of sable. Among the women who filled the tent were some who had coveted these furs and had had similar furs sewn for them. As the Sable-Girl gyrated on the stage, they involuntarily stroked their own furs. Now the tent was as quiet and as calm as could be. This moment of indifference was as innocent as a dove flying through the sky unaware of the letter around its neck.

The mallet descended, the drum resounded. With harsh movements the Sable-Girl would take off her furs. She would be left stark naked. She'd approach the edge of the stage and, making strange sounds, would rain centuries-old curses upon the audience. Like all of her ancestors she fearlessly displayed her monumental ugliness. Like all of her ancestors she was fearlessly ugly. The top half of her body belonged to a woman, and the bottom half of her body belonged to an animal. The mallet descended, the drum resounded. Suddenly, like a caged animal, she would let loose all her rage. With her tail straight in the air, and growling through her clenched teeth, she would crouch on all fours and prepare to attack, looking around wildly for a victim, wearing the ancient anger of nature as a weapon. And at the least expected moment, she pawed at the eyes surrounding her. Unlike her great-great-grandfather the Sable-Boy, she was not obedient.

An ear-splitting voice was heard. 'Close your eyes!' If any of the spectators were still insisting on looking at the stage, they immediately closed their eyes tight when they heard this voice.

Every evening the show was punctuated in the same manner. The Sable-Girl would go, the curtain would come down, but the women with their eyes closed tight would continue to remain frozen in place for a moment. As if there was no place left for them to go except this cherry-coloured tent. They weren't going to go out the door, they weren't going to go down the hill, they weren't going to go back. Who knows how long they would have stayed glued to their seats, holding on to the images of what they'd seen. But the same thing happened every evening. A baby would suddenly cry, or one of the old women would be overwhelmed and suddenly fall into a faint. Then, as if they'd received a command, or as if the owner of the house was chasing them out, all of the women would open their eyes and jump to their feet. They would rush out of the tent pushing and shoving each other, trampling on those who had fallen, trying not to look back if possible, as if they were fleeing from a ghost.

Every evening without fail, a number of children were torn from their mothers' hands and got lost. Some of these children were lost for hours and later were reunited with their mothers in tears, and others would be delivered to angry fathers the next day. It happened that some of these children remained unclaimed, and they would begin to live in the cherry-coloured tent among Keramet Mumî Keşke Memiş Efendi's strange creatures.

The forgotten children in the westward-facing section of Keramet Mumî Keşke Memiş Efendi's cherry-coloured tent would advance, step-by-step, day-by-day, they were bent into shape, through a variety of illnesses, embracing a number of crises, passing from apprenticeship to mastery of ugliness with castrated smiles and nocturnal anger. When the time was just right, they would take their places on the stage and cut through this place of confusion with ear-splitting screams.

Istanbul – 1999

zahir: Zahir, one of the ninety-nine names of God, means 'He who doesn't hide from sight.'

'Don't move!'

I don't know why, but I wasn't at all pleased that the man had said this. And there was no need for him to repeat his warning. I wasn't moving. And I knew what my motionlessness resembled. My motionlessness resembled a hard-working ant running around a dead bee lying on its back at the bottom of an empty water glass; from the same starting point it always watched the world turn, and turn again, with the same delighted amazement. My motionlessness was like a memory that resembled a consumptive spitting out his unforgettable memories into a handkerchief; spending each day in quarantine infecting his sickness with loneliness. My motionlessness was like the warm, yellowish pudding that's poured over homemade cakes; it slowly covered everything with its sweetness. Of course the water glass had an outside; a land where my memory was exempt from coughing or a layer that the pudding had not yet covered. Me, I wasn't outside in that dry, faraway land but: I wasn't m-o-v-i-n-g.

I was waiting motionlessly because I was stuck in a door again. This kind of thing happens to me all the time when I pass through those double doors and only one side is left open. If I have to confess, I don't fit through this type of door. I have to go through sideways. And even then I get stuck.

The front door of the Hayalifener Apartments is one of those double doors. One of the wings was bolted to the floor and ceiling, and only a narrow space was left to pass through. Usually I'm careful going in and out, but today I was in such a hurry to get home that I found myself in a situation where my sweater had been caught on the lock between the two wings of the door. As if that wasn't bad enough, while I was caught there by the threads of my sweater, I was caught by the neighbourhood ladies returning with their bags from the nearby market. As always, they examined me from head to toe. Just to escape their stares I rushed to move aside and let them through, but I didn't think to take off the sweater first, and I became even more badly entangled. The neighbourhood ladies, after talking for some time about how the unravelled strand could never be restored to its former state but should at least be pulled inside the sweater so it couldn't be seen, and about how this might be done, went inside to their homes.

As they were going up the stairs, an old man was coming down. I moved aside to let him pass too. But instead of looking and passing by like the others, he insisted on staying to help and took it upon himself to get me out of the situation and to rescue the strand from my sweater. For close to ten minutes he struggled with his trembling hands and his weak eyes, telling me again and again not to move.

Having to wait without moving, I was reminded of how it was for B–C in the studio. One day a week he modelled there for hours. He felt like a slave, on his way to be sold at a festival, who felt something deep in his heart, knowing that he would never see in the falcon mirror the reflection of the time when he could run free and hunt. He looked hopelessly at the merchants and customers at the auction. It didn't make any difference who bought him; either that one or the other one. So with indifference he posed for people he didn't know. He doesn't know why he goes to that miserable studio, or why he behaves this way; I find it odd that he's so untroubled.

Perhaps I thought it was my duty to take on the anxieties he was neglecting. In his place I would have been anxious. And when I'm anxious I destroy my cuticles.

This is a sensitive matter. First, when hunting, one has to flush the prey out into the open. The devil's wiles made things difficult for me in regard to my cuticles. Anyway, they are as curious as they are wily. To be curious is to want to see; this was the weakest point of my cuticles, the cause of their downfall.

In the drawer where I hid what I saw as a child, there was an attendant from a woman's bathhouse who looked like an ogre. With all her strength, the woman was scrubbing a child who was so thin that you could count her bones. I can't get it out of my mind. As the giant attendant, on her knees, scrubbed off layer after layer of skin and dripped drops of sweat onto the heated marble, she was making kissing sounds. She knew well that, as the skin was made sleepy by the steam and the scrubbing, the rough cloth she was using would soon be black with dirt. Because the dirt loved to have kisses sent to it. It would immediately stick its head out to see who was blowing it kisses. The sound of the bath attendant's kisses was like a siren's call. The dirt that came out of the child's body turned its rudder without thinking and didn't even have time to think that this melody was a sad and bankrupt death. When the rocks ground up the huge ships, because of the excitement of the overseas discovery, not a single bone was left behind. The dirt's corpse, draining away with the filthy water of the bathhouse, was rushing with due speed towards an unknown exit.

I laid the same trap for my cuticles that had been used by the huge bath attendant I'd seen when I was a child. I called them with kisses and they stuck their little heads out to see where the sound was coming from. Then I bit each one of them off with my teeth. The taste was unpleasant, but it wasn't about taste. Sometimes it hurt; and sometimes the area around my cuticles bled. Sometimes I completely forgot that they existed; and sometimes I bit them off so regularly that I had to wait a long time for new ones to emerge.

Being fat doesn't just make me irritable, it also makes me anxious.

Whenever I went to see B–C at the studio, I became so anxious that I didn't have any cuticles left. I just couldn't understand. How could a person display himself; and why? B–C would leave my questions unanswered. On top of that he would say, 'That's the way it is, out of stubbornness.' That's how what is? What is stubbornness? Perhaps I didn't want to understand.

zaman (time): When the cruel bullies of the neighbourhood cut off the black cat's tail, she licked her two new-born kittens clean and then abandoned them. One of the kittens was taken by the people on the top floor, and the other was taken by the people on the bottom floor. The one taken by the people on the top floor was robust, and grew quickly; the one on the bottom floor grew, but very slowly. Both cats were eating the same food.

Time passed differently on the top floor and the bottom floor. The people on the bottom floor kept their clocks by the people on the top floor, but they were always late. When they saw the cats, the inhabitants of the house began to believe that they could see time. On the top floor time was sleek and fat, and on the bottom floor time was weak and puny.

Years passed in this manner. The cats grew older. The cat on the top floor soon became ungainly, the cat on the bottom floor aged slowly. Now time was proceeding backwards.

The studio belonged to an artist who was approaching sixty and who spent all of his time and money making himself look more interesting. Except for Sundays, there were different groups of students who came at different hours and on different days. And every evening there was a different model.

Monday was B–C's day. Every Monday evening B–C, wearing a purple velvet cape that I don't know where he found, would climb onto a stage about five hands high, sit on his stool, and commence not moving. While B–C posed, the students would draw his pose onto their canvasses. He got a ten minute break. Afterwards, B–C would climb on to the little stage one more time, sit on his stool, and throw off the purple velvet cape that I don't know where he found. He'd be left completely naked. His whole body was exposed.

I would have fallen through the floor in embarrassment.

His stance on top of the stool was so precarious; it looked as if he could fall down at any moment. I think that by doing this he made the students' work more difficult. Because it forced them to make ephemeral drawings rather than those that might last. His stance was not as lasting as a deeply rooted tree, or as a tick fastened with all its might to its victim, nor a fairytale that's refreshed as it's told. On the contrary, his stance was as aimless as water from a spring that could emerge from any fissure, as wayward as a pole star that wandered from one sky to another each night, as indifferent as moths who don't know the secrets of the dreams of the corners where they flutter. It was as if, even though he was here at that moment, he could get up and leave at any moment. For this reason, the students were gripped by an unnecessary panic, and missed details in order to finish their drawings as soon as possible.

But I think it was the strangeness of his eyes rather than the ephemeral nature of his stance that made the students' work difficult. Sometimes, though not always, B-C's eyes were reduced to two short, thin lines, and it was as if...as if they were closing. At times like these his eyes didn't express anything, and you couldn't put a finger on what he felt. I noticed something. When B-C's eyes were closed, none of the students' drawings resembled any of the others.

I don't think B-C was aware of this, because he didn't see the drawings, or the students. He just looked around with an aimless stare; from here to somewhere else, and from there to the next place. At the same time, the owner was constantly burning heavy incense in the small studio with small windows. When I came home, I stank of oil paint and incense.

Despite these things, I can't keep myself from dropping by once in a while. Every time I go to the studio, I go off into the corner and watch him and the watching. The owner of the studio watches the students with furrowed eyebrows, the students watch B–C with meaningful smiles, and B–C looks aimlessly into the distance. As the studio owner looks at the students, and the students look at B–C, and B–C looks into the distance, I hate this studio more and more. But B–C used to tell me that I should do the same thing. Since I was already fat enough to attract the attention of anyone who saw me, and since I was already being watched, then I should go and display myself out of spite. While even the thought of standing there naked and motionless in front of their eyes was enough to freeze my blood, B–C would insist on repeating, 'That's how it is, out of stubbornness.'

On top of this, the owner of the studio was always insisting that I model: 'Of course, you won't have to use the stool. We'll arrange a sofa for you.'

zarf (envelope): He worked at the post-office for years. For years he licked and sealed the envelopes that elegant ladies didn't want to touch and hurried gentlemen didn't deign to close. He believed that envelopes were essential not because of the addresses they bore but because they concealed what had been written. What made a letter a letter was the fact of its being closed, of being hidden from eyes. On the day he committed suicide he left behind an envelope with its flap open. He put his eyes into it. 'He went with his eyes open,' cried those who loved him. They licked the envelope and sealed it in order that he might rest in peace.

'Don't move!' said the man again. Though there was no need for him to say this. I wasn't moving.

This kind of thing happens to me all the time. Even if I tend to do the right thing in the right place, when I look, everything I touch comes off in my hands; my feet have resisted me, insisting 'I won't come with you, I won't carry you'; my ankles are angrily swollen, my thighs are chapped; my belly has folded itself into layers;

I've blown my top; my blood-pressure has jumped; my ears are not listening to what I say; my mouth couldn't hold its tongue again; my back is covered in sweat; my legs, seeing their own bulging veins, have given themselves a diagnosis of gangrene and then turned purple in their distress; my skin has discovered new food allergies and is swelling all over; my eyes are watering for no reason…before I know it I'm all over the place. I'd bend over and pick up my pieces one by one, but what I've lost is always more than I've gathered. No matter how careful I am, I always leave something behind. Something is always left half-done, unfinished, incomplete.

My dreams are made of sticks and stones. One flick is enough for them to be level with the floor. 'An earthquake' I'd explain to those around me, 'a terrible earthquake.' It helped them to believe that the ground must have shaken. Otherwise the reason for this terrifying shaking was nothing other than my huge body. Indeed that's why all of these things always happened to me. It's all because of my huge body that all my life I've tried to walk as if I'm in a crystal shop, in the best of circumstances knocking over a few shelves and smashing their contents to bits.

zayiçe (astrology): Looking at the state of the sky in order to see fortunes on earth is called astrology. Astrology is the name given to the charts useful for seeing where the lively stars will be at any given time.

It was clear that the man had good intentions, but also that he was old and inept. As he was struggling I was looking at the top floor of the Hayalifener Apartments. B-C was above, and I was below.

I'm down below because the thread that's been caught has neither beginning nor end; it grew longer when it was pulled, like a story that wore out the listener with its endlessness. I'm down below because I can't fit through doors when one wing is closed. I was stuck; if only I could take off my sweater and save my body. But I can't move because of the man. At one point I considered ringing the bell to call B-C for help. But who wants their lover to see them caught in the front door by the thread of her sweater?

Indeed, I still wasn't used to B-C's presence. B-C wasn't the problem; I just couldn't believe I had a lover. Sure, when you're as fat as I am you resign yourself to certain things. That is, the rule that 'A jug of foresight has fewer calories than a sip of disaster' applied here. In short, rather than nursing unrealistic fantasies and suffering later, I had decided from the start that no one would ever want me or love me. But since B-C had suddenly appeared in my life, the rules I'd lived by no longer seemed important. When I was with him waves washed against my entire length; the advice I gave myself was a sharp stone that could slice the calmness of this sweet water into rings. I didn't listen to it either. My life was like a bulky clock that had been left for broken in a corner, and had suddenly started ticking again for no reason. And I was setting the clock. It was struggling like crazy to make up for having been left behind for so long. It was constantly 'ticktockticktockticktocking'. As always, B-C spoke ill of time; he used to say that ' "tick-tock" is the tactic of time.'

I didn't understand his problem with time. In fact sometimes I didn't know what he was talking about. He talked a lot, and liked to say the strangest things. But I didn't complain. I loved it when he was like that.

zehir (poison): A substance that causes death without showing itself.

When at last he succeeded in freeing the thread, the old man's eyes shone with pride. He cleared his throat in order to accept the words of thanks and praise he was expecting. He must have loved heroes. He had spent his life searching for young women who had been attacked in dark streets, little children who had been trapped in burning buildings, palace dwellers whose family keepsakes in the form of pearl brooches had been stolen by pickpockets, ship-owners' sons who had been kidnapped for ransom. And he'd found them; but he'd never put any of these opportunities for heroism to use. Time had been unjust to him; it had not presented new opportunities to make up for those he'd missed. He'd always been one step behind, going home after everything was over, filled with regret when he realised what he should have done. He grew old needing to face the same incident again, but time refused to repeat it.

When I entered the Hayalifener Apartments holding the well-stretched thread from my sweater, the old man looked after me with anxious eyes. Who was I to have behaved so coarsely? During the twenty minutes he'd struggled to help me, he'd only looked at my eyes, my sweater and the stretched thread. In his mind, he'd given me a form to his own liking, and saw himself helping a young woman. Now, looking at me from behind, he finally perceived the whole of me, and saw me as he hadn't seen me before. He was amazed at how I was able to become so fat. 'It must be hereditary!' He was curious about where I was going. Should he stay and see which flat I went into?

On that question it was enough for him to ask his wife. Since the first day, all of the women in the Hayalifener Apartments knew I was going to B–C's flat.

Zeliha: 'The great vizier's wife was burning with passion for a slave,' laughed the ladies. Zeliha didn't understand that she was expected to punish her eyes for seeing beauty. She was curious about how these ladies, instigators of disaster and experts in gossip, saw this world.

Finally one day she invited the ladies to her house to show them what she liked and didn't like. She gave them fruit and knives. Later she presented Joseph to her guests. The ladies couldn't take their eyes off Joseph, and until they left the room they weren't aware that they were slicing their own fingers instead of the fruit.

Zeliha was calm and sedate as she gathered the plates; 'Look,' she said, 'at what my eyes have drawn to me.'

Again I was out of breath when I reached the top floor. Again, my wheezing wouldn't stop. There was no elevator in the building. I wouldn't ride it if there was one. It was better for me to take the stairs. If you're as fat as I am and the elevator breaks while you're in it, it's definitely you who has broken it. Once, the elevator I took got stuck between the second and third floor: half an hour later they took me out of there, and my rescue was the source of much amusement. Even today I can still see the meaningful looks they exchanged.

But it's still better to be stuck in an elevator alone than to get into an elevator with other people. Crowded together in that narrow space, even the politest people look at me from the corners of their eyes, and then at the sign that tells the maximum weight the elevator can carry. They try to guess roughly how much I weigh, and secretly start adding up. Sometimes this secret tension leads to witty remarks from those who are brazen enough to be crowned: 'Lord, I hope the cable doesn't snap!'

It's all so meaningless and exaggerated! Of course I'm not fat enough to put the elevator in danger. But my appearance becomes more important than anything. Those who end up next to me in a narrow elevator begin thinking with their eyes rather than with common sense.

All of this belongs in the past.

There's no elevator in the Hayalifener Apartments.

zenne: A man who plays women's parts in the theatre.

With the key in my hand, I stood in front of the door waiting for my wheezing to subside. I didn't want B-C to hear me coming. Because I wanted to see what he did when I wasn't there, or to intrude on his solitude. For some time now, he's been sitting in front of the computer working when I come home. With an overflowing ashtray next to him, a desk lamp worn out from its own light, the smell of coffee impregnating the room, hazelnut-wafer crumbs everywhere, rows of letters on the computer screen, pages filled with spidery notes... As if it had all been arranged to show that he'd been there for hours, and that all he'd done during my absence was to work. I became suspicious.

As I was trying to turn the key silently, the door opened from inside. B–C met me with a smile.

'Welcome! Eh, what did we do today?'

zevahir: Outer appearance.

Every evening we told each other what we'd done outside that day. Because we couldn't be together outside. If we took even one step outside the Hayalifener Apartments, our love dissolved. Not only did we not walk together outside, but if we met by chance we would greet each other from a distance. We were not to be seen next to each other. Perhaps I was more particular about this than B–C was. I didn't want anyone to see us together. Outside was forbidden for 'us'. It was only 'I' after the point where our secrecy ended. So that was why when we met at home in the evening we related to each other what we'd done separately as if we'd done it together.

I told him about how we'd gone shopping together that day. I told him about the supermarket.

zirh (armour): A person is more quickly defeated and more easily killed on the battlefield if he doesn't conceal what is within from the outer gaze.

The supermarket is the only place outside where I'm not judged for my fatness. I knew all of the supermarkets in the area; and all of the supermarkets in the area knew me. The security guards at the door would greet me smiling as if we were best friends. Whenever I passed in front of the people who sliced the cheese and the salami, they'd always offer me a taste of some new cheese or salami; the man on duty at the fish counter didn't wear the same sour expression when he cleaned my fish as he did when he cleaned other people's fish; the people in the bakery department always offered me *baklava* and pastries, and expected me to buy several kinds of bread; in the produce department they rushed to bring out unopened crates so I could be the first to choose the best and freshest fruits and vegetables; the girls at the cash registers were delighted to make conversation with me. At supermarkets I felt I was being given special treatment. I could fill my cart completely, and in spite of this come back to the same supermarket the next day and be seen buying an enormous amount again, and continue to do this every day, and still not be regarded strangely. I had the right to do comfortably a lot of things that others saw as disagreeable. I could taste as much cheese and as many olives as I wished; I could open and eat packets of biscuits, wafers and crisps; I could drink the cold drinks in the refrigerators. Sometimes I finished what I'd opened right there and then. At the exit, I'd throw the empty packets and bottles into the bin next to the cashier, and they'd smile understandingly and take the money without having to ask for it. I hadn't done anything shameful. Indeed, I could even have been considered well-behaved. My obesity and gluttony were valid. And in the supermarket their validity was accepted.

In time I noticed that children were tolerated in the same way as fat people like me. They were exempt from certain restrictions, they also received preferential treatment that was begrudged adults. They too opened packets before they reached the cashier, and their snacking in front of everyone was met with understanding. And while they were doing this they could be considered well-behaved. In any event these children, just like all fat people, were thought not to have any will-power.

zıtlık (contradiction): They asked the eye: 'What does it please you most to see?' 'Contradiction,' it said, 'Show me contradiction.' They showed him the forbidden love between Aphrodite, goddess of creation, and Ares, god of destruction.

Aphrodite and Ares carried on their love affair in secret, meeting only at night, and parting before daybreak. But one night they overslept. When the sun took its place in the sky, the lovers were discovered lying side-by-side by the sun. (Note: of course the sky has always been the best place from which to watch the earth.) The sun immediately carried news of what he'd seen to Aphrodite's ugly husband Hephaistos. He bound the two naked lovers in a net, and displayed their treachery as a lesson for others.

'Is this what you call contradiction?' asked the eye. 'Do you think it more contradictory for Aphrodite to have an affair with the god of destruction, or for her to remain faithful to the ugly Hephaistos? Show me contradiction, is there no contradiction?'

That day I told B–C how we'd shopped together at the supermarket that afternoon. I related it as if he knew what he'd seen; wide mirrors, security guards, hidden cameras. In this land of freedom and variety, the signs reading, 'Dear customers, our shop is protected by hidden cameras!', wandering among the eye–pleasing counters, the shopping we did with our eyes rather than with our purse, and before I reached how we paid the cashier and our money was taken, and we had to leave some things behind, I told him that on the way we couldn't see the things we'd bought as we had left our eyes behind with the things we didn't buy.

'Now you tell. What did we do outside today?'

B–C returned at once to his Dictionary of Gazes. He hadn't even heard my question. I regarded him with curiosity. How many more states was I going to see him in other that the one he was in here and now?

zihin (intellect): When the intellect is clouded, what is seen becomes clouded.

He sat in front of the computer, lit a cigarette, and read what he'd just written with raised eyebrows. I saw that B–C, who usually loved to chat, wasn't going to give me an answer no matter what I said. From now on, the Dictionary of Gazes came first.

zilzâl: Zilzâl, reminiscent of earthquakes, is the name of the ninety-ninth chapter of the Koran. According to this chapter, the earth was going to throw out all of the weight it was carrying. Then all of the layers invisible under the ground would emerge aboveground and be visible.

The interest in the dictionary had begun at the cinema almost a week earlier. Both of us loved the cinema. The cinema was the only place outside the Hayalifener Apartments where we could be together. Generally, we went in separately, and watched the film separately. But if the cinema was deserted, if there weren't too many curious eyes, we sat next to each other. We would hold hands in the dark throughout the film. Again I was on tenterhooks. I hated the ten minute intermission. Sometimes, when the intermission was drawing near, one of us would get up and go somewhere else, but most of the time we got involved in the film and missed the moment, and as soon as the lights came on we'd shrink guiltily into our seats. During that endless ten minutes, B–C, as round as a ball, would slide well down into his seat. As for me, there was nothing I could do. No matter how much I shrank, I was still too big to escape notice.

This interest began almost a week ago at the cinema. That day the cinema was almost completely empty. We were sitting together, holding hands, watching a film about a haunted house, when suddenly, when there was still a long way to go before the ten minute intermission, B–C jumped to his feet.

'I'm going home. I have to work.'

He left before I had a chance to ask any questions. I stayed behind at the cinema and continued watching the film.

zina (adultery): In order to prove adultery, there must be four male witnesses who saw the act with their own eyes. It is not enough for the witnesses to have seen the same thing, they're expected to state what they've seen in the same manner. If one of their statements arouses suspicion, the other witnesses' statements are considered perjurous, and the accusation is considered groundless.

ELIF SHAFAK

When the film was over, I went out the back door into the back streets. I saw, on the edge of the pavement, the same blind peddler I'd seen before at different times and in different places. There was an endless variety of evil-eye beads arranged on the counter; hundreds of eyes, big and small. A number of cats, most of them still kittens, were wandering around near the peddler. I grew uneasy. A single large dog was more suitable for a blind man outside than a flock of kittens. On top of this, the cats swarmed around him as if he were a large piece of liver that might get up and run away at any moment.

There, on the edge of the pavement, a blind man sold eyes to those who could see. As I was handing him money, one of the kittens on his lap arched its back and hissed at me. I wasn't surprised, because I'd long known that cats don't like me, but it still made me nervous. Clutching the evil-eye bead, I took myself off to the nearest place where I could get Albanian liver.

ziya (light): Light is that which makes all other things visible.

Well, when I came back from the cinema that day I found B-C working at the computer. Excitedly, he called me to his side.

'My love, this is a Dictionary of Gazes' he said pointing to the screen. He was like someone who was at last able to introduce the two people he loved most, expecting them to become close friends right away.

Well it all started like this.

zorba (tyrant): Because he'd lampooned the tyrant's tyranny, the sharp-tongued satirist's head was left impaled for days on a stake in the square. Passers-by stopped to look, and some came back to look again. Because the tyrant's power was the power of display.

In the beginning B–C's interest in this dictionary had to do with the interpretation of his own madness, and I thought it would pass the way it started. But it didn't happen that way. On the contrary, with each passing day it increased gradually. He worked away furiously, and was interested in a number of visual details that were completely unrelated to each other. He generally wrote at night. In time I became accustomed to falling asleep to the clacking of the keyboard, which at first used to keep me awake. At the end of each night, he'd put what he'd written into a transparent folder, and hide it from the sun and from me. When I got up in the morning, he'd just be lying down to sleep. Even though we lived in the same house, we began to see less and less of each other as time went by.

'Now where did this come from?' I asked one day.

'Where did it come from? It was already here. It was always here. Look, our lives are based on seeing and being seen. All of our troubles, worries, obsessions, our happiness and our memories…our very existence in this world too…and also our love…everything, I mean everything, has to do with seeing and being seen. Well, the Dictionary of Gazes is going to demonstrate this entry by entry. At first the entries will seem unrelated to each other, but because they all have to do with seeing and being seen, each entry will be secretly linked to another. In this way the Dictionary of Gazes will be like a shaman's cloak of forty patches and a single thread. I thought of this metaphor just this morning. So, what do you think?'

I smiled. How he loved to make pretentious statements. I went into the kitchen to look for a snack to go with my tea. Anyway, there were still some of those little round cakes filled with apricot jam that I bought at the bakery yesterday. When I went back to the living room with my plate in my hand, he was waiting for me with a long face.

'You'll see,' he said without hiding his hurt feelings. 'I'm going to prove to you how important the Dictionary of Gazes is.'

To mollify him, I wanted to say that he didn't have to prove anything to me, but he pushed my hand away roughly when I tried to stroke his hair. He didn't want to taste the apricot jam cakes either. He was hurt. As I was trying to think of a way to appease him, my eyes strayed to the computer screen.

'All right, you've just started the dictionary. Why didn't you start with the letter *A*?' I asked as pieces of apricot fell out of my mouth. 'All dictionaries start with the letter *A*. Why are you at *Z*?'

Whenever he has that look, his dark, bitter-chocolate eyes turn into shadows painted with a thin watercolour brush. My hands trembled as if they'd been charged with the responsibility of painting those delicate lines again. I was terrified that there'd be too much water, and the paint would drip, and erase his eyes. At times like these, I couldn't take my eyes off the strangeness of his eyes.

Zühre (Venus): They say that love can be forgotten just like everything else. And that love can be forgotten not only when it's over and done with, and the ashes are growing cold, but also at the moment when it's strongest.

Anyway, there was a star called Venus in the third level of the heavens. Those who couldn't remember whether or not they were in love, or who they were in love with if they were in love, would climb to the third level of the heavens to look into the mirror of love that Venus held in her hand. The face they saw would be the face of the person they loved.

They say that some people saw only pitch darkness in the mirror. These people were wrong to suspect their memories. What they lacked was not memory, but heart.

'I decided it wasn't important to go in order,' he said in a dry voice. 'I don't know… I wanted it to be a little more random. But I don't think so any more, you're right. It has to be orderly. I'll proceed from *A* to *Z*. It's better if I go back.'

I didn't understand why his mood had soured, or quite what he wanted to say. But I was still pleased that he'd listened to my idea. I smiled with the taste of apricots.

Adem ile Havva (Adam and Eve): When Adam and Eve tasted the forbidden fruit, they saw their differences for the first time. They became ashamed, and wanted to hide their nakedness with fig leaves. But one had a single fig leaf, and the other had three. Once they learned how to count, they were never the same again.

The following days were all alike. In the mornings B-C stayed at home, and I went to work. When I left he'd still be sleeping. When I came home I'd find him working on the Dictionary of Gazes. According to the day, he greeted me with either with extreme bad humour, extreme indifference or extreme good spirits. Sometimes too he'd narrow his eyes again like that; and I couldn't work out what he felt. The Dictionary of Gazes determined not only his mood, but also what happened to the rest of our day.

But there were things in our life that weren't determined by the Dictionary of Gazes. Like paying the rent. It didn't seem as if B-C was concerned about this problem. He'd dropped all the work he was doing and devoted all of his time to the dictionary. It seemed as if the owner of the art studio was more put out about this than anyone else. Just as he was on the point of suggesting that B-C model every evening instead of just Monday evenings, the man found out that he'd stopped working. From that moment on, he called again and again, telling B-C that he wanted the students to work with him, that anyway this job didn't take up much time, that at this point it was going to be difficult for him to find a model who interested everyone so much, and if necessary he'd raise the fee. To no avail. B-C simply didn't want to be involved with anything except the dictionary.

At this point I'd found a job teaching half days at one of the newly opened nursery schools. It didn't pay much, but the conditions were good. What I had to do was sing with the children, paint with them, make up stories, and kneed coloured clay with them from morning till noon. At one-thirty we had our lunch break. Our cook prepared different meals each day according to the weekly plan given to him by the parents' association. But it seemed to me as if we ate *köfte* and potatoes every day. Sometimes the *köfte* were made of meat, sometimes of chicken, sometimes of fish, sometimes of cracked wheat and sometimes of soy. The potatoes were always the same. And we always drank a lot of milk. It made the children giggle to see the way I drank milk. Every day we had a different kind of pudding that passed for dessert. When lunch was over the little ones would take their afternoon nap. Then after I'd gone back and cleaned up my classroom, I'd turn my post over to someone else. The director of the nursery was always calling me in and telling me that the parents wanted me to work full-time. According to him the parents loved me. The parents wanted it to be me they saw when they came to pick up their children in the evening.

But I wasn't any better than any of the other teachers. I was just much much fatter. My appearance gave the parents confidence. While I was in charge, they were less worried about their children falling and hurting themselves, or being rough with each other, or playing with sharp instruments. Like an enormous balloon filled with dreams that had the taste and consistency of strawberry pudding, I softened all movement around me. When I was there, modelling knives were a little less sharp, the corners of the desks a little less pointed, the pushing and shoving less harsh, even the slides in the playground were less slippery. When I was around, the children were secure. Perhaps I was even made for this kind of work.

But I had such a hard time going to the nursery in the mornings. Actually I didn't want to do anything that would take me out of the Hayalifener Apartments. As soon as the front door opened I was seized by the desire to go back home. I don't like the outside.

Outside is the land of appearances. The children at the nursery were competing with one another to remind me how fat I was. When I got home my hair smelled of the letters f-a-t-t-y the way someone's hair smells in the evening when they've been around people puffing on cigarettes all day. Indeed the first thing I did when I got home was to wash my hair. The letters would wash off me and swirl away down the drain. But no matter how much I shampooed my hair, some of them wouldn't come out. They'd stick to me like burs. Then, B–C would come help me: he'd pick out the f's, the a's, the t's, the y's.

So one day I decided to dye my hair. It was clear I couldn't get rid of the letters f–a–t–t–y. But with the right hair colour I could make them invisible; like a sweater that doesn't show stains.

ask (love): A widow was in the arms of her lover. 'This thing called love should be forbidden,' she muttered to herself, 'and what is forbidden should be kept out of sight.'

However, the young man wanted everyone to see him make love to the widow. He had to prove to others that he was growing up. For this reason he always kept the window open. But no one ever passed down that street.

Then one day as the young man was wandering around the house, he managed to open a door that was always kept locked, and that he'd never once touched before. 'My God!' he shouted. 'Is that why you've locked everyone into this room? Did you do this so no one would see us?' As he stood waiting for an answer, the widow locked the door on the callow young man and left.

The widow met a caterpillar on the road. 'Will you be my secret love?' she asked him. 'Why keep it a secret?' asked the caterpillar. 'If someone's in love with me I want everyone to see her love. Then I'll be thought less ugly.' For a while, the widow watched the caterpillar gnaw on the leaves. Then she locked the whole wide world on the ugly caterpillar.

She came across the cosmos and asked it the same question. The aged cosmos answered, 'If someone's in love with me I want everyone to see her love. Then I'll be thought younger.' The widow shrugged her shoulders. In any event she had a bunch of keys in her pocket. She locked the aged cosmos in on itself.

In order to continue on her way she had to step off and fall into the void. As she fell she took a new key out of her pocket, but there was no lock in sight. 'Are you an idiot? What would a lock be doing drifting through the void? There's nothing here but nothingness,' grumbled the void. The widow looked at the void with great admiration. 'In that case, please let me stay with you. You're the one I've been seeking.'

'That's completely out of the question,' said the void. 'If you stay with me, you'll fill my void, and then I'll no longer exist.'

'Go on back now,' said the void in a sweet voice, as if wishing to ask forgiveness for having been rude. 'Go back and open all the doors. Let them out. You need them.'

The widow did as the void asked, and opened all the doors she'd locked. When they saw that their captivity had come to an end the prisoners rushed out pushing and shoving; as they ran around dazed by their freedom, some of them were injured. The widow was surprised and angry. 'As if things were any better now?' she was heard to have said. She locked herself in her house in order not to have to witness any more of this tumult. And after this she forbade herself love.

The colour catalogue they thrust into my hands at the hairdresser's was wonderful. There were curls of all colours, but I was more enchanted by the names than by the colours. For instance the caption for a copper-coloured curl was 'Farewell to the Train at Sunset', for a loud reddish tone 'Also Known as Seduction', for an ash-coloured curl, 'What the Fireplace Knows', for a yellow curl, 'Natural Blond', for a dark, chestnut-coloured curl, 'Roasting Chestnuts in the Evening'. I stroked the curls again and again with my index finger. If it were up to me, I'd give each of the coloured curls names that had to do with food. Since I was little, colours have always evoked food for me. As I thought, I looked carefully at my index finger. My cuticles were torn and chewed away, and in horror I hid my finger so no one would see it.

After hesitating for some time, I decided on a curl with silver glitter in it. It was called 'Coal-cellar Black.'

'It will suit you very well,' said the hairdresser. 'It will make your face look thinner.'

I didn't say anything. I didn't return his smiles. I looked at him in the wide mirror in front of where I was sitting. He grew uncomfortable and avoided my eyes. I hate those who think fat people are stupid.

ay (moon): For centuries people, thinking that the moon was close to them, gave it a human face. (Note: research the moon's faces!)

When I came back I found B–C striding around the house in an irritable mood. He noticed what I'd done to my hair right away. He said a few nice things, but it was clear his mind was elsewhere. I'd never seen him this troubled before.

'If it keeps going like this it will take forever to finish this dictionary,' he said while I was in the kitchen preparing a snack.

'Excuse me, but it's only been a few days since you started. I don't even really understand what you're doing yet.'

'Come on!' he shouted suddenly. 'Let's not shut ourselves up at home tonight. Let's go out.'

He must have been out of his mind.

ay çiçesi (sunflower): When the sunflower fell in love with the sun, the other plants all broke out laughing, 'The sun never leaves his throne in the heavens even for a moment. He's powerful and inaccessible,' they said in unison. The sunflower said nothing. It planted its passionate eyes on the sun, and looked and looked and looked.

For a long time the sun noticed nothing, then finally one day he sensed the sunflower looking at him. At first he thought it was just a passing fancy, but in time he understood he was mistaken. The sunflower was so stubborn that wherever the sun moved his throne, she simply turned her head in that direction without being daunted or losing hope.

Then one afternoon, fed up with this surveillance, the sun roasted the sunflower with his bright yellow rage. While smoke was still rising from the sunflower, people rushed to see what had happened. 'Wonderful!' said one of them, 'Now we can enjoy cracking this love between our teeth.'

That night, watching a sad love story on television, they cracked their sunflower seeds between their teeth.

'We're going out? We're not avoiding other people's eyes any more? Tell me, what's changed?'

'I've found a solution for our situation,' he said lowering his voice, and squinting his dark chocolate eyes with childish delight. He remained silent for a few minutes just to fan my curiosity, then added smiling: 'Tonight you and I are going out in disguise.'

ay tutulmasi (eclipse of the moon): Sometimes the moon in the sky manages to hide from the gaze of people on earth. As soon as no one can see, she freshens her powder.

As he's getting ready, he continues to explain. To go out in disguise is to change your appearance. All of the Sultans used this method to see in person what their empires really looked like. Now we were going to follow this royal tradition, and change our appearance. If we don't look like ourselves, we'll be able to go out together.

'Fine, but even if we're disguised won't someone recognise us?' Someone would, of course, why wouldn't they? I wasn't at all reassured.

ayn-al-yakin: Ayn-al-yakin, which is understood as seeing God with the eye of spirit, is the second of three levels.

He shaved carefully. When I wiped the foam off his skin, it smelled like peaches. His peach fuzz quivering in the wind of his agitation gave me goose bumps. He undressed behind the screen. When he came out he was wearing one of my bras. As I was trying to figure out what he had stuffed it with, my eyes fell onto his hips. He passed coquettishly in front of me. I watched with alarm. It struck me with terror to see the man I love display an attitude I'd never seen him display before, and behave in a way that seemed not to acknowledge the past, to make a lie of the present, and to exclude me. How could he internalise his new appearance so quickly? As if his personality changed with his appearance.

I became restless. My heart sank at the thought of leaving the Hayalifener Apartments with B-C. No matter what we wore, how much could we hide from the eyes of others, and for how long? We didn't please anyone's eyes. Even if we were in disguise, and even at night, we didn't suit each other.

I was afraid to go outside. I didn't like the outside.

> *ayna* (mirror): The odalisques in the harem couldn't get their fill of looking at their unsurpassed beauty in the mirrors that had been brought from Venice. Their greatest desire was for the Sultan to see what the mirror showed.

He stood in front of me in a filmy, floral dress that swept the floor, and was wearing mascara as black as olive paste, false eyelashes, butterfly glasses, eye-shadow the colour of blackberries and sprinkled with glitter, with bronze foundation and powdered rouge on his face; his lips were smeared with cherry-coloured lipstick and lined with pencil; he wore a wig the colour of boiled corn, fish-net stockings, and shoes that made him much taller, with mind-boggling heels that from a distance looked like two toy towers. There were large hoop earrings on his ears, a coral necklace on his neck, jangling bracelets on his wrists, giant rings on his fingers, a pea-green, snake-skin bag on one shoulder, and a sad, furry animal tail draped over the other.

How and when did he turn into this? When I touched his body to try to sense its secret, he fluttered his false eyelashes flirtatiously. He was in a completely different state of mind, and if I didn't take myself in hand quickly, it was clear he was going to go out in disguise without me.

Babil Kulesi (Tower of Babel): People were so curious about God that they decided to build a tower that would pierce the heavens. The construction proceeded quickly. All of the workers worked in harmony and with mutual understanding. But just as they were struggling to reach the limits of the seventh level of the heavens, God gave each workman a different language. The construction stopped because no one could understand each other.

Because God didn't want to be seen.

I scurried to get ready

basilisk: The basilisk is a poisonous animal, and its poison is fatal. The basilisk was a nightmare for travellers who set their sails for unknown lands. These travellers carried all kinds of protective objects to evade its poisonous looks. But the most intelligent of them felt no need for anything but a mirror.

What else in the world could stop a basilisk except its own appearance?

It took hours. With B–C pulling the corset strings from one side, and me from the other, we succeeded in squeezing in my fat layer by layer. I was covered in sweat. My fat was used to wobbling about freely, and didn't know how to respond to this unexpected pressure. Some of it was weeping with abandon, some of it was swearing heavily, and some of it was begging pitifully for mercy. Some of it, seeking a hole or a rip through which to escape, soon had to accept defeat. The corset squeezed me so tightly it was a miracle I could even move. I was pressed in on all four sides. I was girded in to the north, south, east and west; there was no place for my fat to escape.

The rest of the preparations didn't take long. Indeed after such struggle, I had neither strength nor patience left. I sprinkled lots of hair all over myself. My hands, chest and legs were covered with hair. I combed back my coal-black hair and gathered it under my cap. My moustache wasn't so thick, but it would pass. Besides, there

was no need for a beard. I'd become a coarse young man. I raised
my eyebrows to tell B–C to walk in front of me. As I locked the
door, he was giggling on the stairs.

He was right. No one would recognise us like this.

baykuş (owl): The aunts and uncles used to feed the canaries. They used
to love the doves, fly the pigeons, chase away the crows, and make the
parrots talk. But the child used to love owls. 'That's an unlucky bird. Don't
utter its name, don't call it to your roof,' the aunts and uncles would say.
The owl is an unlucky bird because it sees at night, because it sees the
night.

That night we kept the main avenue in sight while we walked
through the back streets. With every step, smells of food drifted
to me. My nose was constantly following the traces of each smell
in this confusion where the most wonderful smells and the most
dreadful smells were so mixed together that nothing smelled as
it should. The corset was squeezing me, and B–C was pulling me
along. Finally, after passing I don't know how many stuffed-mussel
stands, I decided I couldn't stand it any more. Before long the
stuffed-mussel boy's shoulders were shaking with laughter as he
removed the empty shells two by two. 'Enjoy yourself, brother!'

Meanwhile, B–C was getting out of control. He wanted to stop
and knock back a few beers at every bar we passed, otherwise he'd
make a fuss. The more he drank, the more he lost control, and the
more he lost control the more he drank. When he started trying to
pinch the cheeks of the thuggish bouncers outside the bars, it was
the last straw. I tried to drag him along by the arm. My brain was
throbbing with irritation. As I grew irritable I became more hungry.
While I was thinking about where I could eat some *gözleme*, B–C
was muttering something to the effect that, 'I'm a free woman, I
can do what I wish.' Holding his arm roughly, I tried to drag him
to the *gözleme* stand at the end of the street. At that moment, very
nearby, a newly rolled *gözleme* was sizzling on the dome-shaped

griddle, absorbing the butter, and was just on the point of turning crisp, while I was writhing with hunger because of some stupid argument. I had to hurry. But before I'd taken two steps, a shout from behind made me turn around.

'Leave the lady alone, man.'

'Did you say something?' I blustered to the round-faced man who was walking up to me.

'I said lady, so what? Or isn't she a lady?'

> *cadi* (witch): Before roasting Hansel in the oven, the witch wanted to be certain he'd been fattened enough. Every morning she inspected the child's index finger. But the finger was always bony and thin. Because Hansel was tricking the witch by showing her a twig instead of his finger. Since the witch couldn't see well, she never managed to eat Hansel.

B–C was winding his finger through his corn-coloured wig, and watching us with a smile that froze my blood.

Just as we were about to start fighting, the man and I both stopped to look carefully at what kind of lady we were risking injury for. And both of us decided at the same moment not to drag the matter out. In a hoarse voice I told him to get lost. He made a short speech about not stirring up trouble. We started to back away, without neglecting to give each other dirty looks, until we both bumped into the same invisible wall.

> *camera obscura*: An instrument that reverses images.

I began to feel my way along the invisible wall that enclosed me. When I'd made it half way around the circle, I found myself nose to nose with the round-faced man. As far as I could understand, he too had been feeling his way along the wall, and had made it half way around the circle. This way, when we met again we'd both have completed the invisible circle. A crowd had gathered around us. We were surrounded by eyes that had flocked around to watch a fight.

It was then that I understood that the flame of every street fight is fanned by the eyes that gather around to watch it. Every street fight is caused by spectators.

> cemal: Beauty. A beautiful face. In Sufism, a manifestation of God in the form of goodness and beauty.

I landed my first punch in his stomach. He doubled over and fell to the ground. I didn't think he'd be able to pull himself together quickly, but I was wrong. It was clear he wasn't as inexperienced as I was. He threw his first punch at my nose. My eyes went dark. I tasted warm blood. B-C, who'd been left on the other side of the invisible circle, started to scream like mad when he saw the blood. The invisible circle was a boundary. We, the fighters, couldn't get out, and no one from outside could come in to help. B-C, with tears in his eyes, was trying to climb the invisible wall that separated us, struggling to reach me.

At that moment something unexpected happened. First, the crowd began to exchange meaningful smiles. Then, just to make the fight more colourful, they opened a door in the invisible wall to let B-C through. As if in a dream, I saw B-C dive through the gap with a blood-curdling scream, jump on me, cover me with kisses, then furiously begin destroying his pea-green, snake-skin bag on the round-faced man's head. The rest was a blur.

> cennet-cehennem (heaven and hell): The eyes of those who have suffered their punishment in hell and have then been accepted in heaven must forget what they have seen there before they can enter.

They took hold of my arms and helped me get up. I didn't have the strength to stand on my feet. I looked at B-C, and saw that his tears had made tracks through the thick rouge on his cheeks. In front of everyone, his eyes shone with pleasure at my having fought for him. We sat on some empty crates outside a grocery store. For a while, we didn't talk. As people started to drift away in ones and twos, B-C began to kiss my bruises softly with his cherry-coloured lipstick. 'Bruised cherries,' I whispered. We embraced each other, and swore once again that we would never hurt each other. I was filled with peace. The wind was blowing bruised cherry, I was aching with bruised cherry, my lover was kissing bruised cherry.

> *ceviz asaci* (walnut tree): The walnut tree records everything it sees in the shells of its walnuts. That's why no one wants to make love under this tree.

When we left with our arms around each other, I thought we would take the shortest route back to the Hayalifener Apartments. But B-C dragged me into the first bar we passed. It was gloomy inside. B-C sat at the bar knocking back one beer after another; I couldn't do anything except retreat into a corner, lean my head back, and wait for the blood to clot. When I did this, I couldn't see B-C. As long as I couldn't see him, I was terrified.

As I grew frightened, I grew hungry.

> *cin* (jinn): According to the Holy Koran, *jinns* were created a thousand years before Adam. *Jinns* made of black clay are visible to the human eye, but *jinns* made of smokeless fire are invisible. There are many types and categories of *jinn*. Some among them can cause madness.

As we sat at the nearest *gözleme* place, waiting for the waiter to bring our spinach *gözleme*, I did the best I could to behave well towards B-C. It was clear that I couldn't tolerate a second fight that night. Though he didn't seem to notice how tense I was. He was frightfully drunk. He was provoking passers-by, talking non-stop about things I didn't understand at all, and laughing loudly at his own words. Everyone's eyes were on us. This wasn't my idea of going out in disguise.

çekirdek (seed): Tired after travelling a long way over hills and valleys, a traveller stopped to rest under a plane tree. He had olives and bread in his bundle. As he was eating, just for fun, he started spitting the olive seeds as far as he could.

A giant approached with enormous steps. He shook his fist and shouted, 'Just now one of the olive seeds you flung killed my son. You've murdered my only son.'

The traveller was bewildered. 'How could that be? It's impossible. Think about it. What's a tiny little seed next to a huge giant?' The giant was confused. In order to understand whether or not the traveller was in the right, he started looking at one of the olive seeds that had fallen to the ground. He looked and looked…he looked day and night, through sun and rain, over seasons. He went away, then came back and looked again.

A long time later the giant roared, 'Ah, so, what's a tiny little seed next to a huge giant, ha? Before long I was going to start believing this lie.'

The giant thought it was just for the traveller, who somehow couldn't convince the angry giant of the difference between looking at a seed 'now' and 'looking at it years later', to bow his head for his punishment under the olive tree that was growing next to the plane tree.

'Why are you so uncomfortable, sugar? Or does it frighten you that everyone's looking at us?' B–C asked ill-temperedly. And then, jumping to his feet, he continued talking in a voice that everyone could hear, knowing that everyone was watching him.

'Of course. Within the four walls of home you want us to be playful and flirtatious, even whorish, but as soon as we step outside you want us to be demure and proper little ladies. You have no idea that when you're playing with our appearance you're playing with our pride. Aren't you men? You're all the same. If we went out and did a tenth of what you want us to do at home, you'd cry for blood immediately. Am I lying? Enough! I object to the splitting of my personality.'

If only the earth had opened and swallowed me up, or one of the bus-boys had showed me a secret passage under the table through which I could slip away, or my corset had burst and me and my warmly dripping fat had been flung for miles, if only I could immediately have disappeared forever. By now everyone in the place must have stopped whatever they were doing and were waiting to see what my reaction would be. For my part, I couldn't take my eyes off the stains on the edge of the plate, full of warm spinach *gözleme*, that the waiter had just brought.

> *Dabbetülarz*: The animal that will emerge from the earth on the Day of Judgement. It has the head of a bull, the ears of an elephant, the legs of a camel and the tail of a hyena. It will paint the faces of the believers white, and the faces of the unbelievers black. The good and the evil will be known by the colour of their faces.

When we finally returned to the Hayalifener Apartments at the end of that long night, B-C couldn't wait for me to open the door. And wouldn't you know it, the key got stuck in the lock. While I was struggling with the door, he suddenly threw back his head and made a sound as if he was choking. Just in time I realised what the sound meant, and was able to get out of the way. He vomited all over the walls, the corridor, and his boiled-corn coloured wig. Then, as if that wasn't enough, he went and vomited on the neighbour-lady's doormat. I was hurrying so much I was shaking. In any event, the key didn't give me any more trouble, and the door opened.

As the door opened, B-C pushed me aside and rushed inside in one motion. Just in front of the bathroom he lost his balance and fell noisily off his lofty high-heels. He was so drunk he wasn't even aware he'd hurt himself.

> *Efî*: The female viper Efî first lost the eyes with which she saw. Later, when she encountered the Razyanc tree, she lost her blindness. (Research: The dried heart of Efî, who first lost the eyes with which she saw, and then lost the eyes with which she didn't see, is considered a talisman against any kind of spell.)

When he came out of the toilet he looked terrible. He'd returned to his former height, he'd smeared cherry-coloured lipstick all over himself, all of his make-up had run and mixed together, his fish-net stockings had run from top to bottom, the hair that had been plastered under the wig was sticking out strand by strand, and the eyes that had been so fiery and alive all night seemed wrapped in a sad silence. He stood before me with his oversized hands clasped together and wearing a pouting expression. It was clear he was going to be very ashamed of himself, if he had the strength to be ashamed.

> *Elsa'nin gözleri* (Elsa's eyes): Elsa's eyes are the residue of sadness. Poets sift through the sadness, and children through the residue.

As he threw himself onto the bed he whispered sadly.

'I wouldn't have wanted you to see me this way. In this state...'

But it pleased me a great deal to see him in this state. To tell the truth, it was quite pleasant to see him in this wretched and disgraceful state, because he always seemed to know what he was doing, and took everything seriously, and wore himself out thinking deeply about every problem, and could always guess everyone's story, and so get a fix on their weaknesses, and succeeded and behaved towards everyone, people he knew as well as people he didn't know, with an authority that someone with his small frame might not have hoped for.

> *fal* (fortune-telling): Every method of fortune-telling wishes to see the future. It's not enough just to see, one has to make others believe one can see. (Example: Apollo gave Cassandra the ability to tell fortunes. But when Cassandra turned down his proposal of marriage, Apollo punished her by 'making others disbelieve what she saw.')

In the morning when I was getting ready for work, I looked and saw that he was up, sullenly making coffee. We came face to face.

'Tell your eyes to forget what you saw last night,' he said half-jokingly.

'I don't think so,' I said. 'They won't forget.'

'Anything?' he asked in an annoyed tone.

'Anything,' I said, not knowing why I was resisting him this way.

'I don't think so,' he said. 'They'll forget.'

Fames: Fames, the god of hunger, lived in a land of boundless appetite covered by inedible plants, razor-like ridges of ice and never-melting snow. He was so thin, so very thin, that from a distance he resembled a heap of bones. From his lips, bitten to shreds and blue with cold, emerged the names of the foods of which he dreamed: The agony of hunger could be read in the sharp glances of his lustreless, blackened eyes. His face was yellow and wizened, and his skin was dried out. His fingers were very thin from being sucked on. From time to time he started to eat himself, and had teeth marks all over him.

Fames' breath smelled worse than rotten eggs. Whoever smelled it once would hence remain hungry. Whoever was poisoned by Fames' breath would remain unsated no matter how much he ate. Hunger ate at them even as they ate their food. Because it wasn't their stomachs that could not be filled, but their eyes.

I felt distressed as soon as I left the Hayalifener Apartments. I wanted to go back home and not go out for the rest of the day. The hill seemed steeper than ever, and the route more complicated than ever. The easiest thing to do would be to take a taxi, but I can't be taking taxis every day. To think about wheezing up the steep steps of the bus at this hour of the morning, to make my way down the crowded aisle and push and shove to make room for myself, to think about the eyes that would be watching me the whole way, made my feet want to turn and go back home. There was a minibus route between the Hayalifener Apartments and the nursery school; but minibuses were the worst of all.

When I forced myself to walk again, terrible wheezing sounds emerged from my chest. With every step I felt how chapped my legs were, and I had to stop frequently. I was accustomed to this much. Movement has always been difficult for me. But now, moving in order to do something I didn't want to do, it was not just my body that resisted, but also my soul. As I struggled up the hill, passers-by gave me worried looks.

> *fotosraf albümleri* (photograph albums): Photograph albums are taken out of the closet at regular intervals to remind the eye only of the good things it has seen. Each time, it will examine the photographs with curiosity, as if it were seeing them for the first time; with curiosity and in strict order: infancy, childhood, youth, marriage, infancy, childhood, youth…

When I reached the top of the hill drenched in sweat, I stopped to catch my breath. I'd made a very definite decision. I couldn't go on like this.

I was going to go on a diet.

TWO
'OPEN YOUR EYES!'

Pera – 1885

After the evening call to prayer, the eastward-facing door of the cherry-coloured tent was opened for men.

At that moment the men, who acted as if they wanted to prove that they were there by coincidence, and had come to the tent not out of curiosity but to see what everyone else was curious about, wearing indifferent expressions as if they were just going to take a quick look and leave, entered the eastward-facing door of the cherry-coloured tent with casual steps. The men's section of the tent had been set aside for them. It didn't matter what nation they were from, what language they spoke or what religion they believed in; it was sufficient that they were men. And also that they arrive one by one. Keramet Mumî Keşke Memiş Efendi had laid down this condition: every man had to come here by himself.

Keramet Mumî Keşke Memiş Efendi loved to examine the different faces of the moon. And he used to say that the eastward-facing door of the cherry-coloured tent was the dark side of the moon.

He also used to tell a strange story about this. According to the story, what the dark side of the moon feared most was to not be loved; and also for his eyes to be seen weeping. And if anyone happened to see that he had wept, his male pride was inflamed. For years, he had kept two crystal marbles next to his testicles. He had stolen them when he was a child; at the cost of becoming a thief of his own possessions.

…so his intentions couldn't be read in his eyes…head on the

ground…heart in his mouth…with timid steps…he approached… the most troublesome in the neighbourhood…the biggest…the child who swore most…the truth…so cowardly…to hide…should have come out fighting…by one's own efforts…should have taken it back…the crystal marbles…isn't that so…this gift…a God never seen…or perhaps…at the head of the street…saints in their tombs… given to him…isn't that so…the one under the pillow…two copper coins…however that happened…one multi-coloured morning… two crystal marbles…given…in any event…what to say…not to hold one's tongue…the one who comes to the front…displaying the marbles…snatched from his hands…and for whom?…the most troublesome in the neighbourhood…the biggest…the child who swore most…who shouted at the top of his voice…without any shame…in front of everyone… 'these are mine now'… 'come take them if you can'…it wasn't easy…the dark side of the moon was?…he waited…for how long…the troublesome child…went to urinate…and then…stole…what had been stolen from him…with his heart in his mouth…head on the ground…so his intentions couldn't be read in his eyes…

The dark side of the moon ran for hours with the crystal marbles in his hand; he ran in the direction in which his fear chased him. He hid them in a place where that oaf would never get his hands on them. After thinking it over for a long time he decided that his own flesh was the safest place. He understood that he'd spent his manhood to get the miraculous marbles. Since, having held tight the mane of the horse of passion just like a woman, without thinking about or weighing what he was spurring, without even wanting to think, he'd galloped off at full speed to get back what had been taken from him; since there was no one with even an atom of courage to stand up to the neighbourhood bully, to win back what had been lost; in any event, after this he was never going to go out in the street, he wouldn't run with his friends but would sit in the window just like a young girl. To give due credit, the one who had taken his manhood had to be part of his manhood. The crystal dreams of his first and last act of heroism, his first and last stand against injustice.

Since that day, he would piss his fear as far away as possible. And he was particularly afraid of not being loved; and also of his eyes being seen to have wept. Both of them led to the same result; loneliness. The reason he stayed completely alone was not being loved and his tears having been seen.

The story Keramet Mumî Keşke Memiş Efendi told about the dark side of the moon was something like this. And he wouldn't tell this story for nothing. He knew that men were most prone to loneliness. Simply in order not to be alone, men would rush outside as soon as the sky grew dark, first to find the consolation of the company of others, and then of one another's conversation; but as time passed, the broth of friendship was spoiled. Whenever they came together, especially if they were a little tipsy, gaining strength learning of their strength from one another, they would run after cheap acts of heroism.

So what if men could find the opportunity to prune the knotted branches of the tree of their childhood nightmares once in a lifetime. After the spell has turned copper into crystal, it's gone and won't return. Alchemy was a door that decided on its own who was going to look for it when. For this reason, missed opportunities were never to present themselves again. So when he didn't get what he wanted, the dark side of the moon grew even darker. And if what he wanted belonged to someone else, he would seize the first opportunity to take it. Keramet Mumî Keşke Memiş Efendi knew that men mostly stole from one another; when they saw the opportunity, they wouldn't hesitate to steal one another's happiness. This was the reason they had to come separately. In order to enter the eastward-facing door they had to climb the hill by themselves, and to remain alone until they reached a certain cherry tree.

Some of the men accepted these conditions from the start. Most of them were of noble birth, or wished to appear so. They'd climb the hill like princes. Starting out at the bottom of the hill alone, they arrived at the mouth of the tent by themselves. And some, knowing full well that they would have to separate, climbed together until the last possible moment. Most of these were of the masses, or wished to appear so. They preferred to bend their necks together rather than start out alone. No matter how much they delayed, what they were postponing was waiting for them at the fountain on the hill. When they arrived at the fountain, they would distance themselves from their travelling companions as if they had a contagious disease. The fountain was very pleased with itself; it sprayed water about enthusiastically. The men would lower their lips to the ice-cold water, and drink deeply. When their sweat dried and they started off again, each one remained alone. As their legs shook with the effort like the legs of new-born animals, those who had accepted solitude at the bottom of the hill strode past them haughtily. Those now-alone imitated those who had already been alone; though without letting on that they were doing so.

From here on everyone was by themselves. Thus the lips of conversation between old friends and strangers were sealed. An indistinct fear would seize the shore of their hearts. Keramet Mumî Keşke Memiş Efendi's orders were categorical; since each man had to arrive alone, not even fear could keep him company. For this reason, those who were climbing the hill would loosen the fingers of fear one by one. When they'd dissolved the last finger, fear would roll over a bottomless cliff; taking part of their courage with it. The men, with the cries of their courage as it crashed down the cliff ringing in their ears, thrust themselves with difficulty through the eastward-facing door of the cherry-coloured tent. Even at that moment the men, who acted as if they wanted to prove that they were there by coincidence, and had come to the tent not out of curiosity but to see what everyone else was curious about, wearing indifferent expressions as if they were just going to take a quick look and leave, entered the eastward-facing door of the cherry-coloured tent with casual steps.

Most of them were on foot. Yes, those who insisted on climbing the hill in a carriage could become the victims of unexpected accidents. One never knew. Sometimes everything went smoothly, and the horses succeeded in reaching the top of the hill covered in sweat. Sometimes the carriage would slip on the ice and overturn. It would tumble and slip back down to the starting point of the voyage. Having seen many incidents of injury from this kind of occurrence, most of the men would get out of their carriages at the bottom of the hill and struggle up by their own efforts. Sometimes, pretty gentlemen would be seen in litters. They would climb the hill with dignified expressions on the shoulders of their strong powerful servants. But as is the way of the world, these too overturned from time to time.

Those who turned and looked back when they reached the top of the hill could see the sea. The sea was blue, bluer than blue; it was hostage to its own clear stillness. Once in a while some men got a crazy idea. To their eyes, the sea looked like a still and silent womb. Now...neither complaining about poverty nor earning their living; as if...only but only existing within was enough for all they'd desired, to set out on journeys not taken, to go back and forth between different lands. In any event, the ball of wool that was their common-sense waited in alarm. The loosening thread was soon re-wound. Those who held unrealistic dreams remembered that holding unrealistic dreams was not appropriate. As Keramet Mumî Keşke Memiş Efendi often said: if the ship of men were to sink, it would sink by breaking up in shallow water thinking that the brightest light was a lighthouse.

Even though in time this area came to be called a swamp, no one who had once smelled the heady fragrance of the fig and lemon trees, or seen their delicate purple buds would want to believe this. It is said that the reason the cherry-coloured tent was erected here rather than somewhere else was Keramet Mumî Keşke Memiş Efendi's mulish stubbornness. He would do things out of stubbornness; and hide the reason within himself. And no one interfered too much in the matter. More important than the outside of the tent was the inside. If anyone knew the truth of this, it was Keramet Mumî Keşke Memiş Efendi.

It was possible to meet endless types of men here; speakers of every language and pliers of every profession. There were notorious womanisers, famous toughs, swaggering losers, gentlemen with inheritances, gentlemen who'd spent their inheritances, antique dealers who hid shops within their shops, spies from rival firms, official interpreters from Genoa or Venice, Galata money-lenders, elegant dance-instructors from Pera, tailors who could make whatever was being worn in Paris, purveyors of glazed fruit, impoverished noblemen, decorators, Circassians with fur-hooded black kaftans, Greek taverna-owners with large bellies, English dentists, hard-faced Bedouins, pale-faced Persians, bakers who were now giving their customers Viennese cakes, importers of wine, those who were regularly invited to magnificent balls, those who behaved as if they were regularly invited to magnificent balls, Russian musicians, French photographers, Armenian printers, Italian architects, Albanians wearing pistols, Jewish merchants, Abkhaz, Serbs, well-known pillars of society, experts in Eastern languages, consular attachés, procurers, treasure hunters running after the legends of Istanbul and the dream brokers who ran after them, professional letter-writers, second-hand booksellers who could read the language of the book, gold merchants who could speak the language of gold, calligraphers who adorned the language of letters, ship's officers, opponents of the regime, supporters of the regime, and, finally, everyone else.

There was one only reason these various men, who did not greet each other in the street and who did not pity each other in a fight, gathered at the eastward-facing door of the cherry-coloured tent: to see La Belle Annabelle!

Keramet Mumî Keşke Memiş Efendi was responsible for all of these things. After all, he was a very clever and agile man. Since his birth, this world had considered him strange. He was like this as a child and he's still like this today. He was always in motion, and couldn't sit still. He was quick to develop a thesis in his mind, but once he had developed it he grew bored with it. He liked to surprise people, but grew cold towards them when they were surprised by unsurprising things. He would involve himself in things that harmed the mind, wake from every sleep with new curiosities, talking constantly, always running around. In spite of this, those who looked at him usually thought they saw him motionless. Because his glances were expressionless. His thinly drawn eyes were without feeling, and seemed far removed from any emotion.

When the time came, his six elder sisters saw to it that a suitable wife was found for Keramet Mumî Keşke Memiş Efendi. The bride was more beautiful and proficient a girl than all of the matchmakers in the city could have found. She had only one fault: she was as silent as a stone that had rolled to the bottom of a lake. She was deaf and mute from birth.

On the wedding night, they saw each other for the first time. The bride, her eyes as big as saucers from amazement, looked for a long time into the eyes of the man opposite her. These eyes had neither happiness nor mercy; neither rage nor beneficence. The eyes to which she would wake up every God-given morning were as empty as this orphan girl's trousseau.

The young woman suddenly started crying. She allowed three teardrops to fall from her two eyes. Keramet Mumî Keşke Memiş Efendi lined up the teardrops and read in them what his wife's still mute tongue related:

'My dear sir. Allow me to leave. I have neither a tongue nor ears. I live through my eyes. I hear with my eyes and I converse with my eyes. I read with my eyes, and I write with my eyes. Your eyes, however... I've never seen eyes like yours before. It's as if your eyes are closed. And if they're closed, they can't say anything. My tongue doesn't speak, and neither do your eyes. How could it work, tell me? How are we going to spend a whole life together, husband? I'm still young. My dear sir, release me and let me go! Otherwise your eyes will be my grave.'

Keramet Mumî Keşke Memiş Efendi rose from the bed without uttering a word. He took a mirror. He looked into his eyes.

Without uttering a word, Keramet Mumî Keşke Memiş Efendi broke the mirror.

As day broke, he helped his wife gather her things. The young woman got up and left without a sound or a gesture of farewell. The outer door closed gently.

And it always remained closed. From that day onward Keramet Mumî Keşke Memiş Efendi didn't set foot out of the house. He didn't want to see anyone, he sent back all invitations, he didn't open the door for his worried friends. His six elder sisters were miserable with grief. They worked to get him remarried for fear that his condition would worsen. Each matrimonial candidate they found was more beautiful and more talkative than the last. But to no avail. Keramet Mumî Keşke Memiş Efendi didn't want anyone.

Finally, one day, his paternal aunt knocked on his door. She'd aged a great deal. When she came in, half of her strength was left hanging on the doorknob.

'I didn't know, son,' she said quietly. 'If I'd known, would it have turned out this way? When you were born your face was a drop of wax, I thought that whatever I drew before it hardened would be for the better. I made you a face, even if it's rigid. But the eyes... Time was so short...after all it was about to harden. In my panic it was the best I could do. That's why your eyes are such narrow slits. I drew your eyes, but I didn't have the presence of mind to open them. A curtain of wax remained over your eyes. I didn't know, son. Forgive me. Otherwise I'll die with my last wish unfulfilled.'

Keramet Mumî Keşke Memiş Efendi looked at his aunt's wrinkled hands. These hands were the creators of his face, the architects of his destiny. He could have kissed those hands and touched his forehead to them. He could have folded these hands into his own hands. But he didn't.

His aunt left. As she left, the remaining half of her strength was caught on the doorknob. On the evening of the same day, news spread of the old woman's death. Keramet Mumî Keşke Memiş Efendi didn't go the funeral. He didn't pay his last respects to his face's creator.

He didn't bear anyone any ill-will. It was just that…he didn't care; he didn't care about anything. Indeed he felt as if he could do anything. Since he could do anything, it was better to do nothing. One by one he spat out those who knocked on his door to help. He caused his sisters to weep bitterly, and his enemies to feel inner delight. He threw himself into an ocean of smoke, he swam as far from the shore into this ocean of smoke as he could. As he swam he saw that 'a long distance' itself was an illusion, a mirage, wherever you moved, the vanishing point remained the same.

'Is there any activity in this world that's worth the effort?' he used to say as he drew in the smoke. He would shrug his shoulders indifferently. 'If there is, I'll do it, and my enthusiasm will pass. I need enthusiasm that will never pass.'

'Is there an adventure in this world that's worth living?' he used to ask as his head spun round and round. He would shrug his shoulders indifferently. 'If there is, let me live it, but the story will end. I need stories that never end.'

He made his decision: It was going to end.

He was melting day by day. In order for the wax to be consumed more quickly, he stubbornly subjected it to heat. He would sit on top of the stove, and would surround himself with candles; he would seize his torch and run to every fire that broke out in the city; he would pass out in bakeries and wake up in furnace-rooms; with *rakı* burning at the back of his throat, he would deliver eulogies to the furnace boys; by day he would sun himself for hours, and at night he would sleep with high-carat whores. He wanted to melt as soon as possible, to free himself from this rigidity that confined his heart and to become liquid again. Since he'd come to this useless structure they called the world as a drop of wax, he'd leave it as a drop of wax. He might not have finished all he'd started, but he'd finish in the state he'd started. Later…later perhaps he'd harden and set again, but this time in a completely different guise. What did it matter if they didn't like that one either? He'd flow again. In any event, time was endless, and space was limitless. Why should he stay squeezed into this envelope?

The weather grew cold. Winter arrived.

The weather grew warm. The snows melted.

But he still hadn't melted completely.

He hadn't the strength left to curse wax, to swear at wax, to reproach wax. Since his wedding night, since his will had been broken, he was like a shaman's cloak of forty patches and a single thread in the reflections of the broken pieces of mirror. He shredded the sealed story with his name, and scattered the pieces through time and space. And with all his melting, these pieces somehow didn't melt.

He passed through bad times. But he lived. And much later, on a brightly coloured morning, he went out into the streets again. Not as before though, there was something altered about him when he went out into the street. It wasn't as it had always been, there was something different about the way he looked at his surroundings. His pupils were pin-cushions. They were covered with holes made by evil eyes and evil words pinched into their halo. Water leaked from some of these holes. This was how he wept.

It had been so long since he'd walked that he could neither keep his legs from trembling at each step nor determine where he was going. It was as if every direction was the same, as if every passageway led to the same dead end, and every street looked exactly like the other. It was as if he'd left this world; it was aware neither of how long Keramet Mumî Keşke Memiş Efendi had been absent nor of the crisis he'd passed through.

A man was coming towards him: young and elegant and swaggering. He planted himself in front of the man like a thief blocking the way to the fountain.

'Where are you coming from like this?'

'From home,' said the young man, looking over his shoulder as if someone was coming after him from his house. Keramet Mumî Keşke Memiş Efendi approached the young man with curiosity. His nose detected a sour smell.

'I drank *rakı* in order to suppress the smell of cloves in my mouth. I may have exceeded my measure,' explained the young man. 'I splashed on lots of perfume but I still can't get rid of this unpleasant smell. My mother puts black cumin in my pockets, and makes me chew cloves before I leave the house. I smell of black cumin and cloves all day. Food is tasteless, streets are narrow, days are short. I smell like those dilapidated wooden houses.'

'So how would you like to smell?' Keramet Mumî Keşke Memiş Efendi shouted after the young man, who was walking away as he spoke.

'You know those fancy stone houses that each have a different name engraved on them. I want to smell like they do. Cool and self-assured.'

He must have said more, but his voice was no longer audible. At one point, Keramet Mumî Keşke Memiş Efendi took advantage of the wind blowing from his direction, and shouted again.

'All right, where can houses like this be found?'

He waited, but the wind didn't bring an answer from the young man. Suddenly, just as he was about to turn and leave, a whisper reached his ear.

'In Pera! To Pera! Pera!'

That was when Keramet Mumî Keşke Memiş Efendi understood the state of the men of his country. Had they changed during his withdrawal into solitude, or had they been this way for a long time, and it was he who was late to see it? He understood that he would no longer be able to watch anything in the same way he used to. The wind had no intention of blowing backwards; it was clear that it had changed direction. There were new things happening; it was the new and the European that was in demand. It was clear that the fancy stone houses didn't let in the roasting, suffocating sun; neither the tastelessness of food, the narrowness of streets nor the shortness of days. The fancy stone houses were refreshing after the dilapidated wooden houses that were faded and falling apart from neglect. Even if the one he was addressing didn't know his language, the fancy stone houses loved to talk about themselves; the wooden houses liked to listen to the conversations of those who lived in them, and therefore didn't talk much. The one found the substance of life in solitude, whereas the other found it in the company of others. The stone houses were built to be seen from without, no matter who was living in them, and they were built in a form that could be looked at. Whereas the wooden houses were built to hide those living in them from outer gazes, and enclosed them within their calmness. The stone houses could refresh broken or as yet unformed families; whereas the wooden houses drew the water of their life from the roots of the densely branched family tree. For this reason, while the talkative stone houses still remained sedate, the abandoned wooden houses never recovered.

The stone houses were built to be seen and shown: indeed that's why their facades were always plastered by the glances of passers-by. The wooden houses were built not to be seen or shown; indeed their facades are worn out by the gazes of strangers.

Keramet Mumî Keşke Memiş Efendi didn't care that this was only one man among many. How many more men would he have to meet in order to have met enough men? How many books did one have to read in order to be wise, how many lands did one have to see in order to be a traveller, how many defeats did one have to suffer in order to become discouraged? How much was too much and how much was too little? This was the second example he had seen. And since he'd broken the mirror, two was enough for Keramet Efendi. Indeed, he found Two to be the most extraordinary of numbers.

For the first time since, on his wedding night, he'd broken the mirror that had shown him his eyes, he'd found a reason to live. Wherever a person hurts, that's where his heart beats. Now, Keramet Mumî Keşke Memiş Efendi's heart was beating in his eyes, and he wanted to occupy himself with something that was worth doing; not just something that would become easier with time, but something he would never be able to do to his own satisfaction. Now it seemed he was on the point of finding this. He also wished for an adventure that was worth living, one from which he could distil stories, one whose entirety he couldn't see even when he saw its entirety, an adventure that might never end. Who knew, perhaps when he started on this project he might also find this.

He had found what he was going to do.

Since the cause of his strangeness was his eyes, from now on he would address only the eyes. Whatever he had lost because of his eyes, he would gain as much and more from the eyes of others. Now the pain of the loneliness that his eyes had caused him would be relieved by drawing thousands of people around him. The life that his eyes had made distasteful would become sweet. The eyes that had seen what no one else could see would cause every raised glass to be filled with an elixir distilled from the contagious blindness of the people. For this reason, he would first ascertain the condition of his country, so he could gather those who believed in the situation as if he was picking mushrooms.

Since the minds of Ottoman men were on appearances, he would offer a thousand men a unique world of spectacle. And since the answer to the question he had asked was Pera, then that's where he would do whatever he was going to do.

~

After collecting quite a few ideas, he spent a long, long time thinking them over and then finally made his decision. He would erect an enormous tent. A tent the like of which would be remembered not just for days or for years, but for centuries. A tent that, like a snake swallowing its tail, would begin where it ended.

The colour of the tent would be the colour of cherries.

In the cherry-coloured tent he would present a world of spectacles to thousands of men. Keramet Mumî Keşke Memiş Efendi, who was born to a woman who paid the ultimate price in order to have a little son, who was raised by his six older sisters and crossed the border that separates the two sexes; who for a long time had found himself observing how each of his elder sisters managed her own husband, and thought that there was no coincidence how these methods of management resembled each other, and that there were rules that all women knew but never mentioned, and understanding that he had been brought up according to the same rules, and having lost his mind on the morning of his wedding night and having since birth possessed extraordinary intelligence, clearly had little trouble envisioning this world of spectacles he would present to the eyes of men.

~

These many men who would only grudgingly greet each other in the street or show mercy to each other in a fight had all come to the cherry-coloured tent after the evening call to prayer for the same reason: La Belle Annabelle. The most beautiful, the only beautiful *jinn* of the poisonous yew forest, the shimmering elixir of life, La Belle Annabelle.

~

In order to understand what La Belle Annabelle was seeking in Pera, in a cherry-coloured tent that had been pitched on top of a hill, while the Ottoman Empire was Westernising with the panic of a boy who'd stolen an apple from a neighbour's garden and hadn't the courage to look back, it's necessary to go back some way. Back past all of the glazed secrets. It's necessary to travel in time and space. Not that far back: earlier in the same century. Not that far away either; in the lands of France. Because it is earlier in the same century, in France, that the story of the most beautiful, the only beautiful *jinn* of the poisonous yew forest, the shimmering elixir of life, La Belle Annabelle, begins.

(But to tell the truth it is possible to skip this part altogether. It's possible not to write it; or not to read it. You can jump ahead to the next one without tarrying here, the next number, that is. In any event they may not even have lived it. No matter how beautiful she was, she might not have become a spectacle, and had the right not to be seen, and keep herself distant from curious eyes. Indeed she wouldn't have been so beautiful if she hadn't been seen.)

France — 1868

In a nut-wood, oriental four-poster bed, in a room with a ceiling as high as the sky and a floor as soft as dove wings, life itself was screaming with pain. The sheets were covered in sweat, and in faeces and blood. It was as if there were two stubborn, invisible packhorses in the room. And the huge bed, turned into a carriage, was pulled in two opposite directions by these stubborn packhorses. One of the animals was pulling hard on the rope in order to extract what was in it. It was foaming at the mouth. As it pulled, the babies in the womb were sliding out gently. As it bit the rope and pulled in the opposite direction, the second horse refused to allow the first to defeat it. As it pulled, the babies in the womb were sliding back, retreating from the exit. Both horses' nostrils were flared and pupils enlarged from the effort. Now everybody and everything was focused on their struggle. As the horses struggled against each other, not only did the bed and the high-ceilinged room shake, but also every other part of the magnificent mansion shook; the babies in the womb were thrown this way and that, and outside a frightful storm was raising clouds of dust. In this tumult, the only living thing that remained still was the woman who was giving birth.

Her name was Madeleine. Or, as everyone addressed her, Madame de Marelle.

Madame de Marelle was not pulling either end of the rope, and indeed was doing nothing at all to assist in the birth. She was as indifferent and as motionless as possible. She didn't make a sound. If she could have spoken, she would have asked God for a heavy snowfall. She would ask God to freeze the pain in her body, the feverish commotion around her, the struggle of the horses, the lives trying to break free from her life, and this sinful mansion, forever. Life itself should freeze, so that centuries later she could serve as an example, before which people would fall to their knees, of the sin of being unable to give birth. And when life freezes, the rope will freeze and break exactly into two perfectly equal parts. Then there would be nothing to suffer. Because nothing would be left.

She could not speak. She was wet with sweat. She gazed at the sky-high ceiling. A field of blond sunflowers was painted on the ceiling; a tiny little, cream-complexioned angel was wandering among the sunflowers. While the woman stared at the angel's wings, everybody in the room was overwhelmed by what bad luck it was that the woman had not yelled, or screamed, or moved. Even as the pain abraded her blood vessels, not even a moan passed Madame de Marelle's lips. Her lips… The girls assisting the midwife were frightened to learn how her lips had come to be this way.

Madame de Marelle's lips were torn to shreds. The flesh of a mouse torn apart by the claws of a predatory bird would not have been as badly shredded as these lips.

~

'Give me your lips,' the young man had said.

The river was two steps ahead, the water was two steps ahead. It was only two steps to the thunderous flowing, drizzling, bubbling, to the flowering on the water bank, to being bait for the fish. 'Give me your lips,' he said, this time in a harder voice. The woman's lips were dry. The skin would tear to pieces and bleed, but the woman was still resisting with her last effort. The skin was on the edge. The woman was on the edge. She wanted to withdraw but she couldn't walk. A humming was rising from within her. She did not love herself at all; her heart was being torn like a scaly yew trunk. Her passion emerged from under the bark. Because she knew it was as poisonous as yew leaves, she did not touch it. The poison was flowing in, because it could not find a way to leak out. Then her feelings were numbed. She surrendered herself to this numbness that was flowing through her. The warmer and the more silent the surrender, the colder and more aggressive the flow of the river. And they were only two steps from the river.

As soon as she saw the young man she knew that God wanted to test her. It was all just like the sermons she'd heard. The flesh had to be fresh and attractive; its taste had to be acrid. It was wet. Liquids were disgusting. But humans are so weak; while trying to dry the soul, they have to endure the bodily fluids. Then, the devil was the winner. Here was the devil before her again, disguised as a breathtakingly handsome young man. For Madame de Marelle, the moment she saw him was the moment her troubles began. From that moment on, nothing was as it had been before. Whenever she was alone, she thought of the young man. She hated sleeping because when she slept she embraced sin; she didn't sleep a wink, and welcomed the dawn with swollen and weary eyes. By day she looked at the young man even as she tried not to; even as she struggled to stay away from him, she cursed each moment without him. Her resistance broke so easily. Ultimately, she realised as soon as she saw the young man that she could not pass the test.

The sun was about to set when the young man reached the de Marelle mansion. It had been raining cats and dogs since morning. He said he'd been walking since dawn. Yet his clothes were bone dry. Pressing his black velvet hat against his chest, he saluted; as he gently opened his black velvet cape, he smiled slightly. It was just as the sermons had warned. An emissary from the devil. His black velvet skin unfolded layer by layer just like a bloody rose. It asked to be touched.

'Touch,' he said in a cracked voice. 'Don't be frightened! It will leave no trace on me, no one will know.'

Madame de Marelle was not sure where the voice came from, and she didn't care. The major-domo was complaining about having too much work. Now that the young man was looking for a job, he could help the major-domo. Telling him his duties briefly, she went away in a hurry. After that, she tried to avoid meeting him. But after having seen such beauty, the man no longer saw the world in the same way. He could no longer stand any moment or any creature that did not reflect him. Madame de Marelle had been praying for hours each night, begging God not to allow her to be carried away by that maddening voice. Some mornings she woke to find herself crouching on the floor. Had she never actually gone to bed, or had she fallen out of bed as she slept? She wasn't able to understand. She was frightened of what she was capable of doing, of what she was capable of wishing. She was frightened of limitlessness, of her own limitlessness.

'Sometimes it happens this way,' the bedside candle used to say. 'Sometimes you encounter someone. You know you have a weakness for him. You are made of dough. He can take you and knead you in whatever way he wants.'

To silence the candle, she blew it out in haste. She bumped into things in the darkness. In the morning, at dawn, she found bruises all over her body.

Instead of suffering so much, she could dismiss him at once. She could show him who was in command. Hadn't she managed on her own all this time? As soon as her husband passed away, she'd set out to turn the mansion she'd hated into a place of faith. The first thing she did after the funeral was to replace not only the furniture but also the help, swearing she would not allow anyone of suspect morals to remain at de Marelle. Only the major-domo…of all of them he was the only one she retained.

The major-domo was the only link between Madame de Marelle's past and her present. He was the only one who, years ago, had seen the confusion in the eyes of the new young bride standing hesitantly in the courtyard and staring at the walls, the only one who knew how the fear had grown within her by day and by night. He was the only one who recognised the smell of the ointment she used to salve the wounds from the whip, and the only one who knew that in time she gave up hope that the ointment would help. He was also aware that the woman's husband was very cruel during the first years of their marriage. Although the man softened over the years, the woman grew harder day-by-day. As she grew harder, she forbade herself and those around her everything that people find pleasant in life. In time, the servants didn't even dare smile in her presence.

Madame de Marelle was sure that the major-domo kept everything he knew to himself. Just as this nut-wood bed and this high, painted ceiling never reveal what they've seen, so the major-domo knew how to be blind and dumb. Of course, he didn't do this out of decency. Decency was not even acquainted with him. He probably behaved this way because he preferred to be blind and dumb. He just kept his mouth shut and did his job.

The woman hated the major-domo. Especially because of his hair. The major-domo had rust-coloured hair that flowed over his shoulders in insolent curls. The woman had straight, coal-black hair. Every morning, before leaving her room, she tied her hair into a bun from which, all day, not even a single strand worked loose. But it didn't matter whether or not she liked the major-domo. He'd been a part of the mansion for years. The major-domo was necessary in the same way as a greasy rope or an old plough.

Several times, Madame de Marelle considered ordering the major-domo to dismiss the young man. Each time, she left without being able to finish the sentence she'd begun in such a determined manner. When she realised she couldn't dismiss him, she decided to avoid him. After days of preparation, warning the servants again and again, she finally set out. The horses went as far as the suspension bridge. 'For some reason the river has risen,' said the carriage man, 'but don't worry, we'll manage to get across,' he added. But Madame de Marelle was aware of why the water had risen, and that they would not be able to get across. She told the carriage man to turn back.

It was night by the time she got back. There was nobody about.

Somewhere in the silence, somebody was murmuring. Following the whispers, she found herself in front of the barn. The voices were coming from inside. She tried putting her eye to a knothole to see inside, but it was too dark. Laughter could be heard from time to time; the horses were neighing as if they were frightened of something. Then, suddenly, the door of the barn opened and the major-domo came out. There were droplets of sweat on his forehead. She looked at him with a disgust that she didn't feel necessary to hide. How wretched he looked. Next to the holy beauty of the young man, he was like a demon who had gone astray and was pushing on the doors of heaven by mistake. He did not belong in a place where such holy beauty reigned. But he was still necessary. The major-domo was necessary in the same way as a greasy rope or an old plough.

When Madame de Marelle fell asleep at last towards morning, she found herself once again in a recurring dream. She was in a low, dark cave. Just in front of her the wall divided into several doors, and forked paths lay behind each of the doors. She had learned the way by losing her way several times in previous dreams. She walked as far as an opening covered with moss. There, among statues of the Holy Virgin surrounded by flickering candles, there was a relief in the shape of a face. This was the Innocent Face who bites and breaks off the hands of those serving devil by tasting the seven sins. To know whether or not a person was innocent, it was enough to put their hand into the open mouth of the relief. If the person was innocent, the mouth would stay open and nothing would happen. If they were a sinner, the Innocent Face would shut its mouth at once and the hand in it would never be released.

Every time Madame de Marelle had this dream, she stood in front of the relief, but she avoided testing her innocence at the last moment. This time she plucked up the courage, and, trembling with anxiety, extended her hand. At that moment, she realised that the Innocent Face was slowly changing. She did not care. She took a deep breath and put her entire hand into the mouth of the relief.

Even though she felt an odd shiver on her fingertips, she did not pull her hand back. Suddenly, the face in front of her transformed into the face of the young man. At the same moment, the mouth of the Innocent Face shut loudly.

She was woken by her own screams. Her right hand was throbbing. Sitting up in the bed, she rubbed her hand. Morning was still far off. In fear, she went back to bed.

She was often woken by her own screams. With her lips aching. When she woke in the morning after each nightmare the pink skin was thinner; it was closer to being torn off.

She went to the riverbank in this state, with her lips about to fall off. When she looked into the distance, she thought the young man was with the major-domo, but when she got closer she realised he was alone. She dashed to his side, moved by an instinct she could not explain even to herself; without a word, she collapsed onto the bank, in front of the young man.

'Give me your lips,' said the young man. He was so relaxed, so fearless that it was as if he wanted her to give her lips to the bushes on the riverbank or the far-off yew forest instead of to him.

While the young man was undressing her, Madame de Marelle was thinking that there was no reason to be ashamed. There was nothing to be ashamed of because she would never rise from the grass on which she was lying. After the disaster, as she tried unsuccessfully to flee, the young man would leave but she would remain here forever. Like a dehydrated insect growing drowsy under the sun, she would wait for death, and for the decay that would return her to the soil. While the young man was undressing, she was listening to the sounds from under the grass. The soil was so hungry. In a few minutes, it would swallow her together with her sins. She closed her eyes. After hanging on for so long, the skin of her lips finally fell away as the young man entered her. A thin, rosy ache ran down her mouth.

When the young man's cries of pleasure echoed in the yew forest and rebounded, Madame de Marelle was still lying on the ground.

She had no intention of getting up. At that moment, feeling neither pain nor torment, feeling nothing at all, she waited for the earth to swallow her. She just raised her head for a moment to tell him they were not to see each other again. She spoke as if to herself, or to someone who wasn't there. The young man looked at her attentively, and asked no questions. He seemed uneasy. To hide his uneasiness he began combing his rust-coloured hair with his fingers. When Madame de Marelle saw him do this, she froze, and then turned pale. She was shaking. Suddenly, she jumped up and began running half-dressed towards the mansion.

She did not leave her room throughout her pregnancy. She never saw the young man again, and never asked after him. From time to time the major-domo came to visit her. She did not like him, she did not want him close. However, the major-domo was necessary. The major-domo was necessary in the same way as a greasy rope or an old plough. No one else but him knew the state her lips were in. They were torn to bits. With the sapphire-studded dagger that her husband had always kept within reach throughout his life, she had made deep cuts in the lips that she'd given to the young man. Her lips opened in layers like carnations and each petal of flesh barely hung on.

~

Now, in the nut-wood, oriental four-poster bed, in the room with a ceiling as high as the sky, and a floor as soft as dove wings while life was screaming out its pain, the scabs on her lips were trembling. The sheets were covered in sweat, and in faeces and blood. She didn't make a sound. If she could have spoken, she would have asked God for a heavy snow. She would ask God to freeze the pain in her body, the feverish commotion around her. Life itself should freeze, so that centuries later she could serve as an example, before which people would fall to their knees, of the sin of being unable to give birth.

She was covered in sweat. She didn't blink. She was staring at the wings of the tiny, cream-complexioned angel on the sky-high ceiling. She didn't make a sound as the pain scythed her blood vessels, not even a moan emerged from her lips. Her lips... The girls assisting the midwife were frightened to learn how her lips had come to be this way.

This is how the twins were born. They put one baby into each of her arms. Madame de Marelle looked first at the first-born. This baby was so ugly that it was more of a demon than a human baby. She smiled tenderly. What was more natural than that ugliness should result from such shameful intercourse? At least God would never let her forget the sin she had committed. After that moment, until her last breath, whenever she looked at that child, the clamp squeezing her conscience would tighten, and it would be harder to carry the weight of her crime. Thanking God, she kissed the wrinkled cheek of the first-born baby with her shredded lips. Then she turned her head and saw the second baby.

The second baby was so beautiful that it was more like a lost *jinn* than a human baby. The tiny lips flowering on her rosy skin were moving slightly as if at any moment she would learn how to speak. Madame de Marelle examined it with curiosity at first, and then with hatred. And when she decided that she did not want to see it any more, she pulled her arm away.

Then, with her back to the second baby, and facing the first, she fell into a deep sleep.

~

Marking the page of the book he was reading with the sapphire-studded dagger that he always kept within reach, Monsieur de Marelle sighed with distress. Even holding the babies in his arms a few minutes ago hadn't helped. Whenever he felt distressed like this, he started combing his rust-coloured hair with his stubby fingers. He liked his hair. He'd never seen any one else with such hair. This rust-coloured hair was passed from generation to generation in his family. One of the twins resembled its father, but the other one? Who knows, perhaps later on the other baby's hair would resemble its mother's. Like her mother, she would wear her hair in a tight bun, never allowing a single strand to escape.

His wife was sleeping again, she'd been sleeping since the birth. Sometimes, as she slept, Monsieur de Marelle sat on the edge of the nut-wood bed and watched her. She'd grown strange in the last year. How difficult her pregnancy had been. It was as if she became more filled with hatred with each passing day, as if every pleasure in life disgusted her. Who knew how long it had been since the light of love had been seen in her eyes. Even though he'd known years ago, when he'd chosen Madeleine as his wife, that she was not in love with him, he'd thought that in time this would be solved. Of course, he was aware of his own faults. Indeed he was quite cruel to her at the beginning of their marriage. When he remembered what he'd done to her in those days, he felt pangs of conscience. But later he straightened out completely, and never hurt Madeleine again. But rather than being made happy by this, she became steadily harder.

He was accustomed to his wife's coldness, but what had happened in the last year was a mystery to him. She was growing stranger by the day. Recently, she'd wanted to take a long trip in order to get away from the de Marelle estate. Monsieur de Marelle hadn't objected because he'd thought it would do her good. But even though she'd wanted to take the trip and had spent days preparing, she'd returned almost as soon as she'd set out. When she came back, Monsieur de Marelle was grooming the horses. When he attempted to ask where she'd gone and why she'd returned so soon, Madeleine looked at him in disgust and closed the door of her room without a word. Over time, incidents like this had become so common that Monsieur de Marelle began to wonder whether or not his wife recognised him. As if…as if she mistook him for someone else, someone who wasn't there. And as if she was fleeing from someone nobody else could see, perhaps a ghost. This region was already better known for its ghost stories than for its yew trees.

In fact, Monsieur de Marelle turned a deaf ear to this twisted reasoning. All he knew was that, for whatever reason, Madeleine's condition was growing more serious by the day. However, throughout this period he continued having affairs with the maids rather than trying to discover what was going on. Nothing changed. In any event, ever since the beginning of their marriage he had been rebuffed every time he tried to touch her. To tell the truth, though, he wasn't that put out by the situation. In fact his desire had been quenched the moment he saw the tight bun in which she tied her jet-black hair. However, he deeply wanted an heir. A child with rust-coloured hair just like his!

He'd begun to believe that he would never have an heir when, one day, he found a note from his wife on the desk in his study. The note told him to come to the riverbank the following morning. Monsieur de Marelle went to the riverbank at the appointed time, and began to wait. Madeleine was not too late. But there was something strange about her arrival. For a while she watched her husband from behind a bush, and then approached like a timid animal, sniffing at him. Finally, she sat beside him quietly and obediently. Monsieur de Marelle looked at his wife in astonishment. He tried to understand how this woman who had not let him touch her since they married and looked at him with disgust had changed so suddenly. Then, suddenly, she offered him her lips. The man was astounded; at first out of surprise, and then in a frenzy, he half kissed those lips. His wife behaved as if she wasn't aware of what was happening. She was unruffled. She let herself go completely. Even when she lay stark naked on the grass, she still behaved strangely; putting her ear to the ground and murmuring.

Even after making love, she continued lying on the ground as she had been. She raised her head only for a moment and said they would not see each other any more. It was as if she wasn't speaking to her husband, but to the world in general; or to someone he couldn't see. Then, suddenly, she went pale, and was perfectly still, as if she has seen something terrifying. A moment later she jumped up and ran towards the mansion half-dressed. As he watched his wife anxiously for a while, Monsieur de Marelle tried to understand the dream in which they were struggling so desperately.

But it seemed that it wasn't a dream. It couldn't be, because his wife was getting bigger by the day. Pregnancy made her stranger, and more ill-tempered. In the following months, she never left her room, and spent her days staring blankly at statues of the Virgin Mary. Even though Monsieur de Marelle knew he wasn't wanted, he visited her frequently, to see if she needed anything, and each time he left his wife with a distress deep enough to cast a shadow over the joy his rust-haired heir had brought him

Finally the day of the birth arrived. It was a terrible, stormy night. While the wind and the rain and the thunder raged outside, and the huge mansion shook, Monsieur de Marelle paced back and forth in the corridors, trying in vain to hear his wife's screams. Hours later he tired of pacing, and secluded himself in his library, where he ceaselessly combed his rust-coloured hair with his stubby fingers as he waited. That's how the twins were born. Since that moment, Madame de Marelle had been buried in an endless sleep. She was always sleeping. Sometimes, at the least expected moments, she woke up and looked around with bewildered eyes. Then they would bring the babies to be nursed. It happened the same way every time. She would nurse the rust-coloured baby for a long time, but when it was the beautiful one's turn, she turned her back and went back to sleep. In the end they had to hire a wet nurse for the second baby.

A suitable woman was found in one of the surrounding villages. She was young and robust. She smelled of sheep's wool and cheese and straw. She had recently given birth. She had so much milk that even if she nursed not just one but a dozen babies her swollen breasts still would not diminish easily. The wet nurse loved the beautiful baby as soon as she saw it. She admired the baby as she nursed her; she smiled as if it was her own beauty rather than the baby's that she was so proud of. When from time to time she was asked to nurse the ugly baby as well, she begrudged him the little milk that flowed into his mouth. As for Monsieur de Marelle, he was pleased to see the difference between his wife and the peasant woman; with curiosity, he watched these two different women and the way they became close to the two different babies. As he watched, his belief that women were strange creatures grew stronger.

The wet nurse was quite pleased to feel Monsieur de Marelle's curious gazes. And one day, when the baby was dozing in her arms, she took her chapped nipple out of the baby's small mouth and offered it to the man. After that, she began to neglect the beautiful baby. Although she continued to nurse her, her primary duty in the mansion now was not to feed the baby, but to feed the father.

~

One day the wet nurse, following Monsieur de Marelle, found herself in the room where the bookcases were. She'd never stepped foot in this room before.

As she gazed at the crowded shelves, a painting on the wall caught her eye. There was a hole in the golden relief of the frame. At first sight, it was like a half-open mouth; you know, an opening to the unknown just like the Innocent Face's mouth which bites and tears off the hands of sinners. This frame, this painting… Suddenly the wet nurse screamed. She grew pale and scurried around the room looking about frantically. As she could not see anything else to cover it with, she hurriedly took off her shawl and covered the painting, groping as she tried to avoid looking in that direction. Meanwhile, Monsieur de Marelle must have been flabbergasted since he couldn't say a word or ask what was going on, but simply watched her frantic movements with wide eyes. But the young woman told him anyway.

'I've heard about this painting. All of the women in the village know about it. They all talk about it. Once, a young man lived here. He worked with the major-domo. He was so beautiful that those who saw him lost their senses. The owner of the mansion was a widow; she fell in love with the young man. But the young man didn't want her. The woman suffered a great deal. Then one day the young man disappeared. They found his body in the forest; under a yew tree. No one understood how it had happened. The widow ran to the spot as soon as she heard. She carried the body by herself to the riverbank. Then she embraced the body and didn't leave it. She wept there for days. She chased off everyone who approached. In the end, they had to drag the woman away from the body in order to bury it.'

The wet nurse was breathless from talking so quickly. After gulping down the wine Monsieur de Marelle offered her, she calmed down a bit and began talking more slowly.

'Before the funeral, the widow hired an artist to paint the young man's portrait. She also had a frame made. The hole in the frame was just like the mouth of Innocent Face. Then she hung the picture beside her bed. Every day she suffered terribly when she looked at that picture. It had been a sin to desire the young man so much, and she thought the young man had died because of this. Every night she put her hand into the hole to see if she was a sinner or not. In the end, she went completely mad. The picture was also lost. All of the women in the village know this story. The picture is said to be cursed. Because the young man was very beautiful. He could make any woman fall in love with him. He captured the hearts of virgins in particular. Any virgin who saw him lost her senses. That picture must be covered. It mustn't be looked at.'

After the wet nurse had had a bit more wine, she asked calmly: 'But how did it get here? I thought it was hidden.'

'Last year… Madeleine hung it here. Madeleine…'

Monsieur de Marelle could not finish his words. He suddenly had a terrible headache. Abruptly, he rushed out of the room. He strode towards the babies; he picked up the beautiful baby and ran back to the library. He uncovered the picture against the objections of the wet nurse and put the baby and the picture side-by-side. Without any doubt, the beautiful baby's face was a smaller copy of the young man's. The moment Monsieur de Marelle saw the resemblance, he hated the beautiful baby. From now on, he no longer wanted to see it. Because every time he looked at it, he would see the face of the man his wife had become infatuated with, and he would remember her betrayal.

~

Not all children grow up alike. Some children grow up diluting the dense thickness of time through the existence of those who love them, sip by sip. Some drink the time without mixing it, gulp by gulp. The baby they called the beautiful baby was one of these, and before she emerged from infancy, she had her share of loneliness. First, her twin brother, who left their mother's womb before her, then her mother, then the wet nurse and finally her father all left her. She was to grow up alone, far away from them.

She spent her time wandering around the countryside or getting lost in the yew forest. She also often went to the riverbank. She loved it there. Something about the river drew her to it. She would sit there for hours, dangling her legs in the water: she would strain to see her reflection in the wildly flowing water. Sometimes she was so absorbed in her reflection rippling on the surface of the water that she didn't even realise the sun had set or that it was getting dark. She wasn't afraid to spend the night there; or of the sounds of the night. In any event, no one at home would miss her. Her mother always looked at her face with shame, the wet nurse with doubt, her father with hatred and her twin brother with jealousy. Whoever saw her either made a face or avoided her eyes. Only the river smiled when it saw Annabelle, telling her that there was nothing to be sad about, telling her that her magical beauty was reminiscent of a beautiful *jinn*. And giving her the good news that she could fly away whenever she wished, fluttering her wings just like a *jinn*.

To tell the truth, it was not a strange coincidence that Annabelle could live her life without leaving the de Marelle estate, and that she could grow old watching herself in the river.

It was the beginning of autumn. Yellow leaves were leaping into space and falling onto the water one by one as if they were in competition. There was a fragile and hollow haste in nature. During these days, a wandering theatre company stopped to rest near the river. All the actors seemed to be tired of life. They picked out the lice wearily, memorised their parts, washed their laundry, spooned up cabbage soup without exchanging a word. But one of them stopped working and became engrossed in watching the girl not far away who was dangling her legs in the river. This little, ignorant, unlovable, arrogant man was the owner of the troupe. After watching Annabelle for quite some time, he turned to his friends and said: 'Everybody should see such beauty!'

~

Sometimes a lot of things happen at once. The owner of the troupe left the de Marelle mansion blissfully happy, even though when he knocked on the door he'd had little hope. His luck was better than he'd expected. First he was astounded by the news that Annabelle was not a maid, but the daughter of the owner of the mansion; then he was amazed that even though she was, nobody objected to her joining the troupe. It happened so easily that the owner of the troupe felt anxious that someone might ruin it all, so he decided that it was auspicious to leave the de Marelle estate as soon as possible and he gathered the troupe together and they hurried off. He still didn't know what skills Annabelle had. If her voice was as beautiful as her appearance, she could sing during the intervals; perhaps she could join the dancing girls or a new part could be written for her. However it was, he was sure that this *jinn* faced girl would bring good luck to the troupe that had so much misfortune recently. He'd even found a name for the girl: La Belle Annabelle!

Annabelle's twin brother, her mother and her father lined up in the courtyard and watched the troupe move off into the distance. When the carriages turned the corner and disappeared, the three of them sighed with relief. Only the village woman who'd once been her nurse and who hadn't left the mansion since was concerned about her and called out to them: 'Where are you taking her?' The owner of the troupe replied cheerfully without taking his eyes off her full breasts.

'To the East! To the city of Istanbul.'

Pera – 1885

The men entering Keramet Mumî Keşke Memiş Efendi's cherry-coloured tent through the eastward-facing door one by one were here to see the dazzling La Belle Annabelle, the great beauty, the only beautiful *jinn* of the poisonous yew forest. She was the last to take the stage. Before her there were other beauties.

The opening was performed by the masked woman. The mask she wore was truly marvellous with the lock of hair on its forehead, its almond eyes, arrow eyelashes, inkwell nose, cherry lips, the dimple flowered for its smile and with the candy pink spreading across its cheeks. She stood on the stage without saying a word or doing anything. It was as if she had been told to wait, and she was obeying and waiting without knowing why or for what. Then, at the least expected moment, she dropped the mask on her face. A cry of amazement rose from the audience. The face they saw now was exactly the same as the one they'd seen before. The faint sound of a distant violin was heard. When the violin stopped playing, the beautiful woman whose mask was her face, her face her mask, saluted the audience in a graceful manner. At her sign, the purple-fringed curtains opened slowly.

While the spring breeze was blowing on the ivy swing hanging from the branches of a wild pear tree in the middle of the blood-red poppy field, and the sun was setting on the horizon, a tiny lady star danced *kanto,* rabbits frolicked and butterflies flew around her. Her name was Hayganoş; her voice was shrill.

My pastry is in the pastry shop
I bake it, I eat it
With cheese or with mincemeat
It's all the same to me
Since my heart is on fire.

When the *kanto* ended, the wild pear tree started walking; it stepped aside with Hayganoş swinging on its branches, the blood-red poppy field round it, the rabbits and butterflies following. While Hayganoş was getting drowsy, the three beauties took the stage. The three beautiful sisters, each more beautiful than the other: Lisa, Maria, Rosa. Lisa, Maria, Rosa. All three sisters were so beautiful that whenever they stood side-by-side, they diminished each other's beauty. Even so, they never separated for a moment, and had never known jealousy. Their hearts were as beautiful as their appearance. Arm in arm, smiles on their faces, flowers flowering in their smiles, they sang songs of how beautiful life was, songs that flowed like a thick liquid. At this point of the show, which went on and on, the teeth of the audience were set on the edge, everybody became bored. Everything was so smooth, so clear, that some of the victims of fate whose lives had gone wrong had to restrain themselves from jumping onto the stage and assaulting the three sisters.

Then, Hoyrat Aruzyak jumped onto the stage. Rather she opened layer by layer just like a seducing skirt instead of jumping upon to the stage. Of all of those who performed in the cherry-coloured tent, she was the most experienced on the stage. She was still just a little child when she first appeared in front of an audience; her hair was curly and golden. As she grew up, she became more beautiful, as she became more beautiful, she became more seductive, and was soon famous throughout the huge city. Stepping on the hearts she'd broken, she moved from one troupe to another, from one embrace to another, adding the sugar of passionate kisses to the sulphurous taste of life. She liked glittering jewellery, bright dresses, ostentation and compliments. Not paying attention to what people said, fulfilling every wish of her flesh, she got whatever she wanted in the world, and more. She knew by heart the secret passages, shortcuts and alleyways of the city of love. However, one day, unexpectedly, the gates of this city were closed to her.

When this event that turned her life upside-down occurred, Hoyrat Aruzyak was on stage. Her role called for her to weep at the edge of the stage while two musketeers drew their swords and fought over her. She was in tears on the edge of the stage while two musketeers drew their swords and were fighting for her. As they had performed the same play for months, there was no chance she would forget her lines. But she did; no one ever understood why. All of a sudden, though there was no such part in the play, Hoyrat Aruzyak jumped up with a shrill cry and jumped between the two musketeers. At the same moment, the hostile swords met on her face. Not only in the play, but also in life, the swords of the two men who hated each other because they were in love with the same woman caused wounds along the length of each side of the face of the woman they had been pursuing. Hoyrat Aruzyak fell to the middle of the stage in pain.

The curtains descended, the audience left but the pain remained. Hoyrat Aruzyak could not hold a mirror any more, she could not look at her face again. There was no need though; she could see how she looked in the eyes of her friends and enemies. She attempted suicide many times, but she was always rescued by the former fans who appeared wherever she went. She didn't want to live, but couldn't manage to die. She could not bear that the women who used to smile at her even though they were envious now looked at her face in pain and smiled inside. She was harsh to anyone who showed her compassion. She learned words she hadn't previously known. As her heart grew harder, her words became sharper. Because she spoke her mind without thinking, no one wanted her near. In any event, she dropped out of sight after a while. It was said that from time to time she was seen near expensive restaurants, knocking at the doors of acquaintances and begging, throwing stones at theatre companies whose stages she had once graced, doing anything imaginable in exchange for a drink. Even though the things she did were spoken about, she was being forgotten even as she was being spoken about, and lurched through their memories like a restless ghost.

~

'Sometimes…suddenly, out of the blue, we're wounded. But all wounds heal. In time, a scab forms and covers it. It hides itself. Because no wound wants to be seen.'

Hoyrat Aruzyak was sitting on the pavement. She was apathetic. She did not raise her head to look at the person talking to her. She hated those who gave her advice even though it was none of their concern, the ones who said how beautiful life was in spite of everything.

'At least your pupils weren't damaged. Because if your pupils are damaged, you can never see the world through the same eyes. You begin to see the bad side of everything. You'll even be able to see dirt that's remained hidden. Others will sense that you don't see what they see, and also that you don't love them any more. This makes them uneasy. They can no longer look at you through the same eyes. For this reason, no one wants to see you near them. In fact the picture is the same picture, what has changed is your eyes. If you can remove yourself from the picture, everything will be as it was before, and everyone will be relieved. In my opinion the best thing to do in cases like this is to leave. To leave and to keep going. Out of stubbornness!'

Hoyrat Aruzyak looked in amazement at the face of the man who was talking away at her. It was his face rather than his words that held her attention; or, to be precise, his eyes…his eyes which were like two thin slits, and which seemed as if at any moment they could deny anything he had said as if he believed it with all his heart. His eyes expressed no feeling whatsoever; neither mercy nor bitterness, neither anger nor hope. Because he never sowed any seeds, he never sought to reap any benefits. But at the same time he didn't seem false. He wasn't playing a game. Even Hoyrat Aruzyak thought that of all the people she'd ever met, she'd never seen anyone so far from being false. The eyes of the man standing in front of her were at least as real as those rare scenes in a play that make the audience forget they are in a theatre.

This is how Keramet Mumî Keşke Memiş Efendi entered Hoyrat Aruzyak's life. In the following days, he never gave her a moment's peace, and talked to her without pause. He also brought her acrid-smelling ointments and pastes made of mysterious ingredients. It didn't seem as if these would cover up the wounds, but at least they weren't as raw looking as when they'd been left untreated.

Then Keramet Mumî Keşke Memiş Efendi began bringing her the make-up that was used by the actresses in the tent. He covered the wounds with face powder and lively colours. For the first time in ages, Hoyrat Aruzyak had the courage to look at herself in a mirror again. She looked. She looked, and, like anyone who is seized by a desperate hope just at the point when they've become accustomed to being cowed, she cursed, first herself, then the person who had given her this hope. Nothing had changed. Both of the wounds were there just as ugly as ever. Keramet Mumî Keşke Memiş Efendi picked the mirror up and passed it to her stubbornly.

'Your ugliness is beautiful enough to thrill us. Aruzyak, you are as beautiful as the night of the apocalypse. Take the stage! And play us a life that does not end in death.'

For a moment, Hoyrat Aruzyak was left looking at the inexpressive eyes of the man who was not at all like any man she'd ever met. She didn't understand a word he said, but there was a tart taste in her mouth. As soon as she was alone, she unpacked the dresses she hadn't touched for so long and tried them on one by one. And the next day, dragging her many trousseau boxes behind her, she honoured the cherry-coloured tent on top of the hill with her presence as if she were a princess visiting a palace in a neighbouring country. The first night she appeared on the stage, she was dumbstruck. The eyes of the audience shone like stars on a moonless night. A warmth she thought she'd forgotten long ago spread through her slowly. She hadn't the patience to wait; she drank in the pleasure of winning approval. She was so merry that night!

From that day on, she waited her turn with a dignified smile and when the time came, she opened layer by layer just like a seductive skirt. The audience was thrilled. Hoyrat Aruzyak presented a night of the apocalypse on which life was killed and death was resurrected, on which men, women and children, indeed the entire population of the ruined city were massacred while its riches were being plundered, and while a baby lizard scurried about scattering seeds of hope that were as tender as its skin.

After Hoyrat Aruzyak, it was the turn of the snake-charmer. Every evening the snake charmer behaved as if he'd had to do something somewhere else first, and had come running at the last moment. As soon as he appeared on stage, the audience was invigorated to see the silver amulet on his biceps, the hoop on his ear and the silver belt round his waist. Even the scrawniest and most timid of them dreamt of rushing out into the streets and bellowing savagely. As the men daydreamed, the snake-charmer proceeded to the middle of the stage, frowned distractedly, bowed his head in salute, and lifted the lid of the basket. The snake emerged from the basket, slithered towards the edge of the stage, and stared with its emerald-green eyes. As it stared and stared, the audience began to see.

In the snake's eyes, the world was reflected in reverse.

In the mirror of its eyes, widows were virgins and slaves were masters. The soil was playful; it tickled the souls lying beneath it. As long as hail flowered on tree branches, the cheeks of the birds with raindrops trembling on their feathers became redder with each glass, and copper coins were gems, and sack-cloth was satin. Rays of light that pierced the clouds tenderly embraced the old and the young, the rich and the poor alike. They were everywhere. They left a faint glitter on all they touched; they could use this faint glitter to weave golden crowns for their uncombed, unwashed heads. There was beauty even in the name of the most wicked man on earth, and a piece of heaven even in the most ravaged land. A startled silence echoes at the heart of every tumult. In the heart of all troubles a timid quietness echoes, at the end of every tunnel there's an unexpected breath of freedom. Life begins as it ends; sometimes falling into the sky; sometimes rising up to the ground, stopping to catch its breath, warming itself in its own ashes. And when it was warm enough, it moved forward again; trudging on like a complex puzzle that did not like its own answer. As it remained, the people could continue to live. It didn't matter whether the stay was long or short, because time wasn't the issue.

This was a portrait of heaven; not of an afterlife but of the heaven at the heart of life.

At this point in the show, all of the men who had seen the reversed world in the eyes of the snake began sobbing; they wept more than they'd ever wept before, and in a way they'd never wept before. Most of them fell to their knees in remorse. The cool smell of cistern water filled the room. It was as if all evil would end, and all would be well. Even if for the briefest moment, all of the men in the tent felt they had the unique chance to be absolved of all their sins, and in order to demonstrate the sincerity of their desire for purification, they threw all of their money onto the stage. Then, the mirror closed just as it had opened. The snake-charmer bowed with a slight smile, deliberately picked up the money that had been thrown onto the stage and put it into his basket, and then, in contrast to his slowness of a moment before, rushed off the stage as if he was fleeing. The snake slithered after its master like a whistled melody.

After the snake-handler, Betri Hanım came on with her puppets. She had ten small puppets on her ten fingers. She would represent the natural world through them. She would become rain, and rain down blessings; become a rainbow and open a passage for the impossible; become a dew droplet and stroke the cheek of the grass, become a breeze and thrill the foot of the mountains, become herbs and restore to health; become snow and spread consolation in large flakes; become sun and cause swan-necked flowers to open; become fog and lower silvery curtains of mystery; become climate and have all of its conditions loved, become water and increase life. There was no favour that nature could not bestow on man.

After this pleasant show, a deep silence filled the tent. Now it was time for La Belle Annabelle to appear.

When it was time for La Belle Annabelle to appear, all of the men were as thrilled as if they'd been tempted by the devil. They were thrilled by the sense that they would now see beauty beyond all of the beauty they'd already seen. If there was something beyond heaven, who would want to linger in heaven? La Belle Annabelle made death meaningless, unwittingly and unintentionally. At the point where death was rendered meaningless, life was unravelled stitch by stitch. And life loved to be amazed. There was a moment when even the most talkative would fall silent; when even the bravest would shake with fear. A moment when someone posing at a joyful celebration feels heart pains at just the second the photographer pressed the button… As if a burnt photograph was deliberately trying to darken the moment of happiness it witnessed… A moment when even the most fainthearted would find courage, when even the most eloquent stammered, when even the most insensitive felt the cry of terror within them… The name of that moment was a word even the most ancient languages under the sun had forgotten to embrace; unwritten and unspoken. For this reason it didn't exist until it approached; and by the time it approached it was too late. Because La Belle Annabelle was on the stage.

The moment Keramet Mumî Keşke Memiş Efendi saw Annabelle he knew he'd found what he'd been seeking for the eastward-facing section of the cherry-coloured tent. He decided to act at once, and began thinking of how to convince the owner of the troupe. However, he would not have to go to too much trouble. It happened that the peevish little old man, who had come here with dreams of earning a fortune, had run into debt soon after reaching the East, and was in need of money. Moreover, Annabelle had been a disappointment to him, because she could not learn even the shortest parts, could not dance properly and was unable to sing. In short, the owner of the French troupe was eager to get rid of Annabelle, who he'd once thought would bring him luck.

When La Belle Annabelle arrived, she was as silent as mud drying in the sun. She met Keramet Mumî Keşke Memiş Efendi's offer with a surprising silence, as if what's called living was something to be scattered randomly. The rest was easy. A little money was pressed into the troupe owner's hand, and the next day Annabelle took her place in the cherry-coloured tent. In the early days, she wandered around idly, and didn't make any effort to learn the language. The words spoken around her hit her randomly, and some of them stuck to her. In this way, without even wanting to, she learned how to speak this new language. But she never spoke.

To tell the truth, no one really expected her to speak. Keramet Mumî Keşke Memiş Efendi didn't want her to dance or sing either. He wanted nothing more than for her to be on the stage, to stand on the stage; more accurately, it was enough simply for her to be seen. She also held a tambourine; but would anyone have noticed whether or not the cymbals jingled or the tassels moved? No one paid attention to anything except La Belle Annabelle's face.

Her face had forty rooms and forty doors like the mansion in which she was born. Forty different visitors were welcomed through forty separate doors. Each visitor, thinking himself the only one, could wander through the magnificent gardens and the cold store-rooms, under the ornamented ceilings, through the cobwebbed attics, and the glittering salons, and the velvet-covered corridors and among mirrors that reflected each other endlessly, without meeting any of the others.

When she was on the stage, each man heard a faint voice whisper in his ear. 'Open your eyes!' And everyone in the audience opened their eyes wide.

La Belle Annabelle's face was a frontier without borders, in the days when the West didn't take its eyes of the East, and still no one could make out where the East ended and the West began. Her face belonged to neither West nor East. For this reason, any man who looked at her felt himself both at home and abroad. There was something very familiar about this face…as familiar as the sweet smell of childhood. Everyone wanted to rush to embrace her. But when they took their first step, they'd feel they were approaching something strange and unfamiliar. This face both repelled and attracted; it repelled without permitting retreat. The face of La Belle Annabelle was as briskly fluid as the river she had left behind. As it flowed past wildly, its expression and condition altered from moment to moment. But whatever happened, she continued to be the most beautiful *jinn* of the poisonous yew forest.

All the men gathered in that tent wished that the ever-moving *jinn* face would regain her breath for a moment; put her head on their shoulders. It was a dream; everybody saw the love they had been longing for secretly on the face of the most beautiful La Belle Annabelle.

Everybody suddenly became a master artist in order to paint her likeness. As their daydreams darted back and forth, each man trembled with the desire to have the honour of being La Belle Annabelle's only love, even if just for the briefest moment. Then the moment ended, and La Belle Annabelle bowed and left the stage. The audience applauded her absence until their palms were red. But despite their insistence, La Belle Annabelle did not return to the stage.

Every night the show ended in the same way. Each night when the eastward-facing door was thrown open, all of the men who had entered separately now rushed out together, pushing and shoving.

They went back down the hill so dazzled by the beauty they'd been able to witness that they didn't know where they were or what they were doing. At the fountain halfway down the hill they washed their faces with ice-cold water. The water didn't help a bit. When they reached home, their faces darkened involuntarily because the women who would spend the night in their arms were not La Belle Annabelle. Some of them felt remorse for thinking this. They tried to behave more tenderly than ever to their wives. Then they wanted to go to sleep at once. Anyway, as Keramet Mumî Keşke Memiş Efendi often said: whenever men want to be free of borrowed dreams, they take refuge in the regularity of sleep.

As they slept, their wives walked anxiously through the house. The image of the Sable-Girl did not leave their eyes. Those who were pregnant didn't dare sleep. They were afraid of seeing that they'd given birth to sable-children in their dreams, and of not being able to find the right interpretation of their dreams when they woke.

Then, the night closed over them. The night was as hungry for consolation as a broken promise; needed renewal as much as a snake trying to shed its skin. Night was the only time in this world of spectacle that no one could see.

Istanbul — 1999

gölge (shadow): Once upon a time, an elderly ship-builder lived in a fishing village where the houses were white and the women wore black. Everyone recognised the elderly ship-builder who had no shadow, but no one knew him.

Many years ago, when he was still very young, he used to dive into the sea all the time, and in order to see what lay beneath the depths, he dove even deeper. One day he dove so deep he knew he'd never reach the surface again. Then the sea granted him a chance out of pity for his youth. He could trade his shadow for his life. From that day to this, the elderly ship-builder has lived without a shadow. He never told anyone his secret.

Anyway no one had a shadow in the fishing village where the houses were white and the women wore black, and everyone had been swallowed by the sea. But because no one noticed the absence of shadows, no one was aware of the situation. Everyone kept their secret to themselves, even though everyone had the same secret and therefore it was not a secret.

'Take these away from me!' I said to B–C.

In front of me there were three slices of *börek*, three cheese and three ground meat. They looked good. On top of that they must have just come out of the oven. Every day of the week, without fail, the neighbour-ladies in the Hayalifener Apartments all went to visit one or another of their number in turn. Every day without fail, cakes and pastries were being baked in one of the apartments, and a wonderful smell filled the building. We regularly got our share of these delicacies. These neighbour-ladies not only put something aside for us on the regular days when they baked for guests, but also when they baked on holidays and special occasions. According to B-C, it had been this way since he moved into the building. The first to see him the day he moved in was the irritable woman from next door. She examined B-C from head to toe, and, on learning he was a bachelor, asked how he was going to look after himself. Within half an hour, all of the neighbour-ladies in the building had come bearing welcome gifts of food. From that day on, the women were constantly bringing him food or sending their children to bring it to him. B-C laughed and said, 'I suppose they think that if I eat more I'll grow bigger.'

According to him, during one period only, the week I moved in with him, did the food sent to him by the neighbour-ladies diminish. But later, after seeing me coming and going to work and labelling me a 'working woman', and after noticing that I didn't cook at home on weekends, and also perhaps thinking that because I was so fat I must have a large appetite, they started to send even more food than they had before. On top of that, the portions were three times larger.

Today's potato *börek* had been sent to us by our downstairs neighbour. I thought she was the best cook of all the ladies in the Hayalifener Apartments. But this time I didn't even taste her *börek*. I was on a diet.

gölge oyunu (shadow play): In many cultures, the existing shadow plays are divided into two parts called 'the shadow's plays' and 'the play's shadows'. Which part is to be seen depends upon the spectator.

In Java, those who go to see the *wayang kulit* shadow plays at the king's palace divide themselves into two groups. Men would sit facing the east and women would sit facing the west. The border between them was called *Pringgitan*, and this was where the curtain was drawn.

Because everyone in Java knew that the sun rose in the east, both the puppets and the *dalang* who manipulated the puppets took their places in the men's section. This way, while the men saw the puppets and the puppet-masters themselves, the women saw their shadows.

Glaucon didn't know this. He was listening carefully to the philosopher sitting across from him.

'Imagine that a number of creatures are crossing a road, and a light is shining from behind them that projects their shadows onto the wall of the cave,' said the philosopher, and then continued. 'Well, my dear Glaucon, the world we see with our eyes is the wall of that cave, and it's a wise man who can look at the light behind and see with reason rather than with the senses.'

'This is why women, who cannot see anything except the shadows, will always think dreams are reality.'

'I understand,' said Glaucon. 'Indeed this is why women can't become philosophers.'

'Of course,' said the philosopher. 'Indeed that's why philosophers can't become women.'

'Is there a new dream?' asked B–C as he took the *börek* away from me.

He always wants me to relate my dreams. And I do relate them; sometimes as they were, and sometimes with changes. I didn't open my eyes right away when I woke. I stayed a while halfway between sleep and waking, and tried to fix my freshest dream in my memory. I season what I've seen with herbs, sauces and spices; I fill in the gaps with my strong imagination, and plaster the cracks with lies. Of course, since I'd started my diet, the dream meals I described to B–C were obliged not only to address the eyes but also the stomach. Perhaps like most people who are trying to loose weight, I wanted to see those closest to me get fatter. Though B–C was one of those annoying people who stay the same no matter how much they eat. Neither my efforts nor those of the neighbour-ladies caused him to gain even a fraction of a kilo.

In order for my dreams to be well-fried, I didn't get out of bed even though I'd woken up, and on the weekends I went back to sleep. Then I would wake up forgetful, or thought I hadn't dreamed at all. Then I would search for ready dreams; dreams that had been interpreted in books, or that I'd heard spoken of here and there. One can find them if one looks. I would change the labels, and present other people's dreams as if they were a meal I had prepared myself. 'Bravo!' B-C would exclaim with a teasing smile. I would look anxiously at my hands. My chewed, shredded cuticles were swimming in the salt water of pain.

He loved films as much as he loved dreams.

Films and dreams provided material for the Dictionary of Gazes. Or perhaps I ought to put it this way: He loved dreams and films because they provided material for the Dictionary of Gazes.

> *gözbası* (legerdemain): To trick the eye by showing, with the aid of speed, something that isn't there as if it actually is there is called legerdemain. If the same action is performed more slowly, the audience's eyes will be opened, and they will see the trick. The magic will be broken and the mystery will be solved.
>
> Ageing causes one to slow down. When ageing conjurers perform their last tricks, they make their own selves disappear.

B-C often used to fall asleep in front of the television. He'd start snoring in the middle of a film he'd wanted very much to see; from time to time, without opening his eyes, he would ask questions about the film, and then would wake suddenly from the deepest sleep, wearing a hurt expression as if he'd been forcibly thrown out of the house, and continue watching the film as if nothing had happened or could have happened during his absence. Perhaps he also thought he was the only one watching the film. As soon as he closed his eyes, he would take all of the actors aside and give them a cigarette break. When he opened his eyes the film would resume at the point where it had stopped.

When B-C was asleep in front of the television, I would take the opportunity to watch him. I would watch the hands that were too big to belong to a dwarf, the toes that all looked as if they belonged to different feet, the tight black curls of his chest hair, his puffy nipples, at the red tongue in his open mouth, and the boldness of this red, the freckles on his face and how very tiny they were. Whenever he fell asleep, and I took off the glasses that were sliding off the end of his nose, I would always try them on before I put them aside. What did his little eyes see through this glass? He knew so many amazing things, so much about people's stories, how did he see it all? Whatever I looked at through them, the lenses of these glasses didn't solve the mystery.

Whenever I put on B–C's glasses, I went to the mirror to look at myself. There would be nothing different about me; my face was always the same face, my body the same body. I was carrying the illness I knew myself to be carrying; my obesity was like an amulet that had mistakenly been sewn to my skin when my form was being put together. Though in the past, quite a long time ago that is, there was a period, a phase of my childhood, when I wasn't at all fat. But this wasn't important right now. It didn't help my present obesity one bit whether or not I remembered that I'd once been a thin child. The past is gone forever. But B–C didn't think this way.

gözbebesi (pupil): Round in humans and generally an upright ellipse in animals, it changes size according to the amount of light that reaches the iris. Darkness and distance dilate the pupils; light and nearness make them contract. That is, this indecisive circle gets smaller if there is light and larger if there is no light. Because it gets smaller when it looks at something close, that which is close is light, and is in the light. That which is far is in darkness. Anyway, no one wants to see darkness up close.

Being in love makes the pupils dilate; this means that the beloved is always far away. The pupils dilate in order to ease the pain caused by this distance.

'The past, the present, the future…we line them all up and draw a straight line. That's why we believe that the past is gone and the future hasn't arrived yet. And worst of all, we're obliged to walk through time along this straight line we've already drawn. But perhaps he's so drunk he can't see as far as the end of his nose,' said B-C, waving the scissors he was holding at the television.

He'd started again. He loved to talk about time. This was his favourite subject. While I just wanted to watch television calmly and quietly. I was watching a film with a large bowl of popcorn on my lap; it was one of those haunted house films. B-C, on the floor, on the carpet, was lost in a mass of daily newspapers and weekly magazines; he was drinking wine and cutting out pictures, articles and advertisements.

He was gathering material for the Dictionary of Gazes.

'If only time never came to its senses. If somehow it wouldn't succeed in walking a straight line. If it would only lurch, behave nonsensically, fall to pieces. And we would watch, and, condemning its actions, would never have to refer to it again.'

Whenever he started talking excitedly like this, he would wave his hands about wildly. As if every word he uttered was lacking something, and he would try to express what was missing with his hands that were too big for a dwarf.

'Yes, if only time wouldn't come to its senses. If it would make lots of mistakes…if it couldn't succeed at any plan it had made beforehand…if it always realised its mistakes afterwards…when it was too late. If it couldn't match its own speed. If it gave up and went backwards, in completely the opposite direction. First spending the future penny by penny. And then find its consolation in novelty. Then it would be the past's turn. For the old that somehow couldn't be made old. If it would vomit its selfishness, all of its knowledge. If the past's order was turned upside down. If there was no order left at all…'

This was one of those moments when he didn't stop talking. I think he didn't really know what he was talking about, and just wanted to hear the sound of his own voice. In trying to make time drunk, he'd become drunk himself.

'So what if it comes to its senses?' I said, throwing a handful of popcorn into my mouth.

The film wasn't that important. B–C's enthusiasm was a match for my passion. I was prepared to ask any question at all just in order to see his enthusiasm. In fact perhaps I don't listen to what he says, but rather watch how he tells it. I loved the way that, when he spoke, he was as excited as if he was solving the terrifying mystery of a cursed tombstone.

'If it comes to its senses it will remember. What use will it be to remember? None. Remembering won't be of any damned use except to cause pain.'

I shut up. At moments like this I don't know what I'm supposed to do, and I couldn't bring him back from wherever he'd gone. 'Say whatever you have to say now or hold your peace forever,' a voice deep within me would say. I would speak up right away in order not to miss the 'now'. I would speak up, but still be unsure of what to say. I knew there was definitely something I had to say, but I couldn't find what it was. Because I had remained quiet 'now', B–C would hold me to the part about holding my peace forever. He'd been talking nonstop. My fingers were blistered by his flaming lips. At times like this it went so far that it defied understanding; his thin little eyes turned into mysteries, and he never showed what he was feeling.

'When you remember, you become frightened of solitude. Those people who remain in stagnant relationships from fear of loneliness, who give birth to children in order to refresh stale love, those are the people with the strongest memories.'

He was sitting in his rocking chair again, holding his purple-fringed blanket tightly, rocking back and forth and talking at the top of his voice. It seemed as if he'd already forgotten how the irritable next-door neighbour had come to complain about the noise we made and had threatened to make a complaint to our landlord. As soon as the women entered her house and carefully examined how messy it was, she couldn't keep herself from making a comment to me. I didn't want to have to see her again tonight. But B-C was having a talking fit again. And at times like this he somehow couldn't moderate his voice. And anyone who heard his voice would have thought it came from an enormous man. He jumped down, came to my side, and took hold of my wrist.

'The past doesn't pass and go away. It doesn't go anywhere. The past always flows into today. That's why being able to forget forgetting is important,' he said.

'To forget is to clean the eyes. It definitely has to be done every spring. If we don't forget we can't live! If we don't forget we can't cause anything to live!'

'I prefer to make my eyes an archive,' I said shrugging my shoulders. He let go of my wrist and pulled back. Was there a mocking smile on his lips, or did it just seem so to me?

'Is it you who's saying this?'

Why wouldn't I say this? What was wrong with my saying this? Instead of answering me, he went back to his rocking chair and squeezed his purple-fringed blanket. This sudden silence distressed me. When I'm distressed I become hungry.

I thought about getting up to pop more corn. I'd forgotten I was on a diet!

gözcü (watchman): One of the greedy jewellers in the Grand Bazaar had a door built into the back of his shop, believing it would lead to eternal life. He intended to slip away through this secret exit when the Angel of Death came for him. For this reason, he needed a watchman to sit in front of his shop to let him know when the Angel of Death appeared at the edge of the market. But no matter how much he offered to pay, no one wanted the job.

The Angel of Death became bored. He took the form of a poor miller and planted himself in front of the jeweller. In exchange for bags and bags of gold, he accepted the job of sitting in front of the shop to inform the jeweller as soon as he saw the Angel of Death. This game went on for some time. The Angel of Death wanted both to take the jeweller's life and to keep his word as a watchman. He'd got himself into a bind.

Finally one day, he thought of a trick that would solve the problem. He placed a full-length mirror on the back door, facing the front door. Then he stood at the front door and told the jeweller that the Angel of Death was coming. The jeweller, with an agility that wouldn't be expected of someone his age, seized the handle of the back door. When he opened the door he thought would lead to immortality, he saw the watchman at the front door in the mirror. He was astounded but quickly realised his mistake. (Who else could accept to be death's messenger except death's watchman?)

I was becoming increasingly anxious. I was anxious because I thought that everything B–C did and said had to do with the Dictionary of Gazes. Since he didn't show me what he'd written, the Dictionary of Gazes was an enigma to me. And with every passing day this enigma distanced him further from me. I also suspected that all of those strange things were taken from the Dictionary of Gazes. As if his contact with me and with life itself was through the vehicle of, and by leave of, the Dictionary of Gazes. I didn't like this.

On top of this, he'd started seeing everyone and everything as material. He said that stories resembled water, and that only in miracles did sweet water and salt water flow together without mixing. He asserted that because the Dictionary of Gazes was not a miracle, it could mix completely with everyone and everything. With a stick in his hand, he was constantly stirring up stories; putting the end at the beginning and the beginning in the middle. He cut up films, dreams, newspaper cuttings, encyclopaedia articles, put the pieces together, and used them as material for the Dictionary of Gazes.

I was anxious because once he used material, he never looked at it again.

gözlük (glasses): Glass placed in frames in order to see better or to see at all.

The next day when I got back from the nursery B-C wasn't at home. Lately he often went out without leaving word. On days like these, one of the neighbour-ladies would always open her door, either to put out the trash or to give me some food; and when they opened their doors they would always let me know when and how B-C had left. But not even the neighbour-ladies knew where he had gone or what he was doing.

I ate my supper alone. When I say supper, it was only grapefruit. I'm punishing myself today because yesterday I forgot I was on a diet. All day I've eaten nothing but grapefruit. As I piled up the grapefruit peels, I carefully examined my belly. I have to confess, I didn't have one belly, I had three bellies. And not one of them had melted even the smallest bit.

halüsinasyon (hallucination): For thousands of years, people had been drinking infusions of mushrooms in order to see what they hadn't seen. Later, they became frightened of what they could see.

I suppose if I wasn't as fat as I am, I'd be able to keep better track of the weight I've lost. When something small becomes smaller it's noticeable right away, but when something large become smaller the loss remains invisible. Just as I used to in the old days, I suffer pangs of hunger all day. Since I couldn't fill my stomach, I suppose my eyes tried to fill themselves by watching all of the cooking programmes on television, and reading food articles in magazines, and gazing at bountiful displays in restaurant windows and at high calorie products in the supermarket, learning recipes from skilful cooks wherever I went, and since I was talking about food all day, when I finally did eat something it somehow didn't fill me. Then I could put away at least thirty grapefruit in one sitting. The pile of grapefruit peels became as high as a mountain. It made me irritable to see them. Dieting made me an irritable person.

Eating that many grapefruits one after the other made me feel quite heavy. I curled up on the sofa. Not long afterwards, I heard the door open. B–C had come home. But I was so sleepy I couldn't get up. My eyes were closing. I fell asleep looking at the mound of grapefruit peels.

> *harem asası* (chief palace eunuch): In the Ottoman harem, as well as, in their time, in the palaces of Assyria, Persia, Rome, Byzantium, Abbysinia and the Mameluks, well-known figures served as chief eunuch. After becoming eunuchs, the gravest sin they could commit was seeing.

'Come on,' I said to B–C as soon as he came in. He looked tired.

'Come on what?'

'Let's go out tonight. It's been a long time since we've gone out in disguise. We haven't seen the mood of the people. Come on, let's go see.'

> *hay* (fantasy, dream): The boy used to climb up into the apple tree and lose himself in his dreams. He wouldn't come down from the tree all day; sometimes he stayed in the tree through the night and into the morning. In the end, the elders of the family, unable to bear the situation, decided to cut down the tree. The boy crawled into the hollow where the apple tree had been and dreamed he was an apple tree. Every year he produced crisp, juicy apples. The elders of the family wept as they spooned up the stewed apples.

This time we changed our appearance more quickly. Two hours later the two of us were unrecognisable. This evening I was a hardened, cold-blooded thief. B–C was my sidekick, an unemployed, shiftless adolescent who had gone to work for his elder brother. Just like the first sprouting of a moustache, he had no idea which way he was going. From the sparse hair on his face he looked like a chick that had had difficulty breaking out of its egg. B–C was confused.

This evening he was an impatient, over-sensitive, ill-tempered and penniless young man. I wanted to take him into my arms, carry him on my back, spin him around, but mostly I wanted to throw him into the air. I wanted him to laugh and enjoy himself in the firmament, to ask why the sun oppressed sunflowers, to stroke the moon's face, to memorise the locations of the stars, and for him to know, as he fell like a lump of metal, that I might not catch him. Perhaps I'd gone and left, out of boredom, or forgetfulness, or perhaps for no reason at all. I wanted him to fall with the malevolent thrill of 'perhaps'. Not wafting down like a leaf, but with the speed of lead.

He'd put a dirty, wrinkled beret on his head. He'd put gel on his hair, and his earlobes, pink from the cold, stuck out from under his beret. He pattered after me with his hands in his pockets. His right kneecap was protruding through a hole in his greasy trousers. His face was dirty and small enough not to show the misgivings he was feeling, but the pursing of his sore-covered lips gave away his fear.

'Don't be frightened,' I said. 'You'll be fine, little one.'

hayalbilim (the study of fantasy): The favourite theme of writers on the study of fantasy is seeing strangers. A stranger who comes from outside the present time and place. Sometimes he doesn't come, and one has to go to him. In any event, a journey is necessary.

The restaurant was very bright. It was a big place bathed in blond light. The light shone superficially and amply in order to provoke the stubbornness of those who flowed deeply and methodically; it jumped enthusiastically from the silverware arranged according to size to the rows and rows of customers, from food that was pleasing to the eye to conversation that was pleasing to the ear, from the salmon-coloured ribbons on the table-cloths to the black bow-ties on the waiters, from the pastel-toned paintings to the shrill tones of the seasonal salads, from the overwhelming smell of perfume to the heavy smell of anise. The light shone like a filled sail in this glittering seaside fish restaurant that defied the night.

I was the one who chose this place. This evening B-C was quiet and obedient. We thrust each other forward and looked in through the glass wall that separated the restaurant from the street. For a time it didn't seem as if anyone noticed us; that is, until an almond-eyed woman eating across from a well-dressed middle-aged man raised her wine glass and made eye contact with B-C. Then, some things began to change on the other side of the glass wall. From where we stood we could see that the mouthful the woman had been chewing daintily somehow wouldn't go down her throat. She was right to be uneasy. It must have been unpleasant to eat with us watching. We wondered what she would do. A little later, the almond-eyed woman, with a dejected expression, nodded her head forward; and found herself looking at the eye of the dead fish on her plate. Perhaps she too was thinking about what she would do. When she lifted her head again, she'd gone pale, and her eyes were lifeless. First the well-dressed middle-aged man and then the head-waiter became aware of the situation. After telling them to get rid of us, she didn't take another look; neither at us nor at the fish on her plate. That evening, in that bright restaurant, for reasons I didn't know, I felt a closeness to the almond-eyed woman who had informed on us.

Hümay: The green-headed Hümay bird who was well-known for avoiding the eyes of the earth and of men was so devoted to the firmament that she would lay her eggs in the air. From time to time Hümay would come within forty cubits of the earth, and let its shadow fall on a person. Whoever Hümay's shadow fell upon would never be defeated in life.

The head-waiter was inclined to settle the matter quietly, but the well-dressed middle-aged man wanted to kick up a fuss. Thanks to him, the whole restaurant was soon aware of our presence. Before long, two enormous men had come up to us and told us not to press our noses to the glass and watch the restaurant. When we objected, we were quickly sent on our way.

But since we were in disguise that evening, we had to return to the place where we mustn't be seen.

Unseen, we lay in ambush in a cul-de-sac from which we could watch. Because the diminishing halo of light from the restaurant ended not far away, we remained in darkness. B–C was constantly repeating it. These overgrown men had taken him by his wispy moustache like a dead rat and had sent him flying. Now, his narrow eyes burning with anger, he watched the restaurant intently. With his nose, he watched the smells of food and drink that wafted on the breeze; with his fist he watched what his fingertips hadn't been able to touch. He watched with his grinding teeth.

'All right, they'll do!' exclaimed B–C, seeing a couple who had left the restaurant and were waiting for their car to be brought. Both husband and wife were wearing a sour apple-green. I ignored him. We continued waiting. Before long, a family wrapped from head to toe in orange emerged from the restaurant. A mother, a father, and two grown-up girls.

B–C and I emerged silently from our hiding place.

isne delisi (eye of the needle): In a neighbourhood where silence was as valuable as gold, a woman and her daughter sat in front of the window embroidering the daughter's trousseau. 'Your dreams have to be small enough to pass through the eye of a needle,' said the woman to her daughter. 'If you see that a dream is too large to pass through a needle, forget it. Dreams that don't pass through the eye of a needle are empty dreams. They won't bring anything but disappointment.'

The poor girl listened carefully to what her mother said. Then she lost herself in her dreams. Whenever she started to entertain a dream, her embroidery fell from her hands, and the needle with it.

'Knife!'

B–C, excited, extended his knife. The orange coloured family passed down the dark street quickly. I hadn't known beforehand which one I would choose. They were shaking. Each one was shaking differently. I chose the wildly trembling mother.

The woman didn't stop begging us to let them go. But when they saw the knife, their fear silenced them. This evening I'm not just hardened and cold-blooded, I'm a practised and experienced thief. I went calmly about my work. I stripped off the orange peels the woman was wearing, without injuring her at all. After I'd taken off her outer orange peels, she stood before us wearing only a light-coloured, dainty lace inner orange peel.

Then I dragged the man into the middle and asked him to look at his wife. Squinting his eyes stupidly he looked first at the orange peels on the ground, and then at me. Finally his eyes caught sight of his wife, though in fact looking and seeing happen at the same time, but because the brain is slower than the eyes it's necessary to wait a little. If it had been a stranger in front of him everything would have been easier. It's easier to see strangers than it is to see those we know. But a little while later, the man knew what he saw. He saw his wife's irredeemable nose, her sagging double chin, her flaccid breasts, her spreading fat, her varicose veins, hair that should have been dyed long ago, the crows-feet between her eyebrows. 'How the years,' he murmured, 'wear a person out. How beautiful she was when she was young. Has it been easy? All these years she's been sacrificing herself for us.'

The sediments of mercy darkened the night.

'Dagger!'

B-C had overcome his excitement and brandished the dagger calmly. Meanwhile, the woman had started sobbing pitifully. I'd stripped off the inner peels, without injuring her at all. The man had to become accustomed; he looked at once. He saw that his wife's lips had shrunk from pursing them at everything, that her mouth was turned down from constantly nagging, that her eyes were wrinkled from regarding everything with malice, that her expression had darkened from seeking other's faults, that her evil heart had drained her body of life, that even though she said malicious things about the beauty parlours she continued determinedly to spend time and money shaping her body, that as her unhappiness grew she tried to get more control over her children and wouldn't let them out of her sight for a moment, and secretly went into their rooms to sniff their clothes and read their diaries, and that for years she had been watching him in the same secret ways. And he didn't like what he saw. With a sour expression, he took a few steps back. At this point the woman had covered her face with her hands, but the man wasn't looking any more.

It was much easier to strip the man of his orange peels. His rough outer orange peels were an amazing optical illusion. When I cut away the thick outer orange peels, a tiny little body appeared. All of the water in his body had melted away. There was no water left to melt, and his body was getting smaller every day. But because of his outer peels, nothing was apparent from outside. His inner, second layer of peels had become separated thread by thread and had taken on a spongy appearance. What we touched broke off in our hands. Meanwhile, before we could say anything, the woman approached the man and looked at him. Years ago she'd married the man with the certainty that he was the right choice for the future, the father of her two daughters, but now with his outer orange peels gone she looked at her diminishing husband appraisingly. 'What a shame,' she whispered to herself. 'How he's collapsed. Was it easy? He worked himself to the bone all these years. All for us.'

The sediments of mercy darkened the night.

'Dagger!'

B-C brandished his dagger in a threatening manner. When the second layer of orange peel was gone, the woman looked again. She looked and saw. She saw that he deferred to anyone stronger than him, or even to anyone of his own strength, that he fills his wallet and his stomach through trickery, that he spends money on pretty boys, his favourite game to play with them is be-the-other-hit-yourself, he dresses the boys in his own clothes while he dresses as a woman, then derives great pleasure from having the boys abuse and humiliate him, then he wants the boys to beat him but constantly cautions them that these beatings must leave no marks, how amazing it is that he's been playing these secret nocturnal games all these years without them leaving any trace on him, that when the beating starts going too far and the blows become harder he takes off his garters and beats the boy hard enough to make him bleed all over, that whatever dirty business he enters, he emerges smelling like roses, that if anyone were to learn his secrets, he would be compromised, that he had risen to his position by compromising and stepping on others. And she didn't like what she saw.

jaluzi (Venetian blind): Inner curtains that are jealous of outside eyes.

B-C was really enjoying himself. He wanted to bring forward the girls who had been watching their mother and father with anxiety, though I was tired and bored. After a short argument he was convinced that we should return to the Hayalifener Apartments. But he insisted that we burn the orange peels before we left. I didn't say anything. With B-C's beret in my hand, I withdrew to a dark corner to watch.

B-C was circling the burning orange peels, which gave off a wonderful smell. It was as if his excitement was rolling down a steep hill, gaining speed and strength as it rolled. He was banging on what looked like the lid of a garbage bin, though without a handle, and was making enough noise to wake the dead. He dropped the lid and held the knife in one hand and the dagger in the other, lifting them both into the air. He moaned as if he was wounded, and trembled like an epileptic. I held my breath, and watched him. I'd never seen him like this before. I watched in amazement as the light of the flames played in his hair, and his lips curled, and his burning eyes refused to witness the world. B-C was a witch who had lost not only the recipe for poison but also the recipe for the antidote as the wind ruffled the pages of the book of spells; who turned into a fly and infuriated the ox from around whose neck the world was hanging; who poisoned all of the cisterns of the city with his anger; who cursed the goddess just before the moon turned full but would not allow anyone else to do so.

Each member of the orange-coloured family watched him, their eyes wide as saucers with surprise. Their pupils were dilating moment by moment from their delight in the knowledge that they would soon be set free from the struggle with the darkness of the pain of the moment; and also…and also a barely visible stain…a stain as small and unimportant as a flea that had bitten, a tick that had attached itself, a caterpillar that had chewed, a leech that had sucked, a moth that had eaten, a worm that had emerged from an apple remained in the pupils of each member of the orange-coloured family.

Janus: Janus, the ancient Roman God, had two faces, one that looked forward and one that looked behind. Because of this, he could see both the future and the past.

Tonight, pruning his bright yellow hallucinations with the sharp edge of his heart, hopping and jumping on the flames, making the most of being someone else on a night of disguise, B–C extinguished with his own sweat the fire he had lit with his own hands. When he left the orange-coloured family in the cul-de-sac, he was still holding the smoke deep within himself. Later, we walked arm-in-arm through the side streets; we walked calmly, without saying a single word. At one point I looked, and saw that he had filled his pockets with orange peels. 'Why did you do it?' I asked.

'Since we'd disguised ourselves as thieves, we had to steal something from them,' he answered. 'How much do you think these orange peels are worth?'

Kalipso (Calypso): The goddess whose name derives from the ancient Greek verb '*kalyptein*', which means 'to hide'.

I smelled of oranges. As if everything smelled of oranges. The first thing I had to do when I got back to the Hayalifener Apartments was to throw myself in the bath. This time I'd spent so long in my corset that my body was rebelling. It was an effort to move or to speak. I felt worse from moment to moment. I asked B–C for help as loudly as I could, but he didn't hear me. He'd long since started working on the computer. From the way he was writing, he had to have found new material for the Dictionary of Gazes.

kedi (cat): Cat's eyes can see what people cannot see.

My body was waiting for me in the bathroom. I stepped in front of the mirror and took off my disguise. The corset was causing me a lot of pain. I unfastened the straps and opened the clasps one by one. The fat that had been confined all night should have started spreading out as soon as I opened the corset, but I didn't feel any difference. Something strange was going on. I took the corset off completely. There was another corset underneath.

I didn't remember having put on another corset like this. I hurried to unfasten it. There was yet another corset underneath it. I was struck with terror. Each time I unfastened a corset, there was another one underneath it. And each corset resembled a grapefruit peel. Just like the orange-coloured family, I was stripping off peel after peel. But at least their bodies appeared after two layers of peels; whereas I seemed to be made up only of peels. I wept as I stripped them off in front of the mirror. As I stripped off layer after layer, mounds of grapefruit peels were accumulating around me.

Finally, after stripping off I don't know how many layers of peels, I was left with something that resembled a fish skeleton. It was so frightful that I didn't have the courage to look at myself in the mirror. I turned my head. It was then that I realised I was standing in front of a restaurant again. But this wasn't like the fish restaurant of earlier; nor was it chic. In the wide display window, rows and rows of chickens were turning on spits. A little behind them there were kid goats, and behind these there were lambs, and at the very back huge cows were turning. All of the animals were turning with the same slowness. Suddenly, I saw my usual body among the meat. It was enormous. It was sticky and glutinous. It was as pitiful as vanilla ice-cream melting under the sun. Wearing an apron, and with a fork in its hand, it was testing each of the cooking animals. At one point it turned and winked. 'Our evening meal,' it said when it came to a large animal that, from its hump, was apparently a camel. 'I'm on a diet,' I said in a low voice. 'Of course, of course,' said my body. 'I forget so quickly. You're on a diet.'

Later, looking deeply into my eyes, it tore off one of the camel's legs and started eating it ravenously.

I heard B–C's voice from afar. It was coming closer. I opened my eyes a little. I'd fallen asleep again, and again at an inappropriate time. He was perched on the edge of the armchair I was sitting in, looking at me. Right behind him were the peels of the grapefruit I'd eaten as soon as I'd come home. I didn't want to see any peels. I tried to say something but B–C brought his finger to his lips.

'Quiet, don't speak,' he whispered. He was smiling. 'It's not a good idea to leave you home alone. How many kilos of grapefruit did you eat?'

I smiled bashfully.

'I don't know what you dreamed tonight, but from the look of you it was nightmare. It's passed now. Don't tell anyone what you saw, keep it to yourself.'

I looked at him with surprise. As if he wasn't the same person who was always pestering me to tell him my dreams. But I was very pleased that he didn't ask any questions, that he preferred calmly and quietly stroking my hair to talking.

kem göz (evil eye): In a frilly white dress that went down to the ground, the young girl was smiling. She passed an old woman with whiskers on her chin who was selling pigeon feed. The old woman said, 'You've become like a swan, my dear.' The young girl felt a strange shiver, but still thanked the old woman.

The steps of the square where the pigeons gathered were covered with moss. She slipped on the last step and landed face-down in a puddle of mud. Passers-by rushed to pick her up, and wiped the blood from her cut lip; but they couldn't clean the white, frilly dress.

'That woman did this,' shouted the young girl. She was standing right behind the old woman with the whiskers on her chin. 'Nonsense,' she whispered. 'Everyone knows that white is soon soiled.' Then she emptied bowl of pigeon feed over the young girl.

The pigeons descended on the feed in a black cloud.

I didn't say anything to B-C, but my dream had left me irritable. I didn't want to see fruit with peels, whether it was grapefruit or oranges, for at least a few days. Of course, I knew that my body was the problem; this is all. Of course, I knew that the problem was my body; and also that I shouldn't be so obsessed about it. But when you're as fat as I am, your body becomes magnified in your mind. As if…as if what you live within, the air you breathe, becomes a place, a place to which you belong. And a person can't easily leave behind a place to which she belongs.

In any event it was I who had been making touching speeches to the children at the nursery about the inner person being more important than the outer person. I told them that their appearance was of no importance at all. They sat and listened very calmly; without making a sound or any comic gestures. They weren't all that interested in what I had to say. They kept turning around to look out the window. That morning we'd all sprayed the classroom windows with fake snow; we'd made snowmen with carrot noses, shrub brooms and coal eyes. It was nice. Their minds were still on the windows.

Only one of them, a likeable, freckled, curly-haired boy, didn't take his eyes off me for a moment and listened carefully to what I said as he was picking his nose. I knew this little boy's family. He had a very young, curly-haired mother. The woman had told the story herself. They'd been married five years, and after the son was born they wanted to have daughters. They did; but the little girl was lame from birth. The woman couldn't hold back her tears when her mother-in-law likened the girl to a three-legged goat. But there was hope, that's what the doctors had said. Because the girl was still very small they couldn't operate. The doctors said that later on, when she was older, there was a chance they could operate. The mother and father did everything they could not to let the little girl understand the situation. They also cautioned the boy constantly. He would have been beaten if he'd done anything to throw the girl's handicap in her face. But there was no need to warn the boy. The woman said that the boy was closed within himself but always behaved lovingly towards his sister. Until now there had been no problem because the little girl never left the house, and no one outside the family ever saw her. But now she was a little older, and she wanted to go outside, she would see herself through the eyes of others…

While I was standing in front of the snow-sprayed windows, talking about how people's appearances were not important, the freckled, loveable, curly-haired boy looked deep into my eyes and picked his nose. At another time this would have made me angry, and I don't know why but I preferred to pretend I didn't see. Then it was time for lunch. The children sat at the round table and ate their *köfte* and potatoes, but because I was on a diet I didn't touch my plate. I just drank milk. One glass of milk. When I turned my head I saw that the freckled, loveable, curly-haired boy was watching me from a distance. With a faint smile he brought his finger to his nose, but instead of picking his nose as usual, he began to pretend to comb his upper lip with his finger. Without taking his eyes off me, he repeated this gesture until he was sure I understood what he wanted to say.

The milk I'd been drinking had left a moustache on my lip. This is what he'd been trying to tell me. Immediately I wiped the moustache off. When I turned my head again, the freckled, loveable curly-haired boy wasn't watching me any more.

To tell the truth, the nursery made me nervous. I wanted to get out of there as soon as possible, and I couldn't breathe easily until I was back at the Hayalifener Apartments. I liked being at home.

kesif (discovery): Hundreds of voyages of discovery were launched on the dark waters out of the desire to be the first to see as yet unseen lands. But in time there were no undiscovered lands left in the world.

At home I'm comfortable, more comfortable than I ever am outside. I loved the newspapers, books and pictures that accumulated day by day, the hundreds of photographs that are scattered willy-nilly throughout this heaven; that no piece of furniture has a fixed or obligatory place; the ability to hide from outside eyes, the privacy, the intimacy. I was comfortable with the confusion created by the daily accumulation of material for B–C's Dictionary of Gazes.

I liked the Hayalifener Apartments. If only there weren't such frequent electricity cuts…

kimlik (identity): Knock knock knock. 'Who's there?' asked the person inside. 'It's me,' answered the person outside. 'I don't know anyone called Me,' said the person inside. 'How could that be?' asked the person outside. 'How could you forget Me? Take one look and you'll remember.'

The face of the person inside clouded. 'Leave here at once,' she whispered in a trembling voice. 'My husband will be coming home soon. I belong to him now.'

Me took one last look at the brightly painted house with the frilly curtains and smoke drifting from the chimney. He'd slept on the mosque porch that night. Towards morning the congregation arrived for prayers. Me thought silently of Us. He had to see her one more time.

Judging from the frequency with which the Hayalifener Apartments were left in darkness, the electric company must have had a grudge against us. Whenever the electricity was cut we would go to the windows and, without rancour, look at the showy lights of the lashless-eyed houses all along the hill. There was nothing that the building supervisor, for whom this was a matter of pride, had not done, no one he hadn't tried to persuade or flatter, no hand he had left unkissed, but in the end nothing changed. 'A simple bureaucratic error, a typical case of negligence,' they said. 'Every problem has a past. Don't you have any respect for the past?' The building supervisor was bedridden because of his distress. He took pride in his past.

Our hands were tied. On the outdated map of the neighbourhood that the authorities were using, there was a swamp where the Hayalifener Apartments should have been. According to the records, this swamp was quite old; at least a century old. 'It's like a wound with a scar on the surface that's festering underneath. It was never drained,' said the garrulous civil servant. Yet he was still hopeful. Funds had been appropriated for the draining of the swamp, and it would be taken care of in the near future.

The authorities accepted the absurdity of the fact that nothing prevented an electric bill being sent to an address they claimed didn't exist, but as they said so many times, 'What doesn't go wrong in this country!' In truth they could have drawn a new map, or corrected the mistakes on the older map. The fact that the swamp had long since dried up and gone, that in its place a large building had been built and that this building had been named the Hayalifener Apartments, could have made its way into their records. But it was an old neighbourhood, a very old neighbourhood, where morally upright families and freethinking single people frequently lived side-by-side. It was so old that, with false teeth and withered gums, dye in its thinning hair, with a clouding memory that retained nothing but tried to remember its youth in the pitiful manner of a flirtatious old shrew, it reminded everyone else of their youth. The reflection of this beauty that was so much spoken of clutched the yellowing map in her ageing fingers. There was no possibility that she would ever accept a new map.

Furthermore, it's not a matter of drawing a new map, but of

working out how electric cables that had been laid according to a map were so incomprehensible. At times like these, as soon as the electricity slowly climbed the hill to visit the Hayalifener Apartments, it saw the ogress of night and went back down. Then, the voltage in the houses further downhill rose so much that people had to turn off their televisions. At the same moment the Hayalifener Apartments were plunged into utter darkness.

'It's like the clogged veins of a forty-year smoker. Once they clog, the blood doesn't flow any more,' said the same municipal employee. 'It climbs the hill, it comes this far easily enough, but the poor thing doesn't flow past this point.'

komsu kadın (neighbour-lady): A neighbour-lady is an eye that never closes. They look through curtains and through lace, from the corners of balconies, over walls, through peep holes, and even into the pudding that they cook in order to distribute.

It wasn't enough that the electricity cuts left us in the dark at night, we couldn't see anything during the day either. There'd been a thick fog in the city for a week. In the meantime, the building supervisor had decided that the Hayalifener Apartments, upon which electricity does not smile, needed to be restored from top to bottom. First he went from flat to flat, convincing us that the facade should be painted in lively colours that would open our eyes and our hearts. And who knows, perhaps with restoration the Electric Company's attitude to us would change.

The painters were working away in the fog. Though B–C didn't really seem quite aware of what was going on around him. In fact it had been a long time since he'd taken an interest in anything except the Dictionary of Gazes. We would neither go out in disguise, nor tell each other in the evening what we'd done alone during the day as if we had actually done it together, nor did we visit each other's dreams. The Dictionary of Gazes was more urgent and more important that anything else. It was as if our relationship grew and developed with the accumulation of material for the dictionary. Now, at the point when the Dictionary of Gazes had become stuck, our love entered an impasse.

korse (corset): A corset deceives the eyes. It shows the body thinner than it is.

He became so irritable... Most of the time he paced about restlessly, picking arguments for the slightest of reasons. The flat was too warm, it was too cold outside; the irritable next-door neighbour's television was too loud, the child upstairs was jumping about too much, the supervisor had found he had too much work to do. It was too messy; or it seemed too messy to him. The cat was shedding too much fur, I was asking too many questions. Everything and all of us were too much for him. The only time he ever calmed down was when he found new material for the Dictionary of Gazes.

koza (cocoon): The refuge in which, unseen by anyone, ugly caterpillars undergo their transformation before becoming beautiful and emerging.

One Saturday afternoon, I couldn't look down from the balcony because of the fog, and I couldn't find peace in the house because of B-C. I had to go to the nursery because this time the meeting that the director arranged at least once a month in the belief that it was helpful for the teachers and parents to meet happened to fall on a weekend. I was late. On the stairs I met the elderly man who'd freed me the time the thread from my sweater was caught in the front door. The fog clinging to his Fedora hat was like a saint's halo. He gave me a blank look. He didn't recognise me. Presumably because of the fog. The fog was pulling layers of leaden curtains between people.

The fog was so thick I couldn't even see a step in front of me. I could only move by feeling my way along. Somehow I managed to reach the foot of the hill, but further along it was frightening. Frightening because I couldn't see.

kör (blind): Once upon a time, a very, very old man lived in a city with golden domes. He was so old that whenever it rained, water meandered for days through the wrinkles in his face. No one could calculate his age, and nothing that happened in the world came as a surprise to him. Whatever he saw, he'd already seen before.

One day, there was a terrible fire in one of the city's schools. The flames spread so quickly that it was impossible to save the children inside. When the fire was finally extinguished, nothing was left of the school building. Everyone was heartsick, except the old man.

'It burned down once before,' said the old man, 'But at that time the building was a prison. All of the prisoners inside were burned. And once it was a hospital, and all of the patients burned. How many fires these eyes have seen, this is nothing!'

A mother who had lost a child in the fire and who had gone mad with grief threw stones at the old man and chased him away.

Many years later, there was famine in the city with golden domes. As people strangled each other for a bite to eat, the old man watched them calmly. 'It happened before,' he said. 'For three springs in a row not a drop of rain fell on this city. And once we were besieged by an invading army, and went hungry again. These eyes have seen so much hunger. This is nothing!'

When a hungry man heard these words, he started slapping and kicking the old man.

Then a war broke out in the city with golden domes. As the war drew on, every household had lost a member. Everyone was speechless from grief. Only the old man, only he kept talking. 'How many wars, how many massacres these eyes have seen. This is nothing!'

The bayonet of a young man who had not returned from battle became so angry at these words that it gouged out the old man's eyes.

This time the old man shouted in amazement. 'Darkness! Darkness everywhere! This I've never seen before.'

He was so surprised by this darkness that he'd never seen before that his tired old heart stopped.

Actually there were two different hills. Because one hill started where the other finished, from the middle it looked as if it was a single hill. And right at the point where one hill finished and the other began, there was an old fountain that had dried up who knew how many years ago. It was completely covered with bills that had been posted on top of one another, and spray-painted slogans and darkened obscenities. But the fountain was still there; even if it was no longer functioning as a fountain, if you looked at it closely, you could see in time, and with a little effort, what it had once been. The strangest thing was that I'd passed this way every day without seeing it, and that I only noticed it when I was struggling to feel my way step by step through the fog.

Below, the fog was thicker, and it was more difficult to walk. I made my way with great difficulty. Finally I made it to the bottom of the second hill, and sat on a wall to catch my breath. Once again I was tired and covered in sweat. A little further along, the bus stops were waiting for me. Today, because of the fog, buses were few and far between, and the traffic was badly jammed. Suddenly, I made a decision that until now I'd been afraid to make. I was going to resign. I wasn't going to go to the nursery. I was going to return to the Hayalifener Apartments right away, and I wasn't going to go out unless I wanted to.

körebe (blind-man's bluff): The person who is 'it' stands in the middle of the circle, blindfolded. (Research songs sung during the game!)

As I was climbing the stairs on my return, the downstairs neighbour hurriedly opened her door to put out the trash. Then she thrust a huge bowl of pudding into my hands.

When I got home I found B-C sitting on the bed with a long face. He complained about not being able to find any new material for the Dictionary of Gazes. 'Why are you in such a hurry? You can take a break.' I said. He looked at me angrily, then lay his head down and slept. Whenever he was distressed, he fell asleep.

köstebek (mole): A land animal whose eyes do not see well.

In any event, the fog didn't last long. One morning when I woke up, the painters were gone and the fog had lifted. The Hayalifener Apartments had been painted from top to bottom in a cherry colour.

The building supervisor had chosen the colour. I was quite happy about the change; B–C didn't seem to care. He'd started getting up and going out quite frequently again.

At times like these I didn't wonder where B–C had gone or what he was doing, because a feeling told me that he couldn't go very far from here, and that he couldn't stay out of the neighbourhood for long. Whether or not it was because of my presence, a deep bond tied him to this place, to the hill that was so difficult to climb and to descend, and to the area around the Hayalifener Apartments. He himself said something like this in the days before he devoted all of his time to the Dictionary of Gazes, when he used to love to chat with me.

'It's just like a murderer returning to the scene of the crime,' he said. 'There are places that get stuck in our memories. Whether because of our dreams or because of our past lives, there are places that keep drawing us back.' Then, in a frightened voice, he confessed: 'Do you want to know something strange? I'm already in the place that I visit in my dreams. In my dreams I'm always wandering around near the Hayalifener Apartments!'

kurban (sacrificial victim): Before monotheism, what was to be sacrificed was bound to whom it was being sacrificed to. In Ancient Greece, female animals were sacrificed to goddesses, and male animals were sacrificed to gods. White animals were sacrificed to the gods of the sky, black animals to the subterranean gods, and red animals to the god of fire.

> *Kurban* comes from the Arabic *krb*, which means 'being close'…
> According to the Koran, when Abraham was about to sacrifice his son,
> God sent him a ram, and in this way the tradition of human sacrifice was
> ended… In addition to rams, camels, cattle, water buffalo, sheep and
> goats are acceptable sacrificial animals… The animal's eyes are bound
> before they are killed.

I didn't worry because I knew that in the end he would think
of coming back here. In any event I was starting to get over my
anxieties. When B-C was out I bought a huge sunshade for the
terrace. A loud, purple sunshade. With a chaise-longue of the same
colour underneath it. Because, except for a few small shopping trips,
I hadn't gone outside since I left my job, I hadn't had to be strangled
by other people's eyes. It was so nice not to be seen by anyone! I
was in good spirits! I no longer chewed my cuticles, and I was no
longer constantly seized by anxiety. And, strangely, but pleasantly, I
was daily drifting deeper into indifference. On top of this, I was also
losing weight.

> *kursuna dizilenler* (members of a firing squad): The members of a firing
> squad bind the eyes of the person who is to be shot.

When B-C finally came back days later, he squinted his bitter-
chocolate eyes at the terrace. He came to my side. He didn't say two
words to me. He turned on the computer and went to work on the
Dictionary of Gazes at once. Not a sound came from inside. I was
aware that he was struggling, and that he wasn't able to write the
way he used to. But since he didn't want my help, I wasn't going to
try to help. Let him thrash about inside while I lay comfortably in
my small world of pleasure. Under my purple sunshade, stretched
out on my purple chaise-longue, I watched people going up and
down the hill; I slurped diet cola and tried to guess which of my
three bellies was melting faster. I constantly calculated how much
weight I'd lost. I kept calculating as if each time I calculated there

would be a few grams less. To tell the truth, my stomach heaved when I saw boiled squash, and I tired more easily than before, and I was very, very hungry, but so be it. I was determined!

kursun dökme (pouring lead): To ascribe meaning to the shapes that appear when molten lead is poured into cold water. If lead poured on a person's head, belly, feet or in the right corner of the room or in the doorway takes the form of an eye, this means that the evil-eye has been cast.

When I saw his eyes I knew that something bad was going to happen. He stood there in the terrace doorway, looking at me in a way I'd never seen him look before. After he'd been sitting at the computer for an hour without being able to work, he started to shout in order to relieve the frustration of the word he hadn't been able to find, or the sentence he hadn't been able to finish, or the story he hadn't been able to tie together. He didn't drink the tea I made him, and wrinkled his nose at the things I said to try to calm him. I went back out to the terrace and didn't pay any more attention to him. For me it was still a pleasant day. I had no intention of going inside and sharing his misery. The edges of the purple sunshade were playing sweetly in the evening breeze. Quite some time had passed. Suddenly, a strange shiver passed through me, and when I turned my head there was B-C. He was standing in the terrace doorway, watching me. Who knew how long he had been standing there watching me, knowing how much I hate being watched.

'I see you're in good spirits,' he said in a hazy voice. I tried to smile but couldn't hide my uneasiness. I couldn't take my eyes off his eyes. His eyes were so strange… His eyes had always been strange, but now…now they'd become unknowable. His eyes were like a dim curtain that had been drawn between us. And this curtain allowed me neither to see him or to see how he saw me. I waited for him to stop talking and go back inside. But he stayed, and continued talking. 'As if your huge body didn't already attract enough attention. With a sunshade of this colour I'll bet you can be seen all the way from the bottom of the hill!'

Sometimes the heart turns upside down. As it makes it's own way slowly, it bumps against the cage of the chest. It feels itself badly broken somewhere depending whether it managed to rise or not. It will examine itself but will not be able find a wound that is apparent from outside. It will shout at the top of its voice. 'I have to get out immediately. I have to get out!' Weeping and moaning it will shake the bars of its cage. And when finally it succeeds in breaking free of the cage of the chest, it will stand looking at the roads stretching in front of it, uncertain of which direction to take; ground as yet not trodden. The roads will become confused with one another. The waters will become cloudy.

The heart is a diamond eye. If it is scratched once, it will always look at the world through a mother-of-pearl-like crack.

Kyklop (Cyclops): Cyclops are giants with one eye. They live in enormous caves; they herd sheep and grow fruits and vegetables. Odysseus and his men entered a Cyclops' cave. They found wheels and wheels of cheese, barrels and barrels of water, mounds and mounds of meat, and bunches and bunches of grapes.

Suddenly the Cyclops arrived. Under a single eyebrow that stretched from ear to ear, he had a single, enormous eye. He ate two of Odysseus' men right then and there. The next day he swallowed two more sailors, and each day from then on he did the same.

One night Odysseus made the huge Cyclops drunk. When the Cyclops became drunk, he began to see double. Because he had only one eye he wasn't accustomed to seeing the world double. At this point Odysseus had little trouble killing him.

B-C went inside, and I stayed out on the terrace. With my enormous body, under the purple sunshade. I watched the sunset, and the death of the clouds, and the rising of the moon, and the thickening of the stars, and all the while I wondered how I had managed to still be motionless. I was burning up. The Lodos was blowing. As the Lodos grew stronger my fever raged. It was our pledge to each other that was burning up.

B-C and I had made an unspoken pledge to each other. What we would say about each other's appearance was decided the day we first saw each other. From that moment on B-C hadn't said a word about my appearance. From that moment on I hadn't said a word about B-C's appearance. Neither of us said anything more about the subject because we had no reason to. And both us found the privacy of our house pleasant, despite the unpleasantness of the roles we were burdened with outside. And whatever the forms of our bodies, we were as fluid and as mutable as water in each other's eyes. For this reason I had never once troubled myself about how I looked to B-C. On the top floor of the Hayalifener Apartments I'd found a peace I'd never found elsewhere; I was free of the weight of the letters f-a-t-t-y. I became lighter here. And perhaps this was why, for the first time in my life, I'd actually succeeded in losing weight.

I finished my diet cola and struggled out of the chaise-longue. In the blink of an eye I was in front of the refrigerator.

Lamia: Before Lamia became a monster with a human head and the legs of a donkey, she was a woman whose beauty was much spoken of. Zeus had made love to her many times. And each time, she became pregnant by Zeus. And the jealous Hera killed each of the babies Lamia gave birth to.

Lamia hated all women whose children were living. She couldn't sleep at night for writhing with this hatred. Then she would go and kidnap the children of others and eat them.

Finally Zeus pitied Lamia, and found the solution of taking out her eyes at night and laying them beside her bed. Then Lamia was able to sleep. As soon as night fell, she slept on one side while her eyes slept on the other.

I opened the door. The light came on. With the light came the smell, a smell that was a mixture of cold and food, and that stroked my face. The refrigerator was smiling warmly.

'Where have you been all this time?' it asked reproachfully.

'I've come,' I said. 'I've come back.'

makyaj (make-up): The roughness of make-up renders stains invisible.

On the first shelf there were several kinds of cheese. There was a big, unopened container of white cheese, a fat wedge of aged *kasar*, a half package of fresh *kasar* that was getting hard around the edges, a tub of cream cheese, and some *tulum*. I took out all of the cheese and lined it up in front of me. On the same shelf there was also some olive paste. I cut a loaf of bread lengthways down the middle and spread lots of olive paste on it. I ate alternately of the bread and olive paste in one hand and the block of white cheese in the other.

When I ate I had to be alone, and away from people's eyes. It was an intimate crisis, or rather a dirty secret between me and what I ate. I squatted down next to the refrigerator. I finished the bread very quickly. I ate the rest of the white cheese without bread. I didn't really want the *kasar* or the *tulum* but they too were consumed before long. On the second shelf I found half of a spicy sausage. I finished this and the rest of the cheese. I was eating so quickly that my stomach, which had shrunk from weeks of dieting, didn't even have the chance to be taken aback. While my stomach was still trying to understand what was happening, my eyes fell upon some stuffed grape-leaves. The rice had all dried out and the leaves had turned a pale colour. I left them all half-eaten. Suddenly, I noticed a bowl at the back of the fridge. This was the pudding the neighbour had given me. I hadn't eaten it because I was on a diet, and B-C must have forgotten about it.

A crust had formed on top of the pudding. When I lifted the crust, I saw the chick-peas, and rice, and figs, and pomegranate pieces, and beans. There were a lot of them, but not too many. When I'd finished the pudding, there was nothing but grapefruits left in the refrigerator. For weeks the grapefruit had been my main staple, and at the moment it was the last thing I wanted to eat. I got up and started to empty the kitchen cabinets. I found a half-eaten packet of crisps in a corner. They were stale, but this didn't matter. Next, I came across two tins of tuna fish. One was for people who were dieting; low fat. I finished both of them. I was stuffed. From time to time I stopped and washed down the food in my throat with milk.

As I ate I felt nothing.

What I ate had no taste. But then I wasn't looking for taste. At the moment what was important was food, not what I ate. Nothing I ate tasted any better than anything else. Everything tasted the same whether it was sweet or sour or spicy.

In one of the cupboards I found a fancy box, from a patisserie, full of anise cakes and walnut biscuits. I'd bought them a long time ago, and had left them half-finished when I started my diet. They'd long since gone stale, but this didn't matter. They still looked good. After eating them, it was time for B-C's favourite hazelnut wafers. Then I came across a paper cone filled with spiced, yellow roasted chickpeas.

As I was emptying the packets one by one in the kitchen, I heard typing sounds from inside. Having mastered his nerves some hours ago, B-C was pounding stubbornly on the keys. He was determined to continue with the Dictionary of Gazes. I hated this sound. I crumpled up the empty packets and threw them away.

masa altı (under the table): Children, domestic animals and others who for whatever reason have problems with the sky, flee under the table in order to hide from eyes.

Suddenly, as I was rummaging through the last cupboard, I found it. Chocolate!

It smelled so lovely…as its bright, tight foil wrapping was ripped open, the dark chocolate smiled coyly. This was chocolate! That which was most forbidden to me.

Because if you are as fat as I am, and after so many diets you have to diet again, eating chocolate isn't the fun it is in advertisements, but is something rancorous. With just one bite of chocolate, the will power that the person has with time and effort wrapped around the spool begins to unravel. And it's too late to reel it back in. Because after you've eaten chocolate, you can eat anything. Just as a sinner who has once committed the gravest sin considers other sins too insignificant to cause suffering, so any kind of food seems harmless after you've eaten a box of chocolates.

> *merak* (curiosity): On the morning after their wedding night, the prince knelt before his wife. 'Wander about as you wish,' he said. 'Live as you wish in this palace of forty rooms. But on no account whatsoever are you to try to open the fortieth door!'
>
> 'As you wish,' said the young woman with a compliant expression. The moment her husband had gone outside, she was standing in front of the fortieth door with a bunch of keys.

The stomach is a mythical land.

Guards made of chocolate wait all along the borders.

Once you've eaten the border guards, there's nothing left to prevent you from breaking your diet. When you cross the border you throw open the doors of a world without rules and restrictions. The stomach is a mythical land. And in this mythical land the distance between man and animals, the elegant and the coarse, the beautiful and the ugly, the civilised and the wild, the attractive and the repugnant is a small mouthful. And this is quickly gobbled up.

> *maske* (mask): A face that shows the face to be other than what it is.

There was nothing left in the kitchen that I could eat. I went to the bathroom. I closed the door. Then counted silently to three.

I was living with my body now. My body was grinding and

digesting the nutrients, tearing them into pieces and piling them up, separating the wheat from the chaff with a mind-boggling speed. I had to be faster than it was. Before what I'd eaten had become mine, that is before it has become part of my system; before it was completely cut off from the outside and digested; I had to act at once to stop this feverish process. Since I'd gobbled everything down in the knowledge that I might vomit, now I had to get back out everything I'd eaten.

mikrop (microbe): An evil too small to be seen with the naked eye.

I started to vomit.

model (model): Praxiteles was in love with the courtesan Phryne, and preserved her exquisite beauty in marble so that even centuries later people could admire it.

From here on I knew by heart what to do. I brought it all neatly to a conclusion. I flushed the toilet. I washed out my mouth. I brushed my teeth. I soaped my hands. I washed out my mouth. I washed my face. I washed out my mouth. I brushed my teeth. I washed out my mouth. I looked at myself in the mirror. I washed out my mouth.

I looked worn out. Worn out and broken. Because there were still something that had stayed inside me. No matter what I did, I vomited less than I ate. I suspected that pieces of chocolate were still trying to work themselves into my digestive juices. Perhaps if I tried harder…perhaps this time I could get them out. I started to vomit again.

Morpheus: Morpheus, the god of dreams, is the offspring of a union between night and sleep (research!).

That's how it started.

That's how my life started going backwards, and returning to what it used to be. When I was in the Hayalifener Apartments with B–C, I thought I'd been completely freed from the claws of my former unhappiness, but now it was manifesting itself again. Indeed it was rapidly growing stronger as if to make up for lost time. Which meant that everything could return to the past, and the old somehow doesn't grow old. B–C was right. Time didn't proceed in a straight line from yesterday, through today, and into the future. Sometimes it went forwards and sometimes it went backwards; sometimes it walked and sometimes it stood still; it staggered about drunkenly.

> *mucizevi göz* (miraculous eye): While the city was grumbling and moaning under a siege, a monk was frying fish beside the Well of the Holy Fish. 'What are you doing?' cried the people. 'Is this a time to be frying fish? They've breached the walls. The city is being taken.'
>
> The monk was very calm. 'It's been a long time since I've stopped believing what people say. But if these fish jump out of the pan, I'll believe the city is falling,' he said. At that moment the moment the fish began jumping one by one, half cooked, into the sacred well.

Within a few days I fell ill. All day I lay about like a pudding. I was delirious, in a state between wakefulness and sleep. B–C had become a propeller and was spinning around me. The top of the commode was filled with sweet syrups and bitter pills. My fever didn't fall. I constantly slept, hid and dreamt. Banging sounds were coming from the centre of the earth, someone was hitting the legs of my bed. Later I understood that in order to keep an eye on me, B–C had brought the computer into the bedroom and was writing the Dictionary of Gazes at my side. He must have found the inspiration he'd been seeking for so long, because the clacking of the keyboard didn't stop.

> *nokta* (point): A single point can blin( )d the ey( )e.

In my dreams I saw multi-coloured balloons. Standing below, I watched them patiently. They climb and climb, and then just at the moment they're about to rise above the clouds, they burst. Pieces of balloon rain down on me.

Oryantalizm (orientalism): A Western traveller was burning with passion to make love just once to an Eastern woman hiding behind her thin veils among her carved, inlaid wooden cages. He continually walked through the back streets in the hope of finding an open door he could sneak through or for the wind to play with a veil so that he could peer under it.

When he returned to his own country, though he hadn't touched any Eastern women nor seen their milk-white skin, their smooth thighs and their fleshy lips, he spoke at length to his friends as if he had. He returned to the East every year without fail.

Years later his fantasy finally came true. An Eastern woman returned his desire. When the traveller arrived at the woman's house, he saw that the door had been left ajar for him. For reasons he couldn't explain to himself, this didn't please him at all. He went inside, and saw that the Eastern woman had begun to undress. In panic he said, 'What are you doing? Don't take it off. By no means take off what you're wearing.' When the woman looked at him with surprise, the traveller fled.

When he returned to his country, he gathered together the friends who were eager to hear his latest amorous adventures with Eastern women. As was the case every year, he had a great deal to tell them.

When I woke my stomach felt as if it had been scraped. I had no idea how long I'd slept; perhaps a few hours, perhaps a few days… Step by weary step, holding onto the walls for support, I wandered through the house. On the living room table, as if it had been left there for me, was a bowl of roasted chick-peas. And right next to it was a transparent file folder… I must have been asleep for a long time. And B-C must have thought I'd sleep even longer, because since the day he'd started writing he'd never ever left the Dictionary of Gazes lying about.

> Pandora: Because she'd lifted the lid in order to see what was in the box, all of the evils were scattered across the face of the earth.

First I finished the roasted chickpeas; after that, I started reading the Dictionary of Gazes.

Darkness was falling. Night was before us. The key turned in the lock. B-C had come home.

> *Pamuk Prenses* (Snow White): The dwarves wept at Snow White's death, and were heartsick to think they'd never see her beauty again. In the end they decided to put her in a glass coffin so they could look at her forever.

'So you've read the Dictionary of Gazes. I haven't finished it yet, though,' he said in a bitter voice. 'There's still quite a bit of material I haven't organised.'

He sat in his rocking chair and started rocking angrily back and forth.

'So, since you've read it, why don't you tell me what you think? To tell the truth I'm not at all pleased that you went and read it without permission, but I suppose that's what relationships are like. You lose your privacy.'

> *paravan* (folding screen): The daughter of the Ambassador of the Two Scillies, Mademoiselle Ludauf, and her friend Mademoiselle Amoureu were invited to visit Hatice Sultan. According to the wishes of their hostess, the two beautiful young women danced gaily all day. They thought they were alone. They didn't know that Sultan Selim III was watching them from behind a folding screen.

He wasn't even aware.

I looked into B-C's face with pain.

Istanbul – 1980

In the afternoons, time used to nap in the back garden. Time never varied its routine. Every day, its eyelids would grow heavy at the same hour, its eyes would stay closed for the same length of time and would always open at the same hour.

While time slept, the child would sit drowsily under the cherry tree, eating the cherries that had fallen to the ground. When the cherries on the ground were finished, she would start to crave the cherries on the branches. But this usually wasn't necessary. Every day, dozens of cherries would leave behind their branches and fall to the ground. If it was that easy, why didn't she do the same thing? Why didn't she leave this house behind?

The house she could not leave behind was the colour of salted green almonds.

The house the colour of salted green almonds was her paternal grandmother's house.

But whenever time took a nap, a person could believe that it was possible to get up and go without leaving a trace, and now, at this very moment, be in a completely different place. Who knew when, following whose trail of cherry pits, without waiting for growth of the cherry trees in the footprints, simply going and going... Not in order to arrive, but simply to leave and keep going.

Until time woke from its nap, she could eat as many cherries as she wished; first the ones on the ground, and then, if she dared, the ones on the branches. Who was going to see her? In any case, everyone and everything fell asleep when time fell asleep.

The lower floor of the house the colour of salted green almonds resounded with her paternal grandmother's snores, and the upper floor with those of Kıymet Hanım Teyze, the landlady. The whole neighbourhood became a giant cradle, and the breeze murmured lullabies. The children slept deeply, and so did cats, and even itinerant peddlers; kites, paper dolls and even nougat. Until they woke, she could eat as many cherries as she wished. She would fling the cherry pits as far as she could. Far, as far as the zinc roof of the neighbour's coal shed.

Open the door, chief merchant, chief merchant
What will you pay as a toll, what will you pay
One rat, two rats, the third escapes to the trap.

The street was calm and quiet. The *jinns* were playing ball. They were always awake during the hours when time slept. And in this deep silence, the *jinns*, in their cracked voices, would sing the same songs the children had sung in the street before going to bed.

In the back garden of the house next door there was a coal shed; with a zinc roof, and two doors. That's where the child would throw the pits of the cherries she had eaten. When the cherry pits made a rattling noise as they fell on the zinc roof, the child would believe hail was falling. Sooner or later, every cherry pit she threw would open a hole. In the end, every cherry pit would become lost in the hole it had opened. Perhaps if she ate enough cherries, that is, if she finished not just those on the ground but those on the branches as well, she would cause the zinc roof to be completely full of holes. Each hole that was opened by each cherry pit would merge with another one just like it, and when there was no place left to make any more holes, any more wounds, the coal shed would make one last effort to hold on to its pock-marked roof. When the flaking plaster had fallen off, and the emptiness beneath it had swallowed it, the coal shed would disappear completely. Forever.

Because the coal shed could not hold its tongue. It talked away as the cherry pits rained down on it. It didn't know that it was necessary for it to hold its tongue. It didn't know that 'the tongues of the talkative bleed.'

Her grandmother used to say that people who cannot hold their tongue will see it bleed. She would say this, and keep her lips, which were as hard and motley as pomegranate rinds, tightly shut. If this rind split open, words would spill out like pomegranate pieces, but it never split. Her grandmother didn't resemble the other women. Because they talked a great deal.

It was the day the women made depilatory wax. Early in the morning they gathered in the lower floor of the house the colour of salted green almonds, and placed the little pans with blackened bottoms on the stove; as they breathed in the heady smell of the wax, they gossiped a great deal to help the wax maintain its consistency. Towards afternoon the women would sit in a row and wince as they peeled the thin layers of wax off their legs; as for the child, she would wander around, licking at a pencil that she had dipped into the wax. She was restless. It was understood that until waxing day was over, she was not to touch anything in the house. As if her fingers would stick even to the wall if she touched it by mistake. The only solution was to sit by the window. It had been raining since morning. She watched the raindrops caress and freshen the back garden as they buffeted it and knocked it about. Soon, the women would wash their hands and legs with soapy water, and turn their attention to the dumplings. The child made an effort not to look in their direction. She knew that there was something shameful about waxing; she didn't want to be party to an unpleasant secret.

When the rain grew much heavier, she got up and walked lethargically into the kitchen. That was when she saw the glass teaspoons. The glass teaspoons were only taken out of their ribboned velvet boxes when guests came. When there were no guests, the child stirred her tea with tin spoons that bent easily.

She leaned against the kitchen counter and looked closely at the glass teaspoons. She hadn't seen these ones before. There were little butterflies made of dark glass at the end of each spoon. It was as if they could take wing and fly off at any moment if they wanted. But also as if, for whatever reason, they had no intention of flying. Right next to the spoons there were two big, round trays covered with newspaper. The women were going to make dumplings. Little pink balls of meat stood on little squares of dough. The mouths of the dumplings had not closed yet. But for whatever reason it didn't seem as if they had any intention to speak.

First the child broke off the wings of the butterflies and put them aside. Then she put the glass teaspoons in the mortar and crushed them thoroughly.

The glass made a crunching sound as it broke. Taking care not to cut her fingers, she placed each piece of glass in the middle of one of the pink balls of meat. The dumplings swallowed the glass as hungrily as dry earth swallows raindrops. In the blink of an eye, all of the pieces of glass had disappeared into the balls of meat. So much so that, even if you looked at them very closely, nothing strange was apparent. The meat and glass dumplings were ready to be cooked. The child didn't feel it necessary to close the dumplings' mouths. Whoever had opened them would close them.

She didn't know why she had done this. But she was aware of what she had done, and of what could happen. If she had wanted she could have stopped what was going to happen. She could have returned to the sitting room right away and told these women who had been hungry for a long time that they were not to eat the dumplings, or else their tongues would bleed. She could have stopped this maddening humming so that no one's tongue would bleed; she could have informed on herself.

As she took another step towards the door that opened from the kitchen into the sitting room, she saw her grandmother's long, thin shadow on the ground. She must have been on her way to close the dumplings. She hadn't noticed the child yet. The kitchen had a back door that opened onto the back garden. The child slipped silently out the back door.

It was raining outside. It was raining as if a plastic bag had been filled to the top with water in order to wash fruit, and then holes had been pierced in the bottom, falling from countless fissures in the grey sky. The child ran about in the mud, falling and getting up again, and stepping on the worms that the earth vomited every time it rained. She ran and ran, and just when she thought she had left the back garden behind, she ran into the coal shed, and fell flat on her face on the ground.

Coalshedevilevilcoalshedcoal.

She looked anxiously at her bleeding knee. She had always feared catching germs. For this reason, she imagined she had a bottle of iodine in her hand. As she poured the imaginary iodine on the wound, she winced exaggeratedly and blew on the place where it hurt. The wound was covered with coal dust. She didn't mind. No harm could come from coal dust. The wind would blow it away, and the rain would clean everything. There wouldn't even be a trace left behind. Coal dust was not like cherry pits, which put out roots wherever they fall.

The child used to swallow cherry pits so that cherry trees would grow inside her. She was little then. She's grown up enough now to know that such things are definitely not possible. She knew well now that no matter how many cherry pits she swallowed, no cherry tree would ever come out of her stomach, because a person had an inside and an outside, and cherry pits didn't belong to the inside but to the outside, and cherry pits could only put out roots in places where they belonged. A cherry pit could never be chewed, but it could be swallowed by accident: even then it could not be digested, but would be brought back out. It was what remained after the flesh of the fruit had been enjoyed, and had to be thrown away. Just like a messenger who has to return to where he came from once he has delivered the letter that was entrusted to him, no matter how valuable the letter is. It was an unwelcome guest. Even if by chance it managed to enter your body, it would have to keep its visit short, and go back out immediately.

Suddenly the water in the plastic bag finished. As the last drops of rain fell into the back garden, the sun smiled lazily at an earth that shone like mother-of-pearl.

~

That afternoon, time was napping in the back garden. After the rain, it was as calm and quiet as could be. The bubbling of the dumplings in the pans mixed with the snoring of the women, who had become tired after the waxing. The floor of the neighbourhood had become a wooden cradle, swinging back and forth; the people of the neighbourhood had stretched out on a bed of lassitude, calmly and sweetly wandering through the wonderful forests of their dreams. While they slept, the child leaned her back against the cherry tree and ate the cherries on the ground. The more she ate, the more she wondered how the cherries managed to leave the tree behind.

Suddenly, time's sleep was torn by a sound that resembled the transparent skin being torn off a sausage. It rose to a shrill scream; then another, and another. The screams were coming from the second floor of the house the colour of salted green almonds. Kıymet Hanım Teyze the landlady was leaning over the kitchen balcony that looked over the back garden, shouting at the top of her voice.

The child was seized by panic. Every spring, Kıymet Hanım Teyze gave the tenants on the bottom floor permission to gather three branches of cherries. Grandmother made jam from these cherries, and didn't neglect to send some of it upstairs as thanks. It was forbidden to touch the rest of the cherries. Only Kıymet Hanım

Teyze, and her sons, could eat these. In truth the child couldn't be considered guilty because today she had only eaten the cherries on the ground. But as she thought this, she realized that she wouldn't be able to prove her innocence. And even if she wasn't guilty today, hadn't she committed the same crime just yesterday? Hadn't she secretly picked the cherries on the branches all day yesterday? Was it perhaps because Kıymet Hanım Teyze rarely went outside and usually only saw the tree from above that she only now noticed how few cherries there were on the branches? Was the child going to be punished today for yesterday's transgressions?

Kıymet Hanım Teyze the landlady lived on the top floor of the house the colour of salted green almonds. She was the fattest woman in the world. Her feet were so fleshy, and so big, that she couldn't wear shoes, and went about in slippers winter and summer. Each of her legs was as wide as two children, and covered with purple toned veins. Some of them were as rigid as laundry that had been left out on a cold night, and some hung down in shame like the elastic of a slingshot that had missed its target. The rest of the veins were reminiscent of telephone cables. Once, when the woman was deep in conversation with some of her neighbours, the child knowingly took the opportunity to examine these veins up close. And this was when she understood without a doubt that Kıymet Hanım Teyze was a robot. The veins on her legs weren't real, they were toy veins. The important thing was that they weren't veins, and what looked like veins were clearly cables. And as long as these cables were not cut, there was no possibility of stopping Kıymet Hanım Teyze. Because she was a robot. If she wasn't a robot, how could one explain how, despite her being so fat, no one had ever seen her eat? She might have fed them with oil from her sons' cars or even with grease from the sewing machine. On top of this, she was probably a sleepwalker. And if she walked in her sleep, then a giant robot, with its cables tangled and its eyes hanging out of its sockets, might be wandering the deserted streets everyday while the morning call to prayer was being recited, looking for its creator.

When Kıymet Hanım Teyze climbed the stairs of the house the colour of salted green almonds, the child would stand waiting silently below. Every time, she imagined that when she reached the last step, she would roll back down the stairs. When that huge body came down on her with such speed, she would have to get out of the way at the last minute or she would be crushed like a bug. But Kıymet Hanım Teyze never fell. Every time, she managed to climb the steps, even though it was with a great deal of huffing and puffing and perspiration. And she rarely went outside. She only left the house the colour of salted green almonds at the beginning of the month when she went to collect rents in the upper neighbourhood; and also when Elsa was out of liver.

She worshipped Elsa. She didn't love animals, or even cats, but only Elsa. She'd choose Elsa's liver herself, and cook it herself. Every day, the second floor of the house the colour of salted green almonds would be filled with the smell of liver. Whenever the pain of her varicose veins didn't permit her to walk to the Far Butcher's two streets away, and by using threat after threat she sent the children to buy liver, she suspected that they bought less liver and put the leftover money in their pockets. Sometimes she would think that the butcher, knowing full well who the liver was for, would give inferior meat; if by chance her suspicion increased and the pain of her varicose veins diminished, she would go up to the butcher's and complain. Then the big, moustachioed butcher, while trying to stop the nervously twitching artery in his forehead with his hand, would make a thousand apologies and prepare a new package. Kıymet Hanım Teyze would put on a long face as she took the package, say a half-hearted thank you, and before leaving the shop would not neglect to make veiled threats. As soon as she had turned the corner of the street, the butcher, who had barely been able to contain his irritation, would throw the old package against the wall or on the floor. Then, for the rest of the day, he would tell every customer who came into the shop about his troubles. The customers were well versed on the topic. Every time, they would calm the butcher with a few words, and remind him that he had it all in his stride. Because the shop belonged to Kıymet Hanım Teyze, as did the houses on either side.

When, as always, time took a nap that afternoon, Kıymet Hanım Teyze, for whatever reason, did not sleep. After lying down for a long time, and tossing this way and that, she decided that since she couldn't sleep anyway she would get up and prepare some food. She was going to prepare stuffed aubergines. Her middle son Nurettin had loved stuffed aubergines since he was little. The dried aubergines were hanging from the kitchen balcony. The kitchen balcony looked onto the back garden. After Kıymet Hanım Teyze had filled her apron with dried aubergines that were hanging from a string, it occurred to her that cherry syrup might go well with the meal. As she thought this she turned to look at the cherry tree just below her. She looked and was astounded. Suddenly, there was a sound that resembled the transparent skin being torn off a sausage. It rose to a shrill scream; then another, and another.

While Kıymet Hanım Teyze stood on the balcony screaming at the top of her voice, the people of the neighbourhood, whose sleep had been disturbed just at its sweetest point, and who had rushed out into the street to see what was going on, had long since crowded into the back garden. Not just the people of the neighbourhood, but also the itinerant peddlers who always show up whenever crowds gather. The back garden had never seen this many people. Everyone had gathered underneath the kitchen balcony, and was looking up with curious eyes. They continued staring emptily until finally a few of them thought to go up. Now, an endless conversation began between those wandering around on the balcony and those who had remained below. Those below asked endless questions in order to find out what was going on; those above, unable to gain any information from Kıymet Hanım Teyze's paralyzed tongue and saucer-like eyes, used their imaginations to think up answers. A long time later, it occurred to one of the people on the balcony to look where Kıymet Hanım Teyze had been looking instead of looking at her. That was when everyone became aware of the bloody body hanging in the branches.

The dead body hanging from the branches of the cherry tree was the body of a cat. Once Kıymet Hanım Teyze realized that the others had seen what she had seen, she found her tongue again.

'Ah, my baby! What have they done to you? May they break their hands!'

Those who had climbed up just a short while ago began clattering down. When there was no one left behind on the balcony except one or two women who were rubbing cologne on Kıymet Hanım Teyze's wrists, no one could quite decide who was going to take the dead cat down. In the end, Kıymet Hanım Teyze's little son Zekeriya was found to be the most suitable to climb the tree. The cat's body was near the top of the tree, and the branches of the cherry tree were very thin. Zekeriya climbed quickly, but when the branches that couldn't take his weight began to snap and break, he understood he could not proceed any further. He climbed as high as he could, and started hitting the cat's body with a rolling pin. He hit the animal on the tail, on the nose, and wherever else he could. As he hit, the branches of the cherry tree shook wildly, and the cherries on the branches fell to the ground, and a cloud of dust from the leaves rained down on those waiting below, but somehow the cat's body just didn't fall.

Then the inhabitants of the neighbourhood decided to put a stop to this, saying it wasn't right for anyone's corpse, even a cat's, to be subjected to so much indignity. They all rolled up their sleeves and started shaking the tree, with Zekeriya still in it. Within a few seconds, first dozens of cherries, then the rolling pin, and Zekeriya, and finally the dead cat, came tumbling down in a cloud of dust, accompanied by cries. Everyone bent down to look. Without any doubt, this was Elsa's bloody body. It had been blindfolded with a cherry coloured muslin cloth that had little sea shells sewn into the corners. The cat's open mouth was full of baby flies whose origin no one knew. There were no wounds anywhere, and it wasn't clear where the beads of blood on its whiskers had come from.

When the muslin cloth was untied, everyone bent down and examined Elsa's eyes with curiosity. They didn't look as if they were dead. With the eyes encrusted with sleep, it seemed as if at any moment the cat might get up and stretch, yawn, and then climb into someone's lap.

At this point, the people of the neighbourhood found themselves bringing their hands to their eyes to rub the sleep out of them. No one wanted to resemble a dead body, even if it was that of a cat. Suddenly, a wave rippled through the crowd. Kıymet Hanım Teyze, her wrists tied with cologne-soaked handkerchiefs, cologne-soaked rags wrapped around her head, nauseated from having drunk water laced with cologne, diving into the crowd with an agility unexpected from such an enormous body, with two neighbour women chasing her with bottles of cologne, threw herself on Elsa's dead body. As she wailed in grief, tears began to form in the eyes of the people who had gathered in the garden. After having rubbed the sleep out of their eyes, everyone was now wiping tears from their eyes, and bottles of cologne were being passed from hand to hand. After a long while Kıymet Hanım Teyze raised her head. With a look of anguish and hatred, she carefully examined those who had gathered around. Then suddenly, her eyes, bloodshot from weeping, settled on the child.

'She did it! That bug-eyed child did this! She's treated Elsa badly ever since she got here. She's a devil. A devil, a devil!'

There was complete silence. As if they had received very strict orders, no one moved or spoke. As it drew on, the silence became so deep that you could hear the itinerant peddlers' ice-cream dripping as it melted, their *simits* crackling as they dried, and their balloons hissing as they slowly let out air. Only Kıymet Hanım Teyze, only she had the audacity to break the silence.

'Say it! Tell everyone! Tell them that this muslin cloth is yours! You brat. Talk.'

After the sleep and the tears, 'I wonder' began to gather in the eyes of those gathered in the garden. I wonder if this is true? I wonder if such a little child could do such a terrible thing? Children loved cats, after all. I wonder if this child loves cats? The stern head-teacher of the primary school, who organized frequent meetings as an opportunity to tell people that television was a bad influence on children and that if he had children they wouldn't watch television, was examining the child carefully. 'I wonder' had gathered more in his eyes than in anyone else's.

With difficulty, grandmother managed to convince Kıymet Hanım Teyze to come to the bottom floor of the house the colour of salted green almonds and take a little rest. Meanwhile, the neighbour women were bumping into one another in their haste to prepare the meal. In the blink of an eye, a young girl had put out the plates, a slightly older girl had put out the knives and forks; just behind them, two large-bellied women, carrying the two enormous pots, began spooning the dumplings onto the plates; a step behind, a tall woman poured garlic yoghurt from a long, narrow-mouthed vessel, and another, tiny woman dribbled melted butter over the white dumplings from a little pan. Everyone was called to the table. But it was as if no one had any appetite left. If you don't count a few nibbles from the dough at the edges of the dumplings, no one ate a bite. Kıymet Hanım Teyze, seated at the head of the table, was weeping inconsolably. As she wept, several women, standing by on duty with bottles of cologne that never left their hands, were trying to rub her wrists. Grandmother was looking absent-mindedly at the neglected dumplings. It seemed as if the table would remain the way it was, and all that work would be wasted. But suddenly, at a completely unexpected moment, Kıymet Hanım Teyze stopped crying, and started spooning up the dumplings in front of her. She ate with such speed that the rest of the women in the room were left with their mouths hanging open. She ate noisily. Every time Kıymet Hanım Teyze finished her plate, it was filled again immediately; every new plate of dumplings had lots of garlic yoghurt poured over it, and was dribbled with melted butter.

That afternoon, under the surprised eyes of the others in the room, Kıymet Hanım Teyze ate perhaps fifteen plates of dumplings. When she'd finished the dumplings in the pots, she polished off the plates that the neighbour women insisted on passing to her. Finally, when she realized there was not a single dumpling left, she leaned back, said a half-hearted thank you, and added, 'Elsa would have loved it too.' Before she'd even finished the sentence, all of the women in the room shrieked as one. Kıymet Hanım Teyze's mouth was full of blood.

That afternoon, seeing Kıymet Hanım Teyze eat for the first time, the child became confused. It was clear that Kıymet Hanım Teyze wasn't a robot or anything. She ate food just like everyone else; she was a person like everyone else, after all.

But if she wasn't a robot, how could she eat so many dumplings without exploding?

~

'You and I will become very good friends. And you know that friends talk about everything.'

The doctor was young and had no moustache. He wore thick-lensed glasses, and had bright blue eyes. The child was his first patient.

~

As the lorry loaded with furniture left the neighbourhood, grandmother, who was sitting next to the driver, turned to look back with tears in her eyes at the house the colour of salted green almonds where she had lived for twenty-two years. That morning, she'd knocked on the door of the second floor to try her luck one last time.

'Kıymet Hanım! Please don't throw me out of my house. After all these years as your tenant, what fault do you find with me? Haven't we been good neighbours all these years? We've looked into each other's eyes. Tell me if there have ever been any problems between us. Believe me, she's going to go. I've sent news to her mother and father. They're going to come and get her. "You know, things are a bit confused at the moment. Let her stay with you for a while," my son said, and I didn't say anything. "We'll come and get her later," he said. "She's my grandchild", I said, and I accepted the situation. I'd never even seen her before. How was I to know she'd be such an imp? She must take after her mother. If I'd known, would I have wanted her to stay with me? Please, Kıymet Hanım Teyze, don't throw me out of my house at my age. I swear on the Koran. She'll be leaving soon.'

Kıymet Hanım Teyze didn't go back on her word.

The truck loaded with furniture pulled up in front of a five storey apartment building on the other side of the city. This was where grandmother's daughter lived; with her husband and three children. As she climbed the steps, grandmother cursed the reasons why, at her age, she would have to live as an unwanted extra person in her son-in-law's house. The child followed one step behind.

This house had no garden. It only had a balcony with empty flowerpots. At one point, the child went out onto the balcony and put several cherry pits into one of the flower pots. She knew that there was no earth in the flower pots. This wasn't important. In any event, she was going to leave this place soon.

~

'If something bad happened, you can tell me about it.'

The doctor, whose anxiety increased as the silence drew on, took off his glasses every two or three minutes and cleaned them with a soft piece of velvet. When he took off his glasses there was a glimmer of shame in his bright blue eyes, with which he couldn't even see beyond the end of his nose. The child liked him when he was like this. She liked to watch him.

'All right, all right, OK.' Said the doctor, opening his arms wide in a gesture of surrender. 'But just tell me this. Before you moved out of your grandmother's house you climbed onto the roof. You made everyone very worried. Do you want to tell me why you climbed onto the roof?'

~

When the child arrived at the house the colour of salted green almonds, the summer season was just beginning. Grandmother opened the child's suitcase, and arranged the contents one by one on the divan. Shorts, socks, underpants and hats came out of the suitcase. As well as multi-coloured marbles.

'Don't you have anything else to wear?'

On the evening of the day the child put on the long-sleeved brown dress her paternal grandmother had bought for her.

'Now you look more like a girl!'

Grandmother closed the suitcase and put it on top of the closet. The clothes in the suitcase could be worn neither outside nor inside. The child could understand why she shouldn't wear shorts outside, but she couldn't understand who she would be hiding from inside. Who was going to see her at home, within the four walls? Her grandmother didn't answer this question that day.

~

'What do you see in the picture?'

In the picture, next to a stove on which chestnuts were roasting, there was a puffy cushion and a red ball of wool.

'You didn't even look properly,' said the young doctor as he thrust the picture back into the child's hands. 'Please look more carefully.'

In the picture, on the puffy cushion next to the stove on which chestnuts were roasting, there was a cat playing with a red ball of wool.

'Do you know that I have a cat too? Perhaps I can bring it here one day. Do you like cats?'

~

Grandmother was tall and wiry. She chewed so slowly that when she finally swallowed the mouthful that her toothless mouth had dissolved into strands from which the taste had long since been leached, she'd forgotten what she had eaten. It didn't matter anyway. Being picky about food amounted to ingratitude. That's what she used to say. That's what she used to say sometimes, and she would deliberately cook badly. Sometimes she didn't add any salt, or else put in too much hot pepper, or didn't use oil. The child had to become accustomed to eating everything. And also, of course, to not eating.

Grandmother fasted frequently. The days she had to make up for from past and future Ramadans never lessened. On these days, even though it wasn't stated openly, the child was expected to keep the fast with her. She wouldn't put anything into her mouth when she was in her grandmother's presence, but the moment she went into the back garden she went straight to the cherry tree. But one day, at a completely unexpected moment, she had to give up this mischievous game. Because that day, taking the child's cherry stained fingers and squeezing them tightly, grandmother looked straight into her eyes. When she finally spoke, her lips, which were as hard and mottled as a pomegranate rind, twisted into a mottled smile.

'Let's say, for instance, that you managed to deceive me. Did you think that Allah wouldn't see you secretly eating cherries?'

~

'Don't talk if you don't want to. But if you don't talk that means you're not my friend. If you're not my friend, that means you won't see me again.'

He took off his thick-lensed glasses and set about polishing them. The threat had worked. The child, whose mouth could not until now have been pried open with a knife, started to talk hurriedly. She told the doctor all of the fairy tales she knew. After that, she started to make up her own fairy tales. She talked and talked and talked, without minding that her mouth was drying up and without worrying that her tongue might bleed.

As she talked, the young doctor's bright blue eyes clouded, and his face darkened.

~

The child opened the package her grandmother had given her. She had been expecting a new dress, but this time a muslin cloth emerged from the package. It was a cherry-coloured cloth with little seashells sewn in the corners.

That day she learned how to pray. As she copied what her grandmother did on the prayer rug, she listened to the voices of the seashells. The seashells always spoke with one voice. When grandmother folded up the prayer rug and put it in a corner, the child followed her.

'When does he watch me, then?'

'Isn't God's time different from yours or mine?'

God was timeless. Even during the hours when time naps, he doesn't sleep, and continues to watch people. The child folded up her prayer rug and put it on top of her grandmother's prayer rug.

'Why does he watch, then?'

'This is your mother and father's fault,' said grandmother in an irritated tone. 'They didn't teach you anything. They wanted to make you the way they are.'

It was as if the child hadn't heard what had been said. It was as if her thoughts were elsewhere. Just as her grandmother was about to leave the room, she shouted after her.

'What about the night? When it gets dark? Can he see in the dark?'

Grandmother turned and examined the child from head to toe as if she had never seen her before. That's when she said those words.

'People should hold their tongues. Talkative people's tongues bleed.'

When grandmother left the room, a thousand sentences formed from the letters of the answer she hadn't received flocked through the child's mind. She understood that during the day, whether she was inside or outside, she had to be careful about what she did and to keep in mind that she was constantly being watched. But perhaps the night was different. Perhaps at night God didn't watch the world. This was why the night was so dark. The night was as black as coal. Coal shed black...

After that day, she started to go to bed later at night.

~

'You're eating a lot these days. Isn't that so?'

The child nodded with a heartfelt smile. Because she didn't want to lose her friend, she leaned back and started talking. Without hurrying, and without taking a break, and in great detail, she told the story of Hansel and Gretel, who fell under the power of the world's most wicked witch, while they were nibbling at the glazed sugar windows, and the door made of marzipan, and the chimney of dough, and the lawn of strawberry pudding, the fences of double whipped cream, the rooms of nougat, and the chocolate roof.

As she told the story, the doctor sat with his head in his hands, looking straight ahead. In front of him, on the table, was the child's half-eaten *simit*.

~

'Don't move,' said the strange man. 'Don't move at all, all right?'

There was no need for him to say this. The child wasn't moving anyway. And she'd stopped so suddenly, it wasn't as if she was frozen in place, but as if she had never moved even once in her life, and couldn't move. Her motionlessness resembled a hard-working ant running around a dead bee lying on its back at the bottom of an empty water glass; from the same starting point it always watched the world turn, and turn again, with the same delighted amazement. The water glass had an outside, of course. But the child wasn't there. She was in the coal shed.

'Good for you,' said the strange man. 'Now I'm going to play a game with you. A counting game.'

In the back garden of the house next door there was a coal shed; with a zinc roof, and two doors. One of the doors was always closed, and the other was always open. There was a big padlock on the door that was closed. They kept wood and coal there in the winter. There was no need for a lock on the door that was left open. Thieves couldn't steal emptiness.

There was a tiny window inside. The glass was broken. Two steps from the rays of sunlight that entered there, it was completely dark inside. There were pieces of broken glass, pieces of wood, countless lost marbles, yellowed newspapers, a single lady's shoe with a broken heel, a tattered tea-strainer, rusty fingernail-clippers with a piece of fingernail stuck in them, broken razors, scattered chick-peas from a torn paper cone had all gathered together in the darkness and were whispering to each other. And children stopped by sometimes, children who were playing hide-and-seek.

In truth, the coal shed always confused the person who was 'it'. Because it was the easiest place to guess, no one hid there, but because no one ever hid there, 'it' didn't feel it necessary to look there, and like every place where 'it' is unlikely to look, it remained a favourite hiding place.

'You know how to count, don't you?'

Actually the child had come to the coal shed to escape from numbers. As soon as 'it' turned his head to the wall, she and the other children were off together like a shot. After a brief hesitation, she decided to climb the garden wall and hide behind Red Show-off. Just then, 'it' shouted 'one!' in a loud voice. Red Show-off was Kıymet Hanım Teyze's oldest son's new car. Every time Abdullah emerged without a scratch from accidents that turned his cars into scrap metal, he would throw himself to the ground in tears, and swear to the whole neighbourhood on the Koran that not a drop would ever again pass his lips; managing to keep his oath for a few days, he told everyone he met that he was a completely new man, and on top of this he would say that he had always been a good man and that he was a victim of bad company and wayward friends; before long, forgetting all his promises and all his tears, he would show up in a brand new car; as he drove the young men of the neighbourhood around in his new car, he would advise them that they had to become men, and go beyond what their elders had told them, and he would continue giving this advice at the tavern; at the end of the evening, at best, weeping next to the wreckage of the new car he had wrapped around a tree, he would be making vow after vow. Everyone knew that Kıymet Hanım Teyze had never given any money to her sons. It was a mystery where Abdullah managed to find so much money. Most people thought that he stole the cars; stole them and painted them. They were always the same colour: bright red.

Red Show-Off was a Mercedes. It hadn't been enough just to paint it, it had waves and waves of highlights on the bonnet. Because, for whatever reason, Abdullah had disappeared soon after parking Red Show-Off in front of the house the colour of salted green almonds, for almost two months now Red Show-Off had been dozing sweetly in the middle of the neighbourhood, with a peace that no other bright red car had ever known.

'It' shouted, 'Twooo!' Just at that moment, the child was passing in front of the coal shed. Suddenly, Red Show-Off seemed very far away. She changed her mind. Quickly, she dove into the coal shed and pulled the door closed behind her.

There was someone else inside. Someone who was not part of the game.

There was a man inside. He was a stranger. He was just standing there, under the broken window, where the rays of sunlight shone in. Half of his face was in the light, and half was in the dark. He was leaning his back against the wall, and held his head in his hands. He looked very worried.

Perhaps he was crying. He was well-dressed. His shoes were very shiny despite being covered with coal dust. It was clear that the man was not a gypsy. The child knew that one had to stay away from gypsies. Gypsies' shoes were never like this.

This man is a stranger. (I wonder who he is?) Strangers were to be avoided. (How unhappy he looks!) The best thing to do is to tell someone. (What is he looking for here?) She should leave the coal shed at once. (The moment she left she would become 'it'!) There was a strange man inside. ('It' was outside.)

The child sat near the door, trying hard not to make a sound. She didn't take her eyes off the man. Outside, 'it' was swearing at the children he had found but who were not listening to him. 'It' had such a foul mouth that one child's mother, unable to stand it any longer, rushed out into the street, said she would complain to 'it's' father that evening, and got involved in the children's quarrel. In the middle of this uproar, faint padding sounds were heard in the coal shed. As if someone was walking gingerly across the zinc roof; someone…or else a cat…

A while later, the strange man slowly straightened himself up. His movements were so slow and heavy that a person might wonder whether or not he was alive. Perhaps this man who had lost his way was really one of those puppets that women sewed while looking at fashion magazines. There must not have been enough cloth, because his jacket looked a little tight. The child had a puppet like this in the drawer where she kept things she had seen. A puppet she had seen at the amusement park. A puppet who waited patiently, hanging on a string, among the dolls with yellow hair and painted lips, the electric cars that did somersaults, the multi-coloured tops, the phosphorescent yo-yos, the tailed kites and the jigsaw puzzles that were useless when a single piece was missing. They gave her three balls. If she could knock it down with the balls, the puppet would be hers. She hadn't been able to knock it down.

The man's eyes were an olive green, and much more beautiful than the puppet's eyes. He had no whiskers on his face, and perhaps he was naturally beardless. The child sat motionless, with her eyes on the man, listening to the children fighting outside. Outside, 'it' was wandering around swearing; he kept finding the same children in the same hiding places, and always complained in the same way. As her voice could no longer be heard, the woman who had come out to scold 'it' had probably gone home. It was clear that the game was coming to an end. At this rate, all hell was going to break loose soon. She had to go out soon.

'Will you play a game with me? A counting game? Would you like to play?'

His voice was just as beautiful as his eyes.

'Now we're going to count to three together,' he whispered. 'You know how to count, don't you? What do you say, shall we count?'

Of course the child knew how to count: after a brief hesitation she nodded her head. Then the man caressed the child's cheek. His hands were beautiful, just like his voice and his eyes.

'Good for you! When I say "one" you're to close your eyes. When I say "two" you're to open them. The game isn't over until I say "three". There's no leaving the coal shed until I say "three". Do you understand?'

Outside, the children were calling her. They were going to start the game over again, someone else was going to be 'it'. They were calling her name. She had to go out.

'One!' said the man. 'Close your eyes!'

The moment the child closed her eyes she was in darkness. She looked straight into the darkness, and there she saw the number One. One was not a run-of-the-mill number. It was extraordinary. It was like a pregnant woman; its singularity was only a matter of time. Soon another life would emerge from its life, and its anxiety about what that life would look like was already showing on its face. The child was seized by fear as she looked at One. She had to flee this place right now, without waiting another moment, before it was too late to act on her decision, before it was time for One to give birth. In order to flee she first had to open her eyes, but unfortunately her eyes were fastened on One.

She felt her dress with her hands. It was a great relief to her that she was wearing the dress her grandmother had bought her, and therefore wasn't naked in front of this strange man. The floor of the coal shed was completely covered with broken glass. She was afraid that if she wasn't wearing her dress, the glass would cut her body. But she was even more frightened of sewing needles. A sewing needle entered a person's flesh, wandered through the veins until it reached the heart and pierced it.

'Twoo!' said the man. 'Open your eyes!'

As soon as the child opened her eyes she was in the light. She looked straight into the light and saw the number Two. Two was not a run-of-the-mill number. It was extraordinary. It resembled a forked road; it had split itself off from the route of its main road. It was easy to see where it began, but its length was unknown, and it was impossible to determine where it ended. The child was struck with terror as she looked at Two. She had to flee this place right now, without waiting another moment, before it was too late to act on her decision, before she saw where Two ended. On top of this, her eyes were not closed, but unfortunately her eyes remained fastened on Two. And wherever Two was, there was always another.

That other was a piece of pink flesh. It was surrounded by very curly, very black hairs. It hung down from among these hairs like the tongue of a thirsty animal. The piece of meat must have liked being looked at, because as the child looked at it, it raised its head in a dignified manner. Very slowly, it was changing. It was becoming bigger, and longer, and thicker. It was becoming fat, with bulging veins. These veins didn't resemble the purple cables on Kıymet Hanım Teyze's legs one bit.

Just as the child was thinking that if it continued to grow it would no longer fit in the coal shed, the piece of flesh stopped suddenly. It stopped and waited. Outside they must have stopped playing hide-and-seek, because there was not a sound, and not even a leaf moved. The child felt that somewhere in the depths of this deathly silence, a pair of eyes was watching everything. They belonged neither to her nor to the strange man; neither far nor near…watching from somewhere else. She was being watched; by someone or something unknown. No matter how much she wanted to find the source of the eyes that were on her, she couldn't ruin the game, and didn't take her eyes off the piece of flesh.

Just at that moment the man began to approach. The child told herself that there was nothing to be frightened of. Anyway, the next number was Three. And since Three always came right after Two, it had to be nearby somewhere. Because it was never late. Indeed it came so quickly that anyone who hadn't succeeded in hiding by the time 'it' counted to Two would definitely be caught out in the open at Three. That meant it was not long before this unpleasant game came to an end. She would finally be able to leave when Three arrived. She would leave the coal shed and never step foot in it again. She would never again play games with strangers in coal sheds. She already regretted taking part, and was waiting for Three to liberate her. Just a little longer…she would be free in just a little while.

But before Three, the piece of flesh arrived. It arrived and entered her mouth. It advanced step by step into her mouth. The man was wheezing heavily. This wheezing reminded the child of Elsa. When you stroked her under the chin she made sounds just like this. But the wheezing was continually growing faster. Now the child remembered the retired history teacher who lived in the house across the way. The retired teacher had asthma. Whenever he climbed stairs he wheezed exactly like this. A while later, the wheezing was so fast and so heavy that the child couldn't determine what it resembled. The piece of flesh was moving back and forth in her mouth, but the child couldn't see it now. She didn't see anything now. She didn't even know if her eyes were open or closed. She felt nauseous.

Suddenly, just as her stomach was about to raise the flag of rebellion and she was about to loose hope; just as the cosmos was stubbornly beginning to gather speed to emerge from its motionlessness of a short while ago and the man's wheezes were turning into hoarse moans; just when, like any number that lives out its life and any number that is living out its life, it imitated the next number. Two finally came to an end.

The piece of flesh left her mouth. A strange liquid flowed in the emptiness it had left behind. It was very sticky. It had a terrible taste. The child couldn't bear it, and opened the door to her stomach. She began to vomit. She vomited out what the piece of flesh had vomited into her mouth.

When she realized that she was vomiting nothing but bitter liquid, she lifted her head and made an effort not to cry. She looked directly into the nothingness and saw that the absence of Three was worse than One and Two and even than Three. Because the man had gone.

He'd gone.

He'd left without saying 'Three.'

There was a coal shed in the neighbour's back garden; with a zinc roof, and two doors. A child was stuck inside.

It didn't matter whether she closed her eyes or opened them. Whether she opened her eyes or closed them, all she saw was the blackness of the coal shed. Everything and everyone was painted in the same colour of blindness. The whiteness she'd vomited, the cherries she'd eaten, the veins on Kıymet Hanım Teyze's legs, and even Abdullah's Red Show-Off were coal shed black.

~

'Aren't you tired of telling fairy tales yet? Because I'm fed up. Do you understand?'

The young doctor was pacing about irritably. Finally he grew tired, threw himself into the armchair across from the child, and moaned, 'Enough!' At the same moment a snapping sound was heard. A snapping sound that was reminiscent of a breaking heart. The doctor jumped to his feet in panic; he turned and looked at the place where he'd just sat. He'd sat on his glasses.

~

She was swimming in a lake that was coal shed black. The lake was warm. She wasn't cold. Before there hadn't even been a puddle here, let alone a lake. This meant that she must have created the lake herself. This meant that the lake must have been created from her tears. 'It seems I've cried a great deal,' she whimpered. She felt a great sense of relief at having cried so much. Perhaps if she managed to cry some more, her tears would cover everything, and the door of the coal shed would open by itself. Then, without having to worry about anything, she could swim straight to the exit, and be free of this place.

She was just about to abandon herself to the currents of the lake when an incriminating smell reached her nose. When she smelled it she understood that what she had thought was a lake was in fact a puddle of piss. It seemed she'd pissed herself. In alarm, she touched her eyes. They were completely dry. She hadn't cried, not at all. She felt a deep shame at not having cried. She felt a sharp pain in her stomach. As she twisted about, she felt once again that she was being watched. But this time she was determined to find who was watching her. And she did. Standing right in front of her: Elsa!

Elsa was sitting in the window with the broken glass, watching the child with fixed eyes. The raw green of her eyes was insolent;

the eyes of insolence were a raw green. It was as if she had been there since the beginning of the world; there was no secret she had not discovered, no sin that she had not recorded. She was a witness to everything that had happened in the coal shed. The child jumped to her feet trembling with irritation. She picked up a lump of coal and flung in at the cat. She missed.

She looked angrily at the retreating Elsa. There was no reason to stay in the coal shed any more. The cat had been watching from the very beginning with her eyes that saw everything and missed nothing, and had long since recorded what she had seen, while the child, having consented to take part in evil, and not having shed a single tear in spite of this, knew that all she had done was to piss herself while she was waiting shamefully and in vain for the arrival of 'Three.'

Elsa had seen everything; everything she shouldn't have seen.

When people commit sins, they can't stand to be in the same place with someone who has witnessed this. Witnesses and sinners can't face each other. Even if they want to forget, their memories are refreshed when they look into each other's eyes.

The best thing was to leave as soon as possible; just like the cherries that left the branches. The world was big. It had to be big. There had to be a place, in the East or in the West, where she would neither see Elsa nor be seen by her.

The house she wanted to leave behind was the colour of salted green almonds.

The house the colour of salted green almonds was her paternal grandmother's house.

~

'Now I want you to colour in this picture. You can use any colour you like. But you have to colour in the whole picture. You mustn't leave any of it uncoloured. Come on!'

There was a box of crayons on the table. The child looked at them. Every colour reminded her of something to eat. It made her hungry to look at these colours. But she didn't say this to the doctor who was watching her so carefully.

There was a family in the picture. The father was in the armchair; he was reading a newspaper with his legs crossed. The mother was on her feet; she was ironing on an ironing board. The grandmother was on the sofa; she was wearing her glasses and she was knitting. A boy and a girl were on the carpet; toys were scattered around them, and they were playing a game.

One by one, the child coloured the father's slippers, the mother's iron, everything from the grandmother's wool to the children's toys. She coloured the slippers spinach green, the iron pudding white, the ball of wool candied-apple red, and the toys egg yellow.

'What about the floating balloon?' asked the young doctor. 'Why didn't you colour that?'

The child was bewildered. There was no floating balloon in the picture. It only showed the inside of a house. But when she bent down and looked carefully she saw that the doctor was right. From the window in the room where the family was sitting you could see a tiny patch of sky. There, among the clouds, was a floating balloon. While the child was trying to choose a colour, she kept her finger on the balloon so she wouldn't loose it. At the same moment the young doctor bent to look at her finger. When she realised he could see how chewed and torn her cuticles were, she was seized with fear. In panic she hid her finger behind the crayons.

The child's face was grim. How could she not have thought of this before? She looked up reproachfully. There was a broken light bulb in the ceiling of the coal shed that she hadn't noticed before. Neither this cobwebbed ceiling nor the zinc roof above it could prevent God from seeing what Elsa had seen.

In hell there was a steep hill. Sinners were stripped naked, and after their sins were loaded into baskets on their backs, they began to climb the hill. The baskets were heavy, the hill was steep and the ground was slippery. They all struggled and perspired. Their feet would slip. They would roll back down. The sins in their baskets would scatter on the ground. But each sin knew who it belonged to, and would go stick to its owner's feet. Towards the top the hill became even more slippery. Way below, at the bottom of the hill, cauldrons burning with the fires of hell had been lined up. The sinners would start climbing again to escape the flames. But the hill was sheer ice; even if it was pure fire below. That's what grandmother used to say. That's what she said, and every time she had to climb a hill, she stopped first, and prayed that she wouldn't slide down. That's what she said, and she warned the child to stay away from hills. Hills opened onto hell. Hell was as terrible as its name.

She looked at the ceiling of the coal shed with eyes full of fear. The only help she could hope for was night. Because if it was night, if it was dark enough, that is if this coal shed was coal shed black enough... God might not have seen anything. And if it hadn't been seen by God, she wouldn't roll down the hill, and she wouldn't end up in hell.

She looked at the ceiling of the coal shed with eyes full of hope. If the light bulb was broken and the coal shed was dark, how was it different from night? She became confused. If only she could find a way to climb above the clouds, she could ask God whether or not he'd seen what happened in the coal shed. If only she knew whether or not God had seen.

~

As she went into the house through the back door of the kitchen, she heard her grandmother's voice. They were looking for her; in the garden, in the streets, at all the neighbours' houses, under Red Show-Off, in front of the Far Butcher's, in the upper neighbourhood... It was clear that the game of hide-and-seek was long over, and her absence alarmed everyone. Now everyone, all of the children and neighbours, was looking for her.

She went to the bathroom. She washed out her mouth. She took off her dress. She washed out her mouth. She soaped the sponge. She washed out her mouth. She sponged herself. She washed out her mouth. She shampooed her hair. She washed out her mouth. She rinsed out her hair. She washed out her mouth. She dried herself with a towel. She washed out her mouth. She combed her hair. She washed out her mouth. She put on clean underwear. She washed out her mouth. She took down the suitcase from on top of the closet. She washed out her mouth. She took her favourite shorts out of the suitcase. She washed out her mouth. She put on the shorts and a t-shirt. She washed out her mouth. She put on one of her hats. She washed out her mouth. She took a biscuit. She washed out her mouth. She was ready to leave now. She washed out her mouth. She opened the outer door. Her grandmother was standing in front of her.

When grandmother, who had been searching the neighbour-hood frantically and didn't know how she was going to tell her mother and father she was lost, saw the child, she couldn't control her irritation. She gave her a resounding slap. The child got up from where she'd fallen. She stepped on the biscuit that had fallen from her hand. She went to the bathroom. She washed out her mouth.

~

'If you continue to eat this way you're going to become a very fat lady in the future. Then no one will like you. You know that, don't you? Do you want everyone to call you fatty?'

Ever since he'd broken his glasses, the doctor had squinted and blinked his bright blue eyes when he looked at the child. The child was looking at him too, with a hidden smile.

~

She washed out her mouth. She went into the living room.

When she went into the living room, all of the women of the neighbourhood were there.

All of the women young and old, feeling it was rude to remain standing, had squeezed themselves into armchairs and onto chairs and cushions; waiting there together as if they were uneasily mourning the untasted death of someone they didn't know. The child stood right in the middle of the living room and looked carefully at the women. When she looked at them she saw sacks and sacks of potatoes, tins and tins of oil, combs and combs of honey, barrels and barrels of pickles, cones and cones of sugar, strings and strings of onions, baskets and baskets of fruit, packets and packets of biscuits, wheels and wheels of cheese, boxes and boxes of chocolate, jars and jars of chockella. She was hungry; very hungry.

She was so hungry that, after being raked by the unbearable looks of these unbearable people, she began to chew at the bunches of grapes on the oilskin table-cloth. She was so hungry that, turning purple like a bleeding fingernail, her hunger started eating at the deathly weight that was pressing down on her. But she still couldn't get rid of the terrible taste in her mouth. She urgently had to eat something else.

Grandmother was in a panic. She hadn't made dinner yet. What she'd eaten wasn't even enough to fill the holes in her teeth, she planted her hungry and now lustreless eyes on the wall. Since the house was the colour of salted green almonds, it might taste good too. However, before her hunger had to resort to becoming fond of the walls, one of the neighbour women rushed home and came back with a large pot of food. The woman's *pilaff* had just a little too much salt and oil.

On the television there was Tom and Jerry, and in the pot there was *pilaff*.

(Jerry was very hungry.) She was very hungry. (He has his eyes on a jug of milk.) She pulled the pot towards her. (But Tom was sleeping next to the jug.) She lifted the lid. (Tom's eyes opened slightly.) The pot was full to the top. (Jerry escapes the cat's claws at the last moment.)

'May I have another plate?'

'Of course, my dear. Did you like my *pilaff*?'

(Jerry had changed his appearance.) One of the women brought a carafe of *ayran*. (He had disguised himself as a female cat.) The *ayran* was frothy. (The jug of milk was only a step away.) She pulled the carafe towards her. (Tom was standing guard before the jug.) The women were watching her out of the corners of their eyes. (The milk was very white.) The *ayran* was very white. (Tom was very polite.) Everyone was very polite. (Jerry, dressed as a female cat, drank all of the milk in the jug in one go.) She drank a carafe of *ayran* in one go. (Tom has fallen in love with the female cat.) The women were bewildered.

'May I have another plate?'

(A thread was hanging from Jerry's costume.) It seemed as if they'd put a little less *pilaff* on her plate this time. (The costume was unravelling quickly.) She was eating quickly. (Tom understood that he'd been tricked.) The plate was finished very quickly (Snarling, he leaps at Jerry, who still thinks he's a female cat.) She reached her hand into the pot. (Jerry managed to escape at the last moment.) The grains of rice had no place to hide. (Tom is chasing Jerry.) She began to eat the rice, which had been finely crushed, by the handful. (Both the cat and the mouse are out of breath.) She was out of breath. (Still the chase continued.) The more she ate the hungrier she got.

(While fleeing, Jerry fell into the jug of milk.) She leaned into the pot. (In order not to drown, he started to drink the milk he was sinking into.) She was eating handful after handful. (Jerry was so bloated from having drunk all the milk that bubbles were coming out of his mouth.) Her stomach began to ache. (Jerry had become a balloon and was starting to rise.) She had become very heavy. (Tom catches the mouse's tail at the last moment.) Still she doesn't stop eating. (They both start rising into the sky.) Now she could see the bottom of the pot. (There were snow-white clouds in the sky.) The bottom of the pot was pitch black.

~

'Do you like my new glasses? My wife chose them.'

The young doctor put on his new glasses and smiled. The glasses were square, with dark glass and a bone frame. When he put them on you couldn't see his blue eyes. The child hung her face. It was bad not to be able to see the doctor's eyes when he looked at her. She didn't want to talk to eyes she couldn't see. She didn't say anything.

She never said anything again.

~

The stomach is a mythical land. It is a land of eternal bliss where the finest food is served on golden platters in banquets that last for forty days and forty nights, where holy wine runs in the rivers, where the elixir of immortality cascades down waterfalls, where healing honey flows on top of the mountains. No one knew what hunger was in this land of plenty and of fullness. And in order to understand how pleasant this is it's enough to see the happiness of a healthy baby who smiles with each spoonful of food.

The stomach is a mythical land. At the end of every fortieth day the dragon emerges from the fortieth gate and breathes fire that burns to ashes every grain of wheat and leaves; not a drop of water in the cisterns; an endlessly cursed land where the harvest is dried up by seven year droughts and in whose dark forests evil-hearted witches brew cauldron after cauldron of catastrophe. A land of gnawing hunger where no one knew what it was to be full. And to understand how terrible it was, it was sufficient to see the suffering of a sick old man vomiting what he has eaten on his deathbed.

The stomach is a mythical land.

And like every mythical land, it has secrets in its back garden.

~

'It's been weeks since you've told me anything. You used to tell fairy tales, but you don't even do that any more. I…perhaps it's my inexperience…I don't know… Perhaps a more experienced physician…I mean after this…'

After that day the child and the young doctor didn't see each other any more.

~

The back garden of childhood has the sour taste of cherries.

Remembering leaves stains on holiday clothes.

In any event it's possible to forget everything. It's good to forget, it cleans the eyes. When a person forgets and is forgotten, they behave like a cat who covers up its own faults. It's enough for the memory to grow cold. Sometimes in winter, when despite the white it could be called black because of the misery, it's necessary to go down to the coal bin for fuel. The kindling, the wood and the coal in the coal bin are composed of memories. Kindling can easily set memory afire; when it burns, who knows when and where blood will flow in its petrified veins. The acrid smoke of the kindling makes the eyes water, but it's good to cry. The pupils are cleaned by crying, are purified. With crying, the lime, tar and clay; sticks and twigs, bugs and dusty earth are washed out. It purifies the night. And night is such a big consolation, so very beautiful. It engraves its beauty on the darkness, just like a lover of glitter pulling her silver threads.

The back garden of childhood has the sour taste of cherries.

Those who taste it will have their teeth set on edge.

So it's not possible to forget everything. What we call the eyes may succeed in forgetting all of what they've seen in life, but it's impossible to stop thinking about having been seen. If there are no witnesses a person can forget the past.

If there are witnesses everything changes. Their every look is an accusation, their existence an obstacle to forgetfulness.

After all, this was why she couldn't count from one to three. 'One' was put aside in a corner, 'Two' in another corner. She was constantly staggering between the two; she diminished because she couldn't reach their sum.

Istanbul – 1999

pencere (window): According to the 18th century philosopher Leibnitz, the monad, the smallest indivisible particle, has no window through which to look out. For this reason no monad can be influenced by any other monad. Monads can resemble each other, but can never be identical. Indeed nothing in the universe is identical to anything else.

He wasn't even aware.

I looked into B-C's eyes with pity.

perde (curtain): For years he sold curtains in Beyoslu. He liked the heavy, velvet curtains best, and wanted to sell those. These weren't much in demand among housewives; frilly lace curtains were in fashion. And Venetian blinds had recently come out. He had all of these in his shop. The only curtains he refused to sell were the new transparent shower curtains.

'Is such a thing possible?' he said to his assistant. 'Can a curtain be transparent? If it's transparent, is it still a curtain?'

I looked into his eyes in pain: His eyes that didn't give away what they were feeling, that collected material from every possible source about seeing and being seen, that were interested in the invisible rather than in the visible, that looked more deeply into the visible solely in order to see the invisible; instead of avoiding the eyes of others he concerned himself with eyes, and displayed himself out of stubbornness even in the knowledge that it would subject him to the abuse of other eyes, who liked to fool people by changing his appearance, who has a issue with eyes, and doesn't like the way time is structured and, in fact, his eyes don't accept anything at face value… I looked into his bitter-chocolate eyes that see the people through their stories, and stories through the people in them, that see everything connected to everything else, that see every disunity in its own wholeness and every wholeness in its own disunity, that is, that can see me in a way no one else can see… I looked at these two thin slits of eyes that have sworn not to express what they feel… I looked with pain.

pervane (propeller): The propeller sacrificed itself in order to get a closer look at fire.

There were some things in B-C's eyes that I wasn't used to seeing. And it was because he saw the world through these eyes that his whole being was so peculiar, and that he was so bewildering with all his being. Until now, the only person whose glances didn't make me uneasy was B-C, and he was the only person I couldn't take my eyes off. He was the only person I wanted to be seen by, who I wanted to see even more of me.

If you're as fat as I am, it's difficult to stay out of sight. You can't stay out of people's sight even for a moment. Wherever you go and whatever you do, you immediately attract attention. People like me are directional signs for other people's eyes. Let's say, someone wants to point someone out in a crowded place…well, in situations like this the best way is to use people like me as a reference point. 'You see that fat woman over there, the woman just across from her.' That's how it is. There's nothing I can do about it. I think there must be other people in this situation; for instance, someone as ugly and strange as a freak, or as beautiful and as extraordinary as a *jinn* must face the same problem. Whatever. The strange thing about it, though, is that if you're as fat as I am, people don't see you. They'll look and they'll watch; they'll point you out and talk about you to each other. In their view, you're material for observation. It doesn't even cross their minds that the way they look at me makes me uncomfortable. They always watch. But they never see. Looking at my body gives them an excuse not to look into my eyes. They never see within.

> *portre* (portrait): Generally a painting that shows a person from the waist up. (Research Mehmet the Conqueror's portrait!)

B-C wasn't like that. His eyes didn't look at me that way. The singularity of his eyes struck me even the first time we met, I mean that day…the day we met.

> *prizma* (prism): a transparent substance that bends and fragments light.

The day I met B-C, I was coming back from the other side of the Bosphorus by ferry. I'd set out early in the morning to take a look at an aerobics centre whose advertisement in the newspaper promised that customers would become two sizes thinner or get their money back. I met a number of plump women there, but as far as I could see I was the fattest one among them. Then the skinny little aerobics instructor arrived and shouted, 'Ladies! We're going to melt away those flabby tummies. Are you ready?' And in unison we cheerfully cried, 'We're ready!' I decided to give it a try, and I registered. To tell the truth, it was really quite far from my house, but I thought this would force me to move more. On the way back I decided to take the ferry.

I was sitting in the top section of the ferry with a *sahlep* in one hand and a *simit* in the other. Because it was terribly windy, there was no one but me in this section of the ferry. I was pleased with myself. Even on the first day, the people at the aerobics centre had thrust a strict dieting list into my hands. Suddenly I heard that mechanical voice. I didn't turn around and look at once. If I pretended I didn't notice, perhaps he would go away; go back where he'd come from.

But the voice challenged my indifference step by step. Behind me, right behind me, someone was taking a photograph. Someone was taking my photograph.

When I turned my head, I came nose to nose with a camera. Behind the camera was the smallest person I'd ever seen in my life. He'd climbed onto the bench. He was turning a giant lens, trying to adjust the view, lifting his head from time to time to look with his naked eye. He was completely relaxed. To look at him, you'd think it was customary for passengers on this city's ferry lines to be photographed by dwarfs.

'Please! I don't like having my picture taken.'

rasathane (observatory): In the observatory founded in Tophane in 1587 by Takiyeddin, chief astrologer of the Ottoman Sultan, there were all types of astronomical instruments arranged side-by-side, as well as an extensive library of books about astronomy. The dome of the observatory was covered in lead. Astronomers and assistants worked on a huge table day and night. There were hour-glasses, set-squares, celestial globes, terrestrial globes, compasses, rolls of paper, ink pots, rulers and astronomical instruments on the table.

First, the Sheik ul-Islam Kadızade Ahmed Şemseddin Efendi issued a pronouncement that observing the skies brought bad luck. Admiral Kılıç Ali Pasa, acting on Sultan Murat III's imperial decree, levelled the observatory, with all its books and instruments, in one night.

If only I hadn't said it that way. I regretted it as soon as the words were out of my mouth. To say I don't like having my picture taken is to say that I don't like pictures of me; to say I don't like pictures of me is to say I don't like how I look. If I had been thin, like a feather trembling in the wind, I could grudgingly have considered the taking of my picture as a joke. I smiled and let it pass. Fat people can smile and let things pass, as long as they remain thick-skinned. For my part, I could succeed neither in losing weight nor in being thick-skinned.

renk körü (colour blindness): A disorder of sight that obstructs the ability
to distinguish all or some colours.

He insisted. He sat on the bench he'd climbed onto a little earlier
and took the camera onto his lap. When he sat he looked very small.
His legs were tiny, his feet were tiny; his shoulders were narrow and
his ears were minuscule. But his hands were large. His hands were
too big for a dwarf. I'd never seen a dwarf before. Who knew how
many dwarves there were in the city, I thought, but I never saw
them. Dwarves don't watch passers-by in the street, or go shopping
at supermarkets, or wander around in public. I could imagine a
dwarf sitting at home or putting on a show, but not wandering
about in public, a packet of sunflower seeds in his hand, cracking
the seeds idly between his teeth. Dwarves are trapped in a state of
invisibility; just like many people who are put on display. They don't
want other people's eyes to see them.

Suddenly I shuddered. People who exist without existing, who
are not seen in public because they are put on display; dwarves,
cripples, fat people…all people who are strange to look at… Those
who hide from outside eyes, who embrace the privacy of their
homes, who like to keep their existence private…I was one of them.
Somehow unable to be comfortable outside, day by day becoming
more closed within myself; as I become more closed within myself,
I become somehow unable to be comfortable outside. I chose this
isolation, but it's impossible to know how much I preferred it.

The dwarf across from me looked as comfortable as could
be. I couldn't take my eyes off him. I who was always made
uncomfortable by the glances of others, found pleasure in watching
someone for the first time in my life. As I watched, I began to worry
that he might get up and go, that he would become offended and
withdraw from me. Indeed, perhaps, from the moment I saw B-C,
I feared never seeing him again.

'I didn't mean to be rude… I'm not very good at these things.'

> *röntgen* (x-ray): An instrument that lifts the curtain of flesh and reveals a person's insides.

He raised his head and looked straight into my eyes. That's the first time I really saw his eyes; when he smiled warmly at me. His eyes were two short, thin little lines drawn with Chinese ink; his eyes had the black colour of bitter chocolate. When he smiled they became even smaller and thinner. My heart was in my mouth. It was as if he continued smiling this way, his eyes would be erased completely.

In any event, I had no cause for worry. I was to realise in time that no matter how much he smiled, he was never able to be happy enough to erase his eyes. There was a strange lack of lustre in his eyes that wasn't immediately apparent at first glance, but which at certain times became quite evident. Indeed sometimes his face didn't say anything; it remained completely without feeling or expression; as if they were somehow free of emotion, as if standing there, simply standing there in his transparent calm, he gazed at the world with indifference. At times like these it was as he was looking through frosted glass or a curtain of wax, and I couldn't tell what he felt. But I didn't understand all of this until much later. A long time after the day we met.

> *rüya* (dream): One night, in 16th century Istanbul, Şair Bâlı Efendi sees his friend Piruza Ali, who had died at a young age, in a dream. Piruza Ali wraps some dirt in paper and gives it to him. Şair Bâlı Efendi puts the twist of paper in a fold of his turban. The next day, while telling those around him about his dream, he reaches involuntarily for his turban. There he finds the twist of paper filled with dirt.

He took the camera from around his neck and handed it to me. While he held the camera with one hand, he grasped my wrist with the other.

'If that's the case, try looking through here,' he said. 'You might like this. Take a look!'

sahne (stage): When the actors are on the stage, the audience bury themselves in their seats and watch what it's like to be watched.

I looked, and more than once. I looked at everything I'd seen around me from behind a camera. Suddenly, I took a picture of him, and then another, and another. I took pictures of him without stop until the ferry was approaching the pier. He was looking straight at me in order not to miss anything; at me, the one who was looking at him. I enjoyed taking his picture so much that I didn't want to let go of the camera. His bag was full of film; when it finished he put in more and he didn't object at all to my efforts to catch every moment on film. At one point, while he was changing the film, I moved closer to him. I caught his smell. The strange thing was that it reminded me of something sweet to eat. His breath, his hair, his clothes…from head to toe he smelled like chocolate.

'Sometimes it happens to me too. I want to take pictures of everything. Sometimes it does one good to put an intermediary between the one who's seeing and the one who's being seen,' he said. 'Do you know what the interesting thing about it is, we believe that God does the same thing. He always sees, and we're always being seen, isn't that so? And God puts an intermediary between himself and what he sees. Prophets, for instance, or angels…Azarael, for instance, or Gabriel… As for us, we're afraid both of being seen and of what we can't see. We wait for a sign so we can say it has appeared. That's also why we give so much importance to miracles. We want to see miracles. Indeed, as I think to myself sometimes, it's as if our entire existence, as well as our non-existence, is founded on seeing and being seen.'

He fell silent. A faint smile remained on his lips. Then he brought his face close to mine and whispered as if he were telling me a secret. 'Do you know, sometimes we get our deepest wounds through our eyes.'

I looked at him in surprise.

saklambaç (hide-and-seek): By the time 'it' counts to three, one must be hidden somewhere he can't see.

That day we wandered around together the whole day.

That day while we wandered around together all day, when we were seen together for the first and last time, I didn't want to miss even a single memory of him. In order to remember the bow-legged manner in which he walked as he tried to match his pace to mine, his squat legs, his ill-proportioned hands, the way he found something to say about every subject, the thoughtfulness with which he spoke and explained, the way he squinted his eyes before he started a sentence, the way he used gestures to emphasise what he had said when he had finished a sentence, his indifference to children taller than himself who pointed him out to their mothers or indeed anyone who threw his being a dwarf in his face, the way he didn't judge people's coarseness, his loneliness, his insensitivity, the way he held his head high, his strangeness, the way he was on display in exactly the same way I was, and because I was on display like he was, I took pictures of him all day that day.

samur (sable): *zo.* (*martes zibellina*) Slightly bigger than a house cat (approximately 50cm in height). Lives alone. It eats everything from squirrels to pine cones to insects. Because its fur, with its grey brown and black tones, is dense and silky, it is highly esteemed. They call it the 'Golden Pelt'.

Before the second half of the 17th century, the sable was the magnet that drew the Russians into Siberia. As a sable hunter of the same century said, 'The sable prepares itself for death by lying on its side, raising its back legs, and covering its eyes with its front paws.'

I took perhaps more than a hundred photographs. More than a hundred times I looked through the viewfinder, and tried to see him in different states, to see what his days and his nights were like, and how he was when he couldn't sleep or when he'd just woken. I watched how as he enthusiastically explained something, it came alive in his eyes, and as it came alive in his eyes, he explained it with enthusiasm, sometimes like this and sometimes like that, his unquenchable curiosity, his lack of restraint, his absent-mindedness, his ill-temper. Finally, when the film in his bag was finished, he grasped my wrist.

'Aren't you hungry? I'm very hungry.'

Then I came to my senses. Who knew how many hours we'd been wandering around and I not only hadn't I eaten anything but the thought of food hadn't even crossed my mind. I smiled shyly.

When we entered the restaurant, B-C preceded me and held the door open. As if we didn't look strange enough together, I didn't see the sense in doing amusing things that would attract attention. I passed through the door feeling shy and embarrassed. The moment we were inside, I saw the first bus-boy to notice us nudge the bus-boy next to him. It had begun. Just as I'd guessed it would. One by one every head in the place turned towards us, and conversations stopped, and people started whispering. All I wanted was to sit down at the nearest table, as soon as possible. But B-C didn't like any of the tables, and continued strolling about, knowing that everyone was watching us. By the time he chose a table, I'd long since turned bright red and broken into a sweat.

While B-C drank one beer after another with amazing speed, I ate my fried mussels as slowly and as daintily as possible. I felt too shy to raise my head and look around. I couldn't make the effort to look into the waiter's face, or to make eye contact with anyone.

'Why do you have such a strange name?' I said finally when I'd calmed down a bit and was able to speak.

'It's not my real name, of course. When I was small, the children used to call me 'itty bitty'. Later I used to say my name was 'bee-tee'. You know, I really thought this was a real name. Then I decided to make this name that had stuck to me a little different. Instead of 'bee-tee' I said 'B-C'. I know it's strange, but...I'm so accustomed to it, I wouldn't even turn around if someone called me by my real name. I like B-C. They're also the second and third letters of the alphabet. They look good side-by-side. As if I'm Two and Three. I'm searching for One. The preceding number was lacking something, it wasn't completed, and it's as if that's why I am the way I am... I'm in the process of creating myself. What happened? Why are you so surprised? Does this seem like nonsense to you?'

For a moment I couldn't speak or breathe. It was as if something clicked within me, but I couldn't tell if it was a good thing or a bad thing. Suddenly, unable to explain even to myself why I'd become so irritable, I snapped, 'Yes, I think it's complete nonsense.'

'You could be right! But don't take numbers lightly. Don't forget that numbers have *jinns*. Numbers *jinns* have torches on their waists, and brooms in their hands, and each one is as small as a flea, their tongues are twisted, and their eyes spin...' While he was saying these strange things, he was playing his fingers like puppets and twisting the shape of his face. I watched him in amazement. Despite the fact that it was always moving, there was a stillness and calm about his face. He suddenly stopped talking and looked around as if he were bored. 'Let's go,' he said. 'Let's go and print these photographs.'

'Where?'

'Home! The Hayalifener Apartments.'

---

sarık sandalı (turban boat): Whenever Sultan Selim III went out to wander along the shores of the Bosphorus, the populace would stop working and go out into the streets. At the very back, the boat that was following the six boats that carried the honour guard, was the 'turban boat'. The official in charge of this boat would carry aloft the Sultan's turban, which was studded with priceless jewels. When the boat was passing close to the shore, this official would wave the turban back and forth.

It wasn't done in order for the people to see the Sultan's turban, but to remind them that they were being watched. The sultanate was an eye that saw everything.

At first I liked the name of the Hayalifener Apartments, and when I saw the building I liked it for itself. The building was on one of the two sides of Istanbul, in a neighbourhood where morally upright families and freethinking single people frequently lived side-by-side, at the top of a steep hill that was difficult to ascend and descend. His flat was on the top floor, and there wasn't a useable elevator. B-C, in front, skipped up the steps; I followed, wheezing. To climb these stairs after that long, steep hill, the pain from the chafing of my legs was growing stronger with each step. I was in agony, and my chest was tight. At least B-C didn't say anything about my condition, or ask depressing questions. Instead of asking questions he didn't stop explaining; he talked away without waiting for approval. Perhaps I was more attracted to the way he spoke than to what he was saying. As he talked, I couldn't take my eyes off him.

'Whenever I'm curious about a person, I cut them out of the frame in which they belong and put them into a background that's least like them. To do this gives me a lot of ideas about people. Let's say a woman is walking towards me. Young, and a bit flighty. I'll take her out of the place where she belongs and put her in a time and place that would be strangest to her, into a frame that's as far as possible from her own, and then I watch. Or let's say a man is walking towards me. Young, and a bit slack. I'll try to find a frame that's least like him. When I put him in this frame he'll look completely different to me. In the picture that belongs to him, he's either strong or weak, either handsome or ugly, either unique or ordinary. But in a picture that doesn't belong to him, he tends to lose his role. And then when you look, you see that he's really not so strong, or not so weak. Neither that ugly nor that handsome. You should try it. Put people in the photograph in which they're least likely to fit, and then take a look at them.'

I looked at him lovingly.

'What about me, then? What's the picture into which I'm least likely to fit?'

He looked at me lovingly.

'Most probably above the clouds. For someone as fat as you the sky has to be the most unlikely place.'

I nodded my head. I had fallen in love.

Şems: When Mevlana came out of Pembefirusan's han, Şems planted himself in front of him and said, 'Hey, appraiser of the world, look at me!'

From that moment on I didn't part from him. B-C was a land I somehow couldn't reach because I had delayed so much. It was as if, after years of being stuck, of believing that in this state I couldn't love anyone and no one could love me, a door had opened in front of me at a completely unexpected moment and from a completely unexpected direction. Once over the threshold, we tumbled together into a world of passion. I could have cut my dwarf lover a giant's shadow without hesitation; with him I could go anywhere and return from anywhere without thinking of what lay beyond.

Nevertheless, I had to think, we had to think. Because we didn't suit each other. That is, I wasn't one of those women who, because they are so short, still look like little round balls despite all their weight... It wasn't just my girth, but because I was also taller than normal, when I stood next to B-C both my height and my weight made for a terrifying contrast. When we were side-by-side we looked so out of place that we couldn't even bring up the subject of not going out together. If we went around holding hands and smiling at each other in the streets like other lovers, everyone who saw us would die laughing. As my eighty centimetre lover tried to match his pace to my hundred and thirty-two kilo body, people would point us out to each other and watch us. Without feeling it necessary to suppress the mocking smiles on their lips, they would wonder whether or not we made love. They would find us so amusing they wouldn't be able to take their eyes off us. They wouldn't be able to stop talking about the contrast between the fat lady and the dwarf for days.

B-C and I had both been the objects of people's stares for a long time. But now that we had come together, if we even held hands we wouldn't just be objects of curiosity, we would also be the source of a great deal of amusement. We were strange enough separately, but together we were not only strange but comic. We weren't pleasing to the eye.

For this reason, there was nothing like the Hayalifener Apartments. Here life was private; safe from abusive stares. Of course the neighbour-ladies' eyes were always on us, but once we were inside there was nothing to worry about. I was comfortable here, I was at ease. I wasn't thinking about returning to the house where I lived with my family. I do know how much my family loved me, and I didn't want to mix their love with pity. I was tired of them being distressed about me. For years my mother and father had been struggling to behave as if we were a happy family and that nothing had gone wrong, but I was tired of seeing the pain in their eyes that they would never speak of. Leaving their house was going to be good for me.

So I gathered my things together and moved to the Hayalifener Apartments. I felt that here I could be free both of the body that enclosed me and of the kinds of looks that made me uncomfortable. Indeed it happened from time to time that I didn't even think about how I looked. I who for years had looked at myself and the world around me through the lenses of my body was now momentarily able to take these glasses off. On top of that, as I gained the ability to see through my body and into myself, I discovered new aspects of myself. When B-C looked at me with love, I was able to see myself and the world around me with completely new eyes. Most of the time, I did my utmost to see through his eyes, and to understand what he saw and how he saw it. I saw neither intimacy nor rejection in his eyes. Life was liveable, I was loveable when I looked into B-C's eyes.

sisko (fatty): She was so fat that wherever she went, people would stop whatever they were doing and stare at her. The way people looked at her made her so uncomfortable that she would eat even more and become even fatter. (Research fatty's childhood.)

But now, having read the Dictionary of Gazes, everything looked different again to my eyes. Now I understood that at first I had been the source of this detestable dictionary, its substance, and that later I had become one item among many. That windy day we'd met on the ferry, B-C had gone out with his camera to find something interesting to look at, and had encountered me. In those days he'd probably become bored with whatever he'd been doing and was looking for something new to occupy himself with but didn't quite know what he wanted to do. He went out looking. Then he met me. He found in me the inspiration for a new project; or more accurately, he found it in the way our relationship was kept hidden from the sight of others. Once he'd started working on the Dictionary of Gazes, I stopped being the inspiration and became material; my dreams, my memories and my anxieties. When he'd finished observing me and found what he was looking for, I might have been the most interesting item in the Dictionary of Gazes. I was the fatty whose childhood he was going to research.

B-C says that it's only in miracles that sweet water and salt water don't mix, and he doesn't like miracles. What he wanted was to take bits and pieces of my stories and other people's stories and mix them all together. When he'd done this, there'd be only a single thread holding it all together: himself!

But what attracted him most were the unseen sides of people. B-C is always interested in the unseen, and wanted to make the invisible visible. Just like the prince's wife in the story, who wanted to know what was behind the fortieth door. The most important thing was to pry open the lock. Once he'd opened the door and seen what was inside, there remained no reason to delay there.

Anything forbidden or hidden in the world…anything suppressed or very respected…in short anything that was kept out of sight was within B-C's area of interest. For this reason, whenever he looked at a person he was trying to find their hidden parts; he took great pleasure in discovering their memories, their secrets, the things that were most private to them. Once he'd completed his discoveries he'd got what he wanted, and he'd start looking elsewhere for new discoveries.

As long as there were things about me he didn't know, I remained unprocessed material for the Dictionary of Gazes. That meant he would stay with me until he'd discovered what was left to be discovered. Later…just as he never took another look at material he'd already used, he would soon tire of me. He'd set off in search of new material, something new to occupy himself, and who knows, perhaps even a new life.

taht-ı revan (palanquin): Every Friday morning, the Sultan's only daughter would arrange a palanquin and leave the palace and go to a bathhouse on the other side of the city. Before she appeared at the palace gates, guards with sharp swords would have cleared all of the streets along the route. People would flee to their houses, lock their doors, cover their windows and shut their eyes tight; they would wait in box-rooms, pantries and secluded corners until the Sultan's daughter had passed in her palanquin. No one had the courage to look outside because anyone who saw the Sultan's daughter even accidentally would have their heads cut off at once.

One Friday morning, the city's most capable thief, who was wandering across the rooftops with a curiosity-stone he had taken from an Indian merchant the day before, appeared at the end of the street along which the Sultan's daughter was passing in her palanquin. His curiosity got the better of him, and he opened his eyelids slightly.

Before the executioner cut off his head, the thief turned to the people who had gathered in the square and shouted; 'Your fear of seeing the Sultan's daughter's beauty is misplaced. The palanquin is empty! If it hadn't been empty, why would he have tried to hide it from us?'

Because at that moment everyone was so absorbed in watching the execution, no one heard the thief's last words.

I couldn't digest the fact that in his eyes, I'd been material for the Dictionary of Gazes from the start. All this time I thought we'd been living a love that was resistant to the gazes of outside, and that, in spite of everything, flowered in privacy. I have to confess, I thought our relationship was based on a mutual desire the like of which would be difficult to find. Perhaps with B–C I drank all of the passion I hadn't lived in my life in a single gulp. In that case everything was very simple. Just like him, I have an issue with eyes; with seeing and being seen. I was just as much on display as he was. And all that we had long-suspected separately, about what this chronic disease resembled, revealed itself layer-by-layer when we came together. This is what had attracted B–C. That was all.

So after putting all the pieces together, I knew why he was with me. That is, if there was any love involved in this, I knew the reason for it. And what we call love is condemned to dry out the moment there's a reason for it.

tedbil gezmek (to go out in disguise): The Sultan used to wander in disguise through the winding streets of the city of cities. Sometimes he would give out rewards, but most of the time he gave out punishments. In order for these rewards and punishments to be given out immediately, the Sultan's disguised bodyguards walked in file behind him.

Mustafa III, who went out in disguise regularly, used to like to dress as a dervish. He used to wander over every inch of the city; a dervish on the outside and a Sultan on the inside.

One day Feyzullah, who'd come to Istanbul after losing the governorship of Çorum, recognised the disguised Sultan. He told him what a difficult position he was in and asked for help. He didn't get any response. Another time Feyzullah met the Sultan in the middle of the market in Üsküdar and once again recognised him. This time he couldn't hold himself back, and shouted; 'Either give me my bread or have me killed!'

Mustapha III looked at Feyzullah carefully. The eyes of the Sultan inside the dervish could be dangerous; indeed very dangerous. He made his decision right then and there. He didn't give him his bread.

This is why I was looking into B–C's eyes with pain. When he'd come home and learned that I'd read the Dictionary of Gazes, he hadn't at first been able to discern what had distressed me, but as the minutes passed he began to understand the reasons for the change in me. And now that he'd once again wrapped his face in an inexpressive blankness, devoid of all emotion, I couldn't make out what he was thinking. His eyes had once again fled behind frosted glass or a curtain of wax; I couldn't guess what he was feeling. I don't know how long we sat across from each other without speaking or moving. But his silence was such an unaccustomed thing for me that it hurt my ears. Then he stood up slowly. He came to my side and held my wrist.

'If you want, let's go out in disguise tonight,' he said.

'All right, let's go out,' I said, unable to control the trembling of my voice.

televizyon (television): It is unsettling to imagine that the television at home, which we watch all the time, could watch us for even a moment.

There was nothing to argue about. And we didn't argue. I started looking for the suitcase I'd brought when I came. I couldn't remember where we'd put it away. But B–C's voice stopped me. 'You stay,' he said. 'You know, I was going to leave anyway.'

There was nothing to talk about. And we didn't talk. I didn't turn my head. I didn't look in his direction. I didn't have the heart to watch his departure.

temasa (contemplation): Watching for the enjoyment of looking.

sahne-i temasa: stage.

Love is a corset. In order to understand the value of this you have to be exceedingly fat. It can quickly wrap up and control the fat that's been gathering layer by layer over the years, spreading out in its stickiness, heaping up in a gelatinous mass. Then you can stand outside your own work and watch the power. Love is a merchant of dreams. Worn-out and cast-off dreams will pick themselves up, clean and shine themselves, deck themselves out, and in their new state laugh at their owners. Love makes a person more beautiful. It plays fearlessly with appearances, that is, with qualities, that is, with mirrors. It makes peace between the taking of offence and mirrors, it increases the lonely with mirrors.

Love is a corset. The day will come when, in the least expected place, at the least expected moment, one of the clasps will burst, or its threads will unravel. Before there's even time to understand what's happened, the fat will have long since come out into the open. In the midst of this confusion, your body returns to its former state in the blink of an eye. Love is a corset. In order to understand why it lasts such a short time you have to be exceedingly fat.

Because something will always happen to spoil the fun. An unravelled thread, for instance, that gets caught in the front door of the building, or that can't be completely removed from the article of clothing it belongs to. Like a hole that causes a balloon to leak, or the sudden cessation of continuity, or not turning at the corner…or an unhealed wound, or an unrealised dream, or a stain in one's pupil, or a crack in the plate…or an uncompleted task, or an unformed substance, or an unfinished story…some things are always lacking something. However much we vomit out, at least one mouthful of the cake we've eaten will remain in the seclusion of our stomachs; like a weight that clings to our ankles and won't allow us to levitate, no matter how much we inflate ourselves and no matter how many jugs of milk we drink. And no matter how clean we might be, every cleaning of the eyes leaves some dust hidden under the carpet; a memory we can't forget or cause to be forgotten. There's always something left over. There's always something lacking.

> *theatrum mundi*: According to this belief, the world is a huge theatre with a single spectator.

I could have followed B-C. Because he was unique, because it was worth not breaking it off with him, and not being stubborn about his absence. I could have chased the giant rhythm of his dwarf heart through the streets. Because he's much more agile than I am, who knows how long I could have followed his trail; or…

…I could have decided not to follow B-C. I could have gone far from here, never to see him or to be seen by him, and remain forever unprocessed material for the Dictionary of Gazes; down the steep hill to hell, with the heaven of the Hayalifener Apartments at the top.

But now I…

> *ultrason* (ultrasound): Babies captured on ultrasound will later have their every movement watched carefully.

…was going to do something else. Because I was hungry!

I was so hungry it was as if I'd always been left hungry. As if I hadn't been stuffing myself all my life. I was a big lie, a huge denial. I was a failure. No matter how I tried, I simply couldn't lose weight, I can't be free of the pincers of my body. I was stuck. I couldn't stop thinking about my fatness for a moment. I was alone. I'd become closed within myself, afraid to look within. I was apprehensive. I was apprehensive about everything, but mostly about myself. I was angry. I couldn't control my nerves when people watched me in order to add colour to their lives or to have something to talk about. I was restless. I was bruised by tossing and turning in bed as if my dream was a river. I was unhappy. Like my stomach, my unhappiness grew the more it was fed. Of course it was possible to exist outside of these things; but I wasn't there. Now I am in the belly of hunger.

I'd never been this hungry before.

I opened my mouth wide. I opened my mouth so wide that the hydrosphere was afraid I would drink up all the water and finish it; it decided to sacrifice all of its fish on the wet, mother-of-pearl alter in order to appease my hunger. I ate all of its fish. Before long, I shouted angrily from the top of a mountain of fish bones, 'Where are your oysters pregnant with pearls, your sluggish octopuses, your hideous monsters, your sweet, sweet starfish, your treacherous whirlpools, your sunken ships full of hidden treasure?'

The hydrosphere hurriedly placed a whale stew in front of me.

I opened my mouth wide. I opened my mouth so wide that the earth feared my teeth would sink into its core; the fruit of all the trees came to me quickly on a command from underground. I finished all the fruit. Then, from the bottom of a hole caused by ripping trees out by their roots, I cried angrily, 'Is this the extent of your generosity?' It anxiously covered up the mole hills. I paid no attention. 'How about the mushrooms that don't even know that they are poisonous, your fat and delicious rocks, your wire-haired maize, your bountiful fields, your missing buried chests; your hilarious landslides…where are they?'

The earth hurriedly placed a vegetable garden in front of me.

I couldn't eat my fill. My mouth didn't close. As one corner of my lips collected drop after drop of water, the other corner collected balls and balls of dirt. Neither water nor dirt could satisfy my hunger. I saw that it wouldn't work, so I decided to try air.

I turned on the gas.

I didn't know why I did this, I wasn't aware of what I was doing. Nor of what might happen. Until now, whenever I was seized by an eating crisis, I had eaten whatever I found without thinking, and didn't look for taste in what I ate. If I looked for taste could I be called a glutton? Again, I did what I always did. Now the hydrosphere and the earth must have heaved a sight of relief, seeing that I had turned my attention to the atmosphere. The gas started filling me. I felt myself being inflated. My brain was being numbed. As my brain was numbed, what I knew was being erased, and the numbers were decreasing. As the numbers decreased, ounce after ounce of weight was lifted from me. I was getting light-ter. Time was going backwards. And it wasn't obliged to continue flowing in a straight line from yesterday to today. When time lurched backwards, a person realised that somehow everything could have been different.

Everything could have worked out differently. That means every story can be told differently.

Of course if it hadn't been necessary to see everything, if it had been delivered at the beginning…

'TWO!'

1868 — France

One night, for no reason, Madame de Marelle told her husband she wanted to redecorate the mansion. She got to work right away. Every morning she walked from room to room with maids following her, rearranging some of the furniture, and having the rest removed to make way for new furniture. One day, she entered an unused room in the attic. There, at the bottom of a chest, she found a rather large box. A relief in the shape of an eye glittered on the lid of the box. The box was locked and it seemed the key was missing.

'What's in here?' she asked as she fiddled with the lock.

'There is a picture, ma'am,' the eldest of the maids said. 'Just a picture.'

'A picture, ma'am,' said the eldest of the maids. 'Just a picture.'

'Fine, where's the key?'

At the same moment, she thought of how to open the lock. She took out the long hair-clip she always used to fasten her hair. Her hair fell over on her shoulders. She began trying to pry open the lock with the sharp end of the hair-clip. But the old servant seemed to be disturbed by this. 'Don't take it out of the box' she whispered. 'According to the villagers, the young man in the picture is so beautiful, everyone who sees him suffers. Particularly…virgins in particular loose their heads over him.'

Madame de Marelle hesitated. She felt that she could get the lock open if she tried a bit more. She was curious about this young man and his famous beauty. She wanted to see. She stood silent for a moment, holding her hair-clip. As the old maid watched her anxiously to try to see what she was going to do, she stood looking at the box as if she was spellbound. Then, suddenly, whatever it was that passed through her mind, she let go of the box. She'd changed her mind about opening the box. She already had too much else to do, and didn't want to linger in that unpleasant room.

Then take it out of my sight,' she said, gathering up her hair and rearranging it into the bun she always wore. When she finished arranging her hair, she left the room wearing a stern expression on her face.

'You're right, ma'am. It's not always necessary to see everything. Some things should remain kept out of sight!' murmured the old servant behind her. She seemed reassured.

In time, Madame de Marelle forgot this incident. She was never curious about the figure of this young man who turned heads and caused suffering, and she never saw it. She gave birth to rusty-haired coloured children. She raised rusty-haired children. As the new names echoed through the mansion, and the branches of the family tree grew heavier, the name La Belle Annabelle was never encountered.

If Madame de Marelle had insisted on seeing what she shouldn't see, this sin would in the future result in Annabelle being surrounded by people who wanted to see her terrible beauty. But because the box had never been opened, nothing like this happened. La Belle Annabelle was never born. There was never such a person. She didn't exist. There was never a figure, no matter how beautiful it was, that lived simply in order to be looked at. Even the most beautiful of the beautiful, the most beautiful *jinn* of the poisonous yew forest had the right to remain far out of sight. Without her, the spectators in the cherry-coloured tent had no need to open their eyes wider and wider. Two never was. One number was missing.

'ONE!'

1648 – Siberia

Timofei Ankidinov couldn't believe his eyes when he saw that huge sable go into the basket and disappear. He left the sailor who was in danger of freezing on the sled, and started circling the basket in curiosity.

'Perhaps it would be better if you didn't look. It could be a trap for hunters. Or a Siberian curse!' said the sailor from where he was lying. He was quite the man for groundless beliefs. He'd witnessed so much in Siberia that his mind couldn't grasp, and he was wary of the natives of this land.

Timofei Ankidinov hesitated. When he lifted the lid of the basket, that huge sable's valuable fur would be his. Who knew, perhaps there were lots of sables at least as big as this one under the basket. Indeed he might even have found a way that led to Pogicha. If that was so, he'd return to his home with a fortune large enough to buy everyone. He stood there holding his dagger. As the sailor watched him anxiously to try to see what he was going to do, he was looking at the basket as if he was spellbound. But suddenly, whatever it was that went through his mind, he took a step backward. He'd changed his mind. He wasn't going to open the basket, he wasn't going to look inside. Indeed he already found the place spooky enough, and didn't want to linger.

'If that's the case, let's leave right away.' He said. He sheathed his dagger, and went to the front of the sled.

As they set off again the sailor whispered in a low but self-assured voice, 'You're right, let's go. It's not necessary to see everything. It's better that some things remain well out of sight!'

As the two men moved off into the distance, two souls were about to unite inside the basket. A while later, the basket opened of its own accord. The beardless youth emerged having taken part of the sable's soul and having added part of his soul to the sable's. He was now the tribe's shaman. Until the moment of his death, whenever he remembered that day, he'd remember that, for reasons unknown to him, he'd felt a terrible fear of being seen; he would never take the talismanic power of eyes lightly. He and his descendants lived for centuries and centuries, until the despicable races that chewed up Siberia had dried up. In the family tree of the shamans, which had its roots in the sky and its branches in the ground, the name Sable-Girl never appeared.

If Timofei Ankidinov had insisted on seeing what he shouldn't see, this sin would in the future result in the Sable-Girl being surrounded by people who wanted to see terrible ugliness. But because he didn't open the box, nothing like this happened. The Sable-Girl was never born. There was never anyone like that. She never existed. There was never a figure, no matter how ugly she was, who lived simply in order to be looked at. Even the ugliest of the ugly, the most wretched, plagued creature had the right to remain far out of sight. Without her, the spectators in the cherry-coloured tent had no need to close their eyes so tight. One never was. The number One was missing.

~

Keramet Mumî Keşke Memiş Efendi ran up to the westward-facing door of the cherry-coloured tent. He was out of breath. He looked everywhere. The Sable-Girl wasn't there. He stopped for a moment to try to think where she might have gone, but at the same moment a worse suspicion was aroused. He ran to the eastward-facing section of the tent. He looked everywhere, searched every corner. What he'd feared had come to pass. La Belle

Annabelle was also missing.

That day, he didn't say anything to anyone until evening about his two most popular actresses having run off. He didn't say anything, but in any event the truth would soon come out. And when the truth came out, he was going to have to give up this enterprise. Without the most beautiful of the beautiful and the most ugly of the ugly, it wouldn't be possible to keep the cherry-coloured tent going for even a single day.

Did this grieve him? No one could tell whether or not he was grieved. As always, his eyes were a curtain of mystery. But surely he wasn't all that grieved? In any event he wasn't going to remain in his present form. Time was endless, and space was limitless. Surely one day he would melt; he would melt, and solidify again, solidify and then melt again. In any event he would return to this world at another time, much much later but very soon, and in another place, very very far away but just here.

In any event...one more...and one more...

'ZERO!'

1999 – Istanbul

'Open the door!'

They're banging on the door. I have to get up and open the door but I'm too weak, much too weak. I can't move. And it's not as if I've suddenly stopped and frozen to the spot either, but I am completely motionless for perhaps the first time in my life, and can't move. I am like gelatine. I am in a dense fog. Sometimes I close my eyes, sometimes I open them. It doesn't make any difference either way. The eye doesn't see here.

'What are you waiting for. She's not opening the door. Break the door down. Break it down!'

This voice sounds familiar. It must be one of the neighbours. Which one, I wonder? What did they cook for us this time, what are they bringing us? Is it *börek* or is it a sweet, is it *pilaff* or is it dumplings... I can't make out which of the neighbour-ladies is shouting.

unutmak (forgetting): Cleaning the eyes.

The door breaks with a terrible cracking sound. With the breaking of the door, an uncountable number of neighbour-ladies rush in, pushing and shoving each other and uttering bloodcurdling screams, and jump on top of me.

At the same moment I start rising into the air.

veda (farewell): 'Why did you turn and look at the city that provoked God's wrath?' shouted Lot's wife angrily. 'Why did you look to see what you'd left behind? Tell me, why does a person have to turn and take a last look at what he's leaving behind?' But he couldn't give his wife's petrified lips an answer to this difficult question.

I was so inflated with gas that I was as round as a ball. In this state I look like a huge Zero; the fattest of all numbers, the only number lighter than air. I was pleased. Since I'd counted my way to Zero, since I'd become Zero by no longer existing, I could comfortably rise into the sky and above the clouds.

At first my feet rise only a few inches above the ground. Later I rise further, and approach the ceiling. I open and close my arms and legs as if I'm swimming. By doing this, and moving to the left and right, I'm able to shake off the neighbour-ladies' hands. They don't stop screaming for a moment. Struggling not to loose my balance, I approach the door to the terrace. Since my feet didn't touch B-C's rocking chair, I must be quite high up in the air. At that moment I see the cat. It's looking at me from below, with all of the fur on its back standing on end. I wave to it. It hisses at me. The door to the terrace is wide open as usual. I swish through the curtains, which were blowing back and forth gently like the curtains in films about haunted houses, and go out into the open air. I'm leaving the house, in a way that I've never left the house before.

vitrin (shop window): A section of glass used to display what a shop sells.

I'm level with the roof of the Hayalifener Apartments now. My feet are swinging back and forth in the emptiness. I'm looking at the people climbing up the hill and the people descending the hill. I'm looking at those who slide on the ice and roll down into the flames. As I rise, I see first the hill, then the whole neighbourhood, then the entire city. And the city is completely different when you look at it from above like this. The neighbourhoods spread out fibrously like boiled chicken, the apartment buildings are layered like pastry, the people are like grains of badly cooked rice that stubbornly refuse to stick to each other. As I look at the city I realise that I'm not the least bit hungry. My stomach is so full that I suspect I might not be alive.

From the sky I look down on the tombs of saints, the crosses on pale-faced churches, fountains in peaceful courtyards, wooden houses under whose eaves demons chat at night, street dogs who rush at strangers like thirsty jackals, the people who comb through the garbage for food. I look down on the city that collapsed under the weight of the bolts with which she blocked the door against the possibility of her heart being stolen in the nonchalance of the night, thus causing herself to become more introverted. To my eyes, the city looks like a bird's nest made of twigs and straw. There are millions of newborn chicks in it; and they're all so hungry. They cry out at the tops of their voices to a mother they've never seen because their eyes have not yet opened. The worms that are stuffed down their pink beaks only serve to stop their endless chirping for a brief moment. Every night the city is drawn to this shrewish hunger. And it is never satisfied.

This city has an East and a West. But once a person rises into the air and sees it from above, this compass breaks. There remains neither East nor West. For me now there's only below and above. Because I...

yabanci (alien): A thing or a person the eye has not seen before.

...have finally become a floating balloon.

yaldızcılık (gilding): 1. The art of gilding. 2. To cover an object's bad sides to make it look more beautiful than it is (for example, to gild it with gold or silver dust).

I'm a floating balloon filled with gas. And like every floating balloon, I'm floating in the eyes of a lonely-child. Lonely-children, unlike other children, often turn their eyes inward. When they're not looking into themselves, they usually either have their heads down and are looking at the ground, or else are lying on their backs looking at the sky. For this reason, they're the first ones to notice me. As I swing in the sky, the lonely-children in the various corners of the earth will stop what they're doing and watch me with fixed eyes. Perhaps at the very first moment they see me, they don't think there could be lonely-children other than themselves who are watching me at the same moment. Let them think so. A floating balloon is a show seen by an audience of one. In time she'll learn why this is so.

yalıngöz: Without eyelids.

Yes, it is learnt of in time. Because a lonely-child is so surprised and excited the first time she sees a floating balloon, she'll want to show it to someone else at once. She'll think she can break free of her loneliness by showing someone else this beauty she's discovered by herself. She'll either go home and call someone outside, or pull her mother by the arm, or shout to the children nearby. At first the others won't understand what the lonely-child is saying; then, they'll look at where she's pointing. But they won't see anything there. Because the floating balloon has long since floated away. It's not there. It's not as if it had been there and was gone; it was as if it had never existed. The people the lonely-child has called to see the floating balloon will laugh half bashfully and half angrily. She's understood. She's understood that if you take your eyes off a floating balloon, it won't be where you left it when you look back. This means that, just at the moment you took your eyes off it, the floating balloon ceased to exist at the point you left it. Because it exists when it's seen, but ceases to exist when it isn't seen.

The next time the lonely-child sees a floating balloon, she won't try to show anyone else. She's grown up after all; enough to see that in this world, anything she discovered alone wouldn't free her from loneliness. From now on she'll keep her secrets to herself. The next time, she'll hold her breath, and won't take her eyes off the balloon as she watches it rise. Her heart will soar. She won't tell anyone what she's seen. Because the rise of the balloon addresses only the eye; it is seeing and being seen. Putting it into words wears it out; virtually any word that tries to describe it will be inadequate. As if it's not a balloon, but a silent promise that's floating in the sky. The balloon floats, the child watches; the child watches, the balloon floats. Then, the balloon passes through the sky's satin gate. It disappears. The lonely-child is disappointed. Because she didn't take her eyes off it for a single moment; she hadn't let go of the imaginary string. The floating balloon has still gone. Not because it was invisible, but that in its visible state it had become lost to the eye. Then the lonely-child realises something else. She understands that time is forever chasing its own end. For this reason, every balloon explodes in the end, and every secret gives itself away.

> *yasam* (life): To see life, we hold a mirror to our mouths. Even if we don't see life, we know we're alive from the condensation on the mirror.

So, in the end I became what I'd always wanted to be. I am a floating balloon. And like every floating balloon, I'm floating in the eyes of a lonely-child. My celestial passage will only last for the blink of an eye. And like every floating balloon, I can be considered a miracle. Because I swallowed so much gas without stopping and because I can remain light as long as I'm in the air. On top of this, if I wanted I could eat even more and expand even more, but not become the slightest bit heavier, and still be able to glide through the sky.

It's so nice to fly… It's so nice to be in the dome of the sky, lighter than a feather, more vagrant than a kite, more playful than steam, more carefree than a snowflake. My intention is to climb higher and higher. My intention is to climb miles and miles into the grey sky, and, touching the sun's shadow, sit cross-legged on top of the clouds, watching the world. Because I want to know, can you see everything that's going on down there when you look from up here? I'm curious about whether the hidden secrets of back gardens, the sins that are committed, the unfinished games, are recorded line-by-line, word by word. I want to know, does humanity has any privacy at all? Even if it's only once in a while, I want to know if there's a moment of the night when we can flee from sight, be free from being seen, some dark point, a small gap, invisible rip, tiny crack, minor leak…that is, as if a flea had bitten, a tick had fastened itself, a caterpillar had gnawed, a leech had sucked, a moth had eaten, one of the three apples that fell from the sky had worms, I want to know if there's even the smallest bit of privacy in this world.

There's not much further to go. The clouds are near. When I've climbed a bit more, my head will touch the clouds. Then I'll climb a bit more, and then, finally, at long last, I'll learn the answer about which I've been curious. Soon I'll see the truth, and soon the truth will be seen.

yay (bow): At one time, they used to bury swords that had been used to execute prisoners. So that they would forget what they had seen. If a bow was used, it was definitely broken. It was best to break them because they couldn't succeed in forgetting what they'd seen.

Suddenly, I'm staring into a pair of bulging eyes. They're looking at me with curiosity. They're trying to understand what I am, what I'm seeking here, and why I'm so strange. They're judging me. They know I don't belong here. I'm a stranger in this stratum. This is the picture frame in which I least belong; it too is aware of this. The bulging eyes belong to a bird of prey. If I'd seen it at another time, that is, if I'd seen it when I was looking from below, I might have found it beautiful; but now, meeting it here, it looks terribly ugly. I wait for it to pass me and move on, but it continues to follow me. It keeps making sporadic squawking sounds. The sound is unpleasant and frightening. And suddenly, I don't know why, it begins to attack. Its pointed beak, its beak the colour of raw meat, its beak punctures me.

I'm a floating balloon. I'm deflating now. As I rise I'm losing air. I'm letting out the air that I took in to give back the air I had dispersed. I'm buzzing like a confused fly, zipping from here to there through the air. If there's a lonely-child watching from below at this moment, she'll know that I'm about to disappear from sight. But anyway, she's watched for long enough. Anyway I don't like to be seen too much. Because life is private. And like everything private, it sometimes has to be able to remain far from the eye, from eyes.

I'm not going to be able to stand it any longer. I'm exploding.

yılanın ayası (serpent's foot): 'Try to see a serpent's foot. Whoever sees a serpent's foot goes to heaven,' said the grandmother to her grandchild. 'But there's no such thing as a serpent's foot,' said the grandchild to the grandmother. They gave each other offended looks.

I'm exploding. I'm not going to be able to stand it any longer.

Zümrüdüanka: A legendary bird whose power and beauty depended both on her will to be seen and on her remaining unseen.

'Enough! Since we started out you've been counting onetwothreeonetwothree... What is this? It's making me ill. Isn't there anything after these numbers? Look, if you're going to count honestly, all right, then count. But if you're going to keep getting stuck like that, then be quiet. Be quiet!'

A deep silence fills the minibus. Everyone has stopped, and is looking at me in surprise. Nobody moves, not even to blink. Suddenly everything freezes. Everything, even the eyes as they turn to look at me. I feel myself going red. I'm sweating. The driver's eyes are looking at me through the rear-view mirror. The young man sitting in the front street, who had turned completely around and was looking at me with his arms folded and his face contorted into an exaggerated expression of amazement, has stayed that way. I imagine they're waiting for me to explain why I suddenly started shouting that way. I can't see the faces of the people sitting in the back seats, but I can feel their eyes on me. The two housewives, the well-dressed estate agent and the man next to the window who was clearly on his way to an important meeting are all watching me intently. I don't move my head at all in order not to make eye contact with the schoolgirl and especially the child's mother. But I can still see from the corners of my eyes that they're looking at me.

A red light is burning in the single eye of the silken-haired doll hanging from the rear-view mirror. It seemed that the driver had stepped on the breaks the moment I shouted. The red light in the doll's eye is now looking at me like everyone and everything else on the minibus. Beads of sweat are collecting on my forehead. I'm suffocating. But this terror won't last much longer. The driver is the first to pull himself together. As he starts the minibus, he continues watching me through the rear-view mirror. We get under way.

The next person to pull himself together is the young man sitting in the front seat. He decides not to wait for my explanation, and turns to face forward. Judging from the way they whisper among themselves, it seems that the housewives have recovered from their initial surprise. Meanwhile. The woman next to me has started wriggling restlessly. As for the child...the bug-eyed child had embraced her mother in fear the moment I started shouting, and remained with her face buried under her mother's coat. Now, she too is slowly lifting her head.

She lifts her head, looks at me, makes a distressed sound, breathes in, then, pouting, makes an even more distressed sound, then suddenly starts wailing. At the same moment, the mother and all of the passengers on the minibus jump to console the child. Everyone, talking at once, is uttering phrases like 'Don't cry my dear, there's nothing to cry about, it's all over.' At one point the driver, turning sideways and holding the steering wheel with one hand, makes funny faces to try to make the child laugh. When he sees that this is not going to work, he faces forward again, and gives me dirty looks through the rear-view mirror. As for me, all I did was sit there and sweat.

Knowing that everyone in the minibus was on her side, the bug-eyed child cries even more. She's crying and screaming and kicking up a fuss. As she cries, my brain is throbbing and my limbs are shaking from nerves. I said it before, being fat makes me an irritable person.

I get off at the next stop.

I start walking. I overcome my body's objections, and start trudging slowly up the hill. The sky has grown quite dark, and it's very late. I don't know how long I was on the minibus. But I don't care about time any more. I'm cold. It's cold enough to snow tonight. As I approach home, I sense that something strange is going on. It's as if…there's too much activity. Streets that are usually deserted at this hour are lively. A little further along, a group of people has gathered. The lights of all the houses overlooking the street are burning, and curtains are wide open. Neighbours have crowded onto balconies and are hanging out of the windows. As I approach the place where people have gathered, high-pitched sounds reach my ears. Some people run past me, heading in that direction. It's clear that whatever is being shown there, some people don't want to miss the show.

This is a world of spectacles.

About seeing and being seen.

A little later, when I'm able to find a place in the curious crowd, I can see what everyone else sees. In the middle of the street, under a street lamp, a woman in her fifties, in a flannel night-gown and slippers with pom-poms, is shouting and screaming as she does a belly dance. A group of people in night-gowns and pyjamas, who from the state they're in are clearly the woman's relatives, are trying to get her back in the house by pulling at her and begging her. 'Get her in the house and she can shout as much as she likes. Get her in the house so the neighbours won't see. It doesn't matter if other people hear her, it's enough that they don't see.'

The family is trying to pull the woman away from the crowd's gaze. The crowd are holding their breath, watching carefully, the more they see, the better.

I hold my breath, and watch very carefully.

The Flea Palace
by Elif Shafak

★ From the author of *The Gaze* ★

The setting is a stately residence in Istanbul built by Russian noble
émigré Pavel Antipov for his wife Agripina at the end of the Tsarist
reign, now sadly dilapidated, flea-infested, and home to ten families.
Shafak uses the narrative structure of *A Thousand and One Nights*
to construct a story-within-a-story narrative.

Inhabitants include Ethel, a lapsed Jew in search of true love
and the sad and beautiful Blue Mistress whose personal secret
provides the novel with an unforgettable denouement.
Add to this a strange, intensifying stench whose cause is
revealed at the end of the book, and we have a metaphor for the
cultural and spiritual decay in the heart of Istanbul.

'Once foundations are laid, this novel takes off into a hyper-active,
hilarious trip, with farce, passion, mystery and many sidelights
on Turkey's past. A cast of wacky flat-dwellers lend it punch and
pizazz, from Ethel the ageing Jewish diva (a wonderful creation) to
Gaba, the finest fictional dog in years.' *The Independent*

Translated from the Turkish by Müge Göçek

★ Shortlisted for the *Independent* Prize for Foreign Fiction 2005 ★

NEW £7.99 EDITION AVAILABLE NOW
ISBN: 0-7145-3120-0

four walls
by Vangelis Hatziyannidis

Following the death of his beekeeper father, Rodakis lives a
solitary life in the old family house on a Greek island. One day he
is asked by the village elders to take in a young fugitive woman.

He reluctantly agrees, and the woman soon persuades him to
return to the family business of making honey – using a secret
recipe that everyone on the island wants to get their hands on.

Exploring the themes of jealousy, incest and imprisonment,
with a suspicious death and runaway criminal thrown in for
good measure, *Four Walls* explodes the stereotypes of
idyllic Greek island life.

'Probably the most atmospheric Greek novel of the year' Greek *Vogue*

Translated from the Greek by Anne-Marie Stanton-Ife

ISBN: 0-7145-3122-7 • SPRING 2006 • £7.99/$14.95

THE CIRCUMCISION
by György Dalos

A self-proclaimed 'Hungarian Communist Jew for Christ', twelve-year-old Robi Singer has a lot on his plate. He is a 'half-orphan', he is painfully overweight and what's more, he has yet to be circumcised. With his Bar Mitzvah fast approaching, the pressure is on. To make matters worse, Robi's not sure he wants to be Jewish at all.

As his hypochondriac mother is more concerned about her secret affair with 'Uncle' Moric, Robi's only ally against the teachers at his Jewish school is his eccentric, headstrong grandmother. It seems everyone has an opinion on what he should do, but ultimately Robi must make his own decision.

'Wisdom and humour against the shadows of existence: Dalos, like Isaac B. Singer, is a follower of the great Yiddish literary traditions.' *The Giessener Anzeiger*

Translated from the Hungarian by Judith Sollosy

ISBN: 0-7145-3123-5 • SPRING 2006 • £8.99/$14.95

The Silent Sin

by Anja Sicking

When Anna's family – and with them her fortune – are destroyed in a fire, she finds herself alone and vulnerable in eighteenth century Amsterdam. Orphaned and penniless, she is forced to take a job as a servant girl for music publisher De Malapert.

She throws herself into her work, in the hope that someone will notice she is worth more than the average maid. Anna is intrigued by the mysterious De Malapert, and gradually becomes obsessed with him, occupying her mind with fantasies about his life away from the house.

From the outside, it would appear that De Malapert's only passion is for his music, but one day Anna discovers the secret that he must keep hidden from the rest of the world.
All her hopes are destroyed as she realizes he will never love her.

Translated from the Dutch by David Colmer

ISBN: 0-7145-3125-1 • SUMMER 2006 • Price: £9.99/$14.95